"Julie, are you all right?"

Rigg practically shouted as he grabbed her by the shoulders and pulled her out of the doorway.

"I didn't mean to hurt you, Julie. But didn't you see the van...a black van. It jumped the curb and... Oh my God!"

"What, Rigg? What is it?" Julie insisted.

He ran his fingers through his hair. "Julie, I didn't tell you. I didn't think you needed to know. But whoever called your mother told her it was a black van jumping the curb that killed you."

Julie closed her eyes, her body trembling. This couldn't be happening to her. She opened her eyes. Bits of garbage were blowing down the street now. There was no doubt something *was* happening to her. She looked at Rigg and shook her head slowly. Her voice, when she spoke, was a terrified whisper.

"Welcome to my nightmare, Rigg."

ABOUT THE AUTHOR

Dawn Stewardson lives near Toronto, Canada, on the shores of Lake Ontario, in a turn-of-the-century house built by a retired sea captain. She shares her home with her husband and an array of pets. One of the array appears as the furry feline, Asset, in this book.

Books by Dawn Stewardson

HARLEQUIN INTRIGUE
80–PERIL IN PARADISE

Don't miss any of our special offers. Write to us at the following address for information on our newest releases.

Harlequin Reader Service
901 Fuhrmann Blvd., P.O. Box 1397, Buffalo, NY 14240
Canadian address: P.O. Box 603,
Fort Erie, Ont. L2A 5X3

No Rhyme or Reason

Dawn Stewardson

Harlequin Books

TORONTO • NEW YORK • LONDON
AMSTERDAM • PARIS • SYDNEY • HAMBURG
STOCKHOLM • ATHENS • TOKYO • MILAN

To my mother and father,
who will remember the roastin' ears.
To Marmie Charndoff,
for her wonderful Intrigue editing.
And to John, always.

Harlequin Intrigue edition published May 1988

ISBN 0-373-22090-1

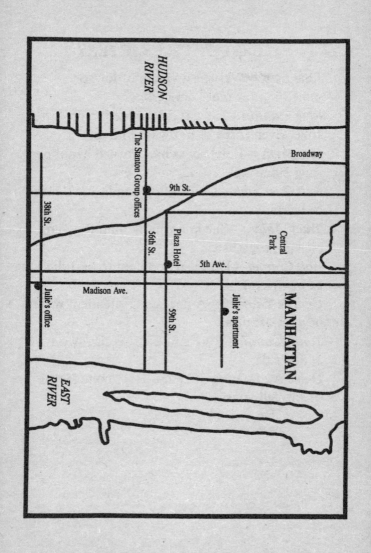

CAST OF CHARACTERS

Julie Lind—Was she a victim of love or something far more dangerous?

Rigg Stanton—He was determined to protect Julie. Even if she didn't want him to.

Ray Brent—Julie's boss had warned her about Rigg Stanton.

Neil Overbach—Could Rigg's right-hand man be trusted?

Tracy Alders—She knew more than Rigg and Neil put together.

Bob Cramer—He wasn't content to be Julie's ex-boyfriend.

Charlie Thomas—A new superintendent with a new set of rules.

John Stanton—Rigg's father was firmly on Julie's side.

Detective Wilcott, NYPD—His "coincidence" theory fell apart.

Chapter One

A gloved hand quietly shut the apartment door. An unseen cat meowed loudly, once, from a room down the hall, then silence prevailed. The intruder moved soundlessly on the thick, white carpeting, across to the living room, appraising the cool, blue-and-white color scheme, the traditional furniture, the antique accents. Along the hall then; the den would be first. Eyes leisurely scrutinized the room, focused on the flashing red light of the answering machine beside the phone. A finger pressed the *Rewind* button... then *Play*. A thick file folder on the desk invited investigation. Fingers flipped its cover open as the phone message began. The intruder smiled, listened to the caller's name, his words, then pressed *Rewind/Erase*... reset the machine.

Her bedroom next; the cat stretching lazily, its body almost invisible against the white, eyelet bedspread; only its green eyes apparent, gazing disdainfully while the intruder searched, handled, chose, took. Then, with feline disinterest, the cat began to groom its long fur.

A drawer was opened, more objects selected. That was everything. Time now for the final touch, the master stroke. And then, one more slow, sweeping glance around the living room. There was no need to hurry; she'd be gone for a long while yet. A sardonic grin curled the intruder's lips as one last item was chosen. And a gloved hand quietly shut the apartment door.

THE CASKET WAS CLOSED, of course. *A .38 pressed against the temple doesn't leave much face for the mortician to work with.* Julie shivered, recalling the detective's remark, his emotionless voice. He'd been delivering a statement of fact, nothing more: a statement of death, an everyday occurrence for officers of the NYPD's homicide division. But for Mark Thompson's associates at Grant and Kellog, his death was a devastating reminder that not everyone dies peacefully in his sleep.

Suicide. Julie tried, for the thousandth time, to convince herself the police were right. She swallowed hard, refusing to face the only possible alternative, telling herself, once again, to ignore her intuition. The detectives had talked to everyone at G and K, had listened attentively to her doubts. And their pronouncement had been *suicide.* They must be right. After all, she hadn't known Mark very well; he'd simply been a colleague. And what did she know about suicide...or murder?

She glanced toward the front of the windowless chapel. Muted, artificial light faded into dove-gray walls. Her gaze came to rest on the back of Mark's wife...Mark's widow. Then her eyes moved to the burnished heads of the two small boys beside their mother and the knot in her throat tightened. She watched the younger child turn around in his seat, his large, liquid eyes surveying the gathering. And she knew, with bone-chilling certainty, the police were wrong. Mark Thompson had not committed suicide.

Julie forced her gaze away from the little boy and focused on Helen, sitting beside her in the chapel pew. The skin around the older woman's eyes was puffy and gray, almost the precise gray of her hair. She twisted a well-used Kleenex tightly between her fingers. The past few days had been harder for Mark's secretary than for the others in the accounting firm. She was the one who had found his body slumped over his desk, head resting in the pool of congealing blood, the gun clenched in his hand. Julie reached across the space between them and touched the secretary's arm. Helen looked over at her, managed a tortured smile, then turned her attention back to the front of the room as the eulogy began. Julie closed her eyes, trapping the tears that were stinging them, wanting to block out reality.

And then the service was over. The mourners lingered uneasily on the sidewalk outside the chapel, assaulted by the raucous blare of Manhattan traffic. Everyone seemed uncomfortable, anxious to escape the aura of untimely death, escape into the bright May sunshine, into the refuge of the Memorial Day long weekend that lay ahead.

"I have to get away from here, Julie," Helen whispered, tears visible in her eyes, threatening to spill over any moment.

Julie took the other woman's hand and gave it a reassuring squeeze. "You'll be all right?"

Helen nodded, cast Julie a weak, trembling smile and headed down the street. Julie glanced around, wondering if she, too, could manage an unobtrusive escape. She'd just decided to try, when Ray Brent caught her eye through the gathering and motioned for her to wait. He spoke briefly to the two men with him, apparently about her, and the three of them started toward her.

Both of the strangers appeared to be in their midthirties. The man to her boss's right was shorter than Ray, not more than an inch or two taller than her own five foot six. His prominent belly tested the buttons of his dark suit with each step. His even more prominent nose supported a pair of large, horn-rimmed glasses. Sparse strands of pale hair were combed carefully over as much of his bald spot as they would cover.

Julie focused on the other man, now more clearly visible behind Ray. The only word that came to mind was *gorgeous*. She felt a sharp pang of guilt for even noticing his good looks at a time like this, but it would have been impossible not to. He defined tall, dark and handsome to perfection. The trio reached her and Julie turned her attention to her boss.

"Julie, I'd like you to meet Rigg Stanton, president of the Stanton Group." Ray nodded toward Tall, Dark and Handsome. "And Neil Overbach, his vice president," he added. "Gentlemen, this is Julie Lind."

Short, Fair and Not-So-Handsome grabbed her hand with his own rather sweaty one and shook it vigorously. "I'm looking forward to working with you, Julie. The circumstances are certainly unfortunate, though," he added quickly.

"I feel as if I know you already, Neil," Julie told him softly. "Mark mentioned you several times. He was impressed by the successful start-up you managed for the Stanton Group in the east."

Neil grinned at her, flashed a glance at Rigg Stanton, obviously wanting to be certain the company's president had noted her comment, and Julie knew she'd just ensured for herself all the cooperation she might need from the vice president in charge of the Stanton Group's eastern division.

Rigg silently appraised this woman who'd been thrust into Mark Thompson's place as external auditor of the division's financials. She'd appeared, from a distance, to be like the women he occasionally saw gazing regally down at him from the cover of *Vogue* on a newsstand. The similarity, he decided, lay in those high cheekbones and the way her blond hair was pulled smoothly back from her face. But, looking more closely, he realized she'd made no attempt to emulate a fashion model. She wore hardly any makeup and her severe hairstyle was softened by a tumble of shaggy bangs, covering her eyebrows entirely, half covered, in turn, by the black veil that had served her as a hat during the service.

It was only when she smiled at Neil that Rigg noticed her mouth and wondered how those sensuously full lips could have escaped his glance for even an instant. The absence of lipstick, he realized. His eyes caught hers. They were, without doubt, the most beautiful eyes he'd ever seen—soft, pale gray in the centers, growing darker toward the outer edges. He smiled at her as Neil released her hand. "You must get awfully tired of being told you don't look like an accountant."

Julie smiled a little in return. He was right. She couldn't count the number of times she'd heard that line. But this man's remark seemed neither sexist nor condescending and his soft, brown eyes told her the statement was meant as an honest compliment.

Before she could reply, Ray rushed to her defense. "Don't let her looks fool you, Rigg. Not many accountants make junior partner at Grant and Kellog when they're only twenty-eight. And she was the top of her class at NYU."

Julie shook her head at her boss's exaggeration. "Not quite the top, Ray."

"Close enough." He dismissed her correction and turned back to Rigg. "We've given your account to Julie because she's had experience auditing property development companies. I'm sure you, your shareholders and the IRS will all be happy with her work."

"I see no reason to doubt that," Rigg said quietly, smiling a slow, lazy smile at Julie, making her incredibly conscious of his attractiveness. "I apologize for the poor timing, Julie, but I'll be heading back to Houston in a couple of days and I'd like to talk with you a little about the audit.

"Once this division's filed a few annual tax returns and the IRS is content that we know what we're doing, I won't give the audit process a second thought. But, this being our first year of operation in New York, I'll breathe a little easier once I've seen an unqualified audit report.

"I'd planned on spending some time tomorrow reviewing things with Mark. Could I drop you off some place now? We could chat on the way."

Julie vacillated, not wanting to offend a client but wanting to be alone, hoping a walk in the spring air would alleviate the sadness that had enveloped her since Mark's death. "Thanks for the offer, but I'm just going straight home and it isn't far. Besides, I wouldn't be able to chat very knowledgeably yet. I haven't had a chance to go through Mark's file. But I do have it at my apartment to work on over the weekend. Why don't I review it tonight and call you in the morning, after I've seen how far along Mark was with things?"

"Fine. But I can still give you a lift now," Rigg persisted, leaving Julie little choice but to accept his offer. "I'm going your direction anyway," he added with a momentary grin.

She glanced at him wryly, amused by his blatant mendacity. "And how do you know that?"

Rigg shrugged, a smile tugging at the corners of his mouth. "Psychic powers."

"You're heading west, then?"

"All the way to the Hudson River."

"So much for psychic powers, Mr. Stanton," Julie teased gently. "I live on East Sixty-ninth." She had to give Rigg credit; he didn't miss a beat.

"Well, this city always confuses me. I'm continually getting east and west mixed up. What I meant to say was all the way to the East River." He smiled disarmingly at Julie, his look challenging her to call him on his game.

She merely nodded solemnly, straight-faced. "You simply have to remember the song. 'The Bronx is up and the Battery's down.' Once you figure out if you're pointed north or south, then east and west are easy. But," she continued, trying to keep from smiling, "as long as I'm not taking you out of your way, then a ride would be welcome, thank you."

"You a native New Yorker?" Rigg asked as they walked toward the chapel parking lot.

Julie nodded. "You a native Texan?"

"Yes, ma'am!"

He grinned broadly at her and Julie smiled at his sudden, exaggerated drawl. "That's the first time I've heard you sound like one . . . or, at least, like the stereotype."

Rigg laughed. "I don't think I like being reduced to a stereotype. I did have a Texan twang when I was younger—until I came east to university. In fact, I got called cowboy about eighty-two times during my first week at classes. After that, I realized if I wanted anyone to bother learning my real name I'd have to temper my drawl. But I reckon I could slip right back into being a good ol' boy if you all would like that, ma'am."

Julie laughed, realizing as she did so that it was the first time she'd felt like laughing in days. "I didn't think Texans ever deigned to go to school in the east."

"Well, I did start off at the University of Texas, but my father found out I was spending more time at Scholz Garten than in class, and the next thing I knew I was in Boston and my drinking buddies were still in Austin."

"Scholz Garten?"

"It's a beer garden on the fringe of the campus—a registered historic site, mind you—but a beer garden nonetheless. I sure did miss Lone Star beer for a while!"

Julie laughed again, glancing over at Rigg as they neared the parking lot. His hair, in the late-afternoon light, wasn't as dark as she'd first thought; its warm brown was streaked with golden glints. He wore it longer than was fashionable in the city and it fell, in a somewhat unruly manner, over his forehead. His evenly chiseled face was tanned—a tribute, she assumed, to the strength of the spring sun in Texas. Rigg stopped beside a silver Mercedes sports car and unlocked the passenger door.

"East Sixty-ninth, you said?" he asked, sliding into the driver's seat next to Julie.

She nodded. "Between Third and Lexington. I hope that actually *is* on your way. The traffic's always awful on Friday afternoons but it's even worse before a long weekend."

Rigg pulled the car up to the lot's exit. "The company keeps a suite at the Plaza, so you're only a minor detour."

The Plaza and a Mercedes, Julie mused. The president of the Stanton Group wasn't a man who skimped on expenses. Rigg pulled the powerful car abruptly into the street and was rewarded by a sharp blast from the horn of the Yellow Cab he'd cut off. Its driver followed up by way of a rude suggestion with his finger through the taxi's open window. Julie grinned. "I'm surprised you bother to drive in New York. A lot of people who live here don't even attempt it."

Rigg shrugged. "I'm used to always having a car. You just can't get around Houston at all without one."

"You live right in the city?"

"No. We have a ranch not far outside."

Julie glanced at his left hand. No ring. That meant nothing; the *we* undoubtedly did. She tried to ignore the strong twinge of disappointment and forced her mind back to business. "I'll go through Mark's entire working file tonight, Rigg. I don't know what stage things were at, but if he was almost done, I can probably just finish up the audit report from the information there. Otherwise, I'm going to have to do some work at your offices."

He nodded without taking his eyes off the street. "Neil's going away for the weekend but I'll be spending some time there if you need anything."

"I think the entire city's going away." Julie smiled ruefully. "I'm feeling extremely deprived."

Rigg glanced at her, uncertain if she was serious or not. Her sense of humor was more subtle than most women's. "I really do apologize for making you work on the weekend, Julie. But with our tax year-end coming up we're a little pressed for time. I imagine," he added quietly, after a pause, "Mark's death has caused quite a disruption at G and K."

"Yes, of course. All his clients still have to be looked after. Things are bound to be a little hectic for a while."

Rigg heard the change in Julie's voice and instantly regretted mentioning the death. He found the whole business of Mark's suicide unsettling and he'd barely met the man. It had to be far more disconcerting for people who'd worked with him. Rigg turned onto East Sixty-ninth and glanced over at Julie for instructions. She pointed to one of the elegant old apartment houses lining the street. "Very nice. G and K must pay their junior partners awfully well," he teased, hoping to make her smile again. He liked that warm smile. But she simply shook her head.

"Rent controls," she explained. "The apartment's been in my family for years. I grew up in it, in fact. New Yorkers never let a good apartment go. My mother and I stayed here after my father died and then my mother remarried and moved out about five years ago. I took over the lease."

Julie glanced at Rigg as she finished speaking and he realized she'd caught him staring at her long, slender legs. The cool look she shot him made him hot. He suddenly didn't want her to escape. "Do you have to go right in, Julie? I realize it's still afternoon but, since I'm ruining your weekend, the least I can do is offer you dinner."

"Thanks, but no," she said firmly. "Dinner's going to be a grilled cheese sandwich and a careful read of the Stanton Group file. Would you like me to call you in the morning and let you know if I'll be needing anything more?"

Rigg merely nodded, hoping his disappointment wasn't obvious. "If I'm not at the Plaza, I'll be at my office. I only come in from Houston about one week a month, so most of that time is spent working." He helped Julie out of the car and watched her walk toward her building. Her hips swayed just enough to be provocative; she was one hell of an attractive lady. He certainly hoped she'd find that the audit needed a lot of work at his offices.

JULIE'S PHONE BEGAN RINGING as she closed the apartment door. She considered letting her answering machine take the call. Then, deciding to answer it herself, walked swiftly to the living room extension. A loud, plaintive meow greeted her from the kitchen. "In a minute, Asset," she called, picking up the phone.

"Julie." The familiar voice made her heart sink. Her answering machine would have been the better choice.

"It's Bob, Julie. I'm glad I caught you. I left a message earlier but you can ignore it now. How've you been keeping?"

"Fine thanks.... And you?"

"Not bad, considering. Julie, I was cleaning house a few days ago and came across some records you lent me.... Thought I'd better get them back to you. Will you be home later tonight, say about nine-thirty?"

"Bob, I will, but I have to work." Why, she wondered as she spoke, did the truth sound like a lie to her own ears? "Anyway," she rushed on, "if I haven't missed them by now, they aren't worth worrying about. Why don't you keep them? You'll probably get more enjoyment out of them than I would."

There was a pause at the other end before Bob spoke again. "I really think I should return them...."

Asset leaped into Julie's lap and began rubbing her long white, fur against Julie's black dress. Julie pushed her away, ignoring her wail of protest. The cat marched stiffly back to the kitchen, muttering loudly, tail twitching back and forth.

"No. Honestly, Bob, my record cabinet is overcrowded anyway. Please keep them."

"Well . . . all right then. Thanks. But I'd like to see you anyway, Julie. Something's come up that I have to talk to you about."

Julie closed her eyes. She didn't want to see Bob. Ex-boyfriends made her extremely uncomfortable. Remaining good friends with them was something she was a definite failure at.

"It's really important, Julie. How about dinner tomorrow?"

She couldn't think of a polite way to refuse—another of her failings, she thought wearily. Maybe whatever was important had nothing to do with the two of them. "That sounds nice, Bob," she lied.

"Wonderful. I'll pick you up at seven-thirty. And dress up, Julie. I want to take you somewhere special." Bob's voice practically purred over the line and Julie knew she'd made a mistake.

"I'll be looking forward to it, Bob." She felt her nose grow, à la Pinocchio. "See you at seven-thirty."

Julie hung up the receiver and sat glumly on the couch, swearing silently over her wishy-washiness. She kicked her shoes off, yanked the silly veil from her head, pulled the pins out of her hair and ran her fingers through it, letting it fall comfortably free onto her shoulders. Then, shoes in one hand, veil in the other, she padded down the hall to her bedroom to change.

She tossed the veil onto her bureau, glanced absently into the mirror above it and her heart stopped beating. Her eyes were riveted to the vibrant, purple letters that had been smeared across the glass. An icy chill swept through her body, leaving every tiny hair on her skin standing straight up. The letters seemed to be flashing on and off like a bright neon sign; she knew that was impossible. Her eyes wouldn't focus. She stared, disbelieving, at the letters, wanting them to not be there, wanting them to disappear from before her eyes. But they continued to stare boldly back at her. She didn't want her brain to turn them into words, didn't want to read the message...GET OUT OF NEW YORK BITCH!

Julie whirled around, her eyes darting about the room, not wanting to see anything else amiss, not wanting to see a person, the person who had done this. No one. And everything looked normal. But someone had been in here, could *still* be in here, could be hiding, waiting, waiting to harm her far more than words could. She turned and ran from the room, shoes still in her hand. She ran down the hall, out of her apartment, slamming the door behind her, raced along the corridor to old Mrs. Benson's, pounded on the door. "It's me, Mrs. Benson. It's Julie," she called, barely recognizing her own voice, hearing only the panic in it. Why didn't the woman answer? She was always home! Julie pounded on the door again. Deathly silence answered her knocks.

Julie glanced frantically down the empty corridor, knowing the other neighbors wouldn't be home from work this early. She breathed deeply, trying to calm herself, bent over and slipped her shoes back on. She looked down the hall, toward the elevators. She'd have to pass her apartment again to reach them. Six floors up. Turning in the opposite direction she ran to the stairs, down five flights, the clickety-clack of her heels echoing the noisy beating of her heart, along the corridor that would take her to the superintendent's apartment. Once there, she banged on the door, sighed with relief at the sound of footsteps inside. A chain was slid, a lock snapped. Julie watched the door open and then heard her own sharp intake of breath when she saw the stranger.

The stocky, dark-haired man stood in the doorway, watching her with a curious expression.

Julie shook her head. "I'm sorry. You took me by surprise." She tried to control her ragged breathing. "I'm Julie Lind...apartment 627. I was expecting Bill Farrel. He was here for so many years I forgot for a moment that he'd retired. I am sorry," she repeated, realizing she was sounding foolish. "But I just had a scare and I'm afraid I'm not thinking too clearly. And, you're the new super...."

"Charlie Thomas." The man's words filled in the blank.

"Charlie Thomas, of course. I am sorry."

"There's no need to be sorry. Please come in." The super grinned; the toothy grin didn't reassure her. She wanted Bill Farrel who'd been here as long as she could remember. She didn't want some middle-aged stranger who'd been the superintendent for barely a week. He opened the door wider. "What can I do to help? Helping the tenants is part of my job," he added when she didn't move.

Julie nodded. "I'll have to call the police. Someone's been in my apartment. I had this horrible feeling they were still there. I didn't phone from upstairs. I just wanted to get out."

Charlie gestured at his phone, his grin replaced by a concerned expression. "Be my guest."

The officer she spoke to sounded bored. A break-in, no apparent damage, was obviously a very insignificant event. An hour, more likely two, he told her. It was, after all, the start of a long weekend. Could she wait where she was? Nothing in her apartment was to be touched until the police got there. Julie glanced at Charlie Thomas. He'd obviously picked up the gist of the conversation, and was regarding her anxiously.

"He told me not to go back to my apartment until an officer arrives," Julie said, hanging up. "It'll be a while. I can sit in the lobby."

Charlie shrugged. "No need to do that. I'm not going anywhere. In fact, I was just about to make coffee. Like some?"

"Thanks... if it's no trouble." Julie surveyed the living room while Charlie was in the kitchen. Bill's overstuffed furniture had been replaced by a modern sofa and the matching chair she was sitting on. Charlie Thomas would likely be a good super. Bill Farrel's living room had always looked comfortably "lived in." Now, the room was so spotless that seeing it made her feel guilty about her own housekeeping. Her apartment was neat enough, but dusting and scrubbing definitely weren't her top priorities in life.

Julie continued her survey of the room. In the far corner sat a large, console television. Along the wall beside it was a bench and a set of weights. As the new super returned, she realized he wasn't so much stocky as muscular.

Charlie gazed, with a worried look, over his coffee at Julie. "Should I be doing something about this break-in? I guess it's sort of my responsibility if someone strange was in the building, got into an apartment."

Julie shook her head slowly. "I think calling the police is about it. Break-ins aren't exactly rare in Manhattan. And you can't be expected to see everyone who's coming and going."

Charlie looked marginally relieved at her reply and lapsed into silence, startling her when he eventually spoke again. "There's a good game show on now." He picked up his remote and turned on the television. They were well into game show number three before the police officer appeared.

Chapter Two

Charlie unlocked Julie's door for them and retreated, Julie imagined, to his game shows. She flicked on the living room lights from the hall, banishing the early twilight. Nothing seemed out of place. Her purse and keys lay, where she'd tossed them earlier, on the couch. Asset howled hungrily from the kitchen.

"It's in the bedroom." Julie pointed along the hall, waiting for Officer Drake to precede her, wishing he were more like the experienced homicide detectives who'd been around Grant and Kellog for the past few days. This lanky, uniformed young man looked about twelve, although she knew he had to be twenty-four or twenty-five.

Drake stared at the message on the mirror, shaking his head. "Someone's been watching too many horror movies."

"Pardon?"

Drake glanced at Julie's reflection in the glass. "Horror movies. You don't watch them?"

She shook her head; he elaborated. "A scary message in lipstick on your mirror. It's a cliché from the horror movies."

"Well, cliché or not, it frightened the devil out of me! I don't even want to look at it *now*."

Drake nodded. "Your own lipstick?"

"No. I'm not into electric grape."

He looked at her directly this time, nodded again, then pulled a tiny camera from his pocket and snapped a shot. "Hope it's bright enough in here. Can't use the flash on the mirror." He scrawled a few lines in his notebook then looked around. "See anything missing?"

Julie shook her head. "I haven't checked all the rooms, though."

Drake continued his questioning as they looked through the apartment. They found nothing gone, nothing disturbed, and returned to the bedroom. "So," he summarized, "the break-in could have happened any time between eight this morning and when you arrived home around five."

Julie nodded. "I went straight from G and K to the funeral. They closed the office at two o'clock." She glanced at the mirror once more, forcing herself to reread the words, trying to make sense of them. She'd lived in New York all her life. Why would someone tell her to leave? Absently, she picked up her veil from the bureau and realized something was missing. Her thoughts whirled. "There's a picture gone." Her voice was barely a whisper. She tried again. "There was a picture on the dresser of my mother and me."

"Describe it."

"Just a photograph of the two of us. My stepfather took it six or seven months ago, the last time they visited. They live in Phoenix. She sent it to me at Christmas."

"What size?"

"Large...ten by twelve, I guess."

"The frame?"

"Silver...it was a Christmas gift."

"Expensive frame?"

"I imagine. It was heavy and ornate. But look." Julie pointed at her dinner ring, sitting on the bureau, inches from where the photograph had sat. "This ring's far more valuable than the frame could have been."

Drake made a few notes and looked slowly about the room once more. "The message and the picture...and that's it?"

Julie shook her head. "It's all I've noticed. Why would someone take a photograph?" She shivered. "That's almost as creepy as the message on the mirror."

"Maybe we could go back to the living room," Drake suggested. "I'd like to ask you a few more questions."

Asset wailed mournfully as they neared the kitchen.

"Do you mind if I take a minute to feed my cat? Otherwise, we won't be able to hear each other." Julie quickly opened a can of chopped chicken and thrust it in front of the cat, giving her furry head a quick rub. "Think you can rough it without a bowl tonight, Asset?"

Drake was gazing at Julie's end table when she entered the room. He glanced up. "There's space here that's not dusty."

Julie looked at the place where her clock belonged. For one tiny instant, she felt guilty about her housekeeping again. Then she simply felt nauseous. She swallowed hard before speaking. "There was an antique clock there."

"Valuable?"

"No, not at all. I bought it at a flea market for six or seven dollars and it was probably overpriced at that. It didn't work. It didn't work when I got it. It was just an ornament, really." She described the clock, still trying to make some sense of what was going on."

"Was it important to you? Have any particular sentimental value?"

Julie shook her head slowly. "No. It was pretty but it didn't have any significance to me."

"The picture would mean something to you ... but a broken clock?" Drake looked puzzled. "That doesn't figure. But, from the fact that nothing really valuable was taken, my guess is that it was someone you know who was in here. Anyone else have a key?"

"Only my mother in Phoenix. And the super has a master key, of course."

Drake nodded. "What about a possible motive? Have you had any trouble lately? Fight with anyone?"

Julie bit her lip, feeling more uneasy by the minute. "No. No fights, no trouble."

"What about your love life? I'm not being nosy," he added at her wry glance. "But people are weird when it comes to relationships and this strikes me as pretty weird. You involved with anyone at the moment?"

"No, not for the past few months."

"And, before that?"

"I was seeing someone for a while last fall—till a little after New Year's. I haven't heard from him since then. No, that's not true." A creepy, crawly feeling wormed up Julie's spine. "He called me today. I talked to him just before I found the message." She glanced at Drake. He was busily writing but looked up at her when she paused. She shook her head firmly. "Just a coincidence. There isn't a more unlikely suspect in the world."

"What's his name?" Drake asked with obvious interest.

"Bob Cramer."

"Address?"

"He wouldn't do anything like this."

"He have a key to your apartment while you were seeing him?"

"No."

"I need his address for my report."

"Wooster...near Spring."

"SoHo," Drake commented as he wrote.

"He likes old buildings, anything old, in fact. He's an archaeology professor. This is silly, you know. He's absolutely positively not the sort of man who would do this."

Drake nodded. "Ex-boyfriends are obvious prime suspects in cases like this. That's all."

"Will you be talking to him?"

"Somebody probably will."

"He'll be mortified!"

"It'll be just a talk. If he's a regular guy, he'll be glad we're doing our job. You can't think of anyone else that might have had a reason to do this?"

"I can't think of *anyone* who might have had a reason."

"Well, you may find other things are gone. If you do, give me a call. I'll add them to the report. Maybe the motive will be clearer if there's something else missing." Drake scribbled a phone number on a piece of paper and handed it to her. "Talk to your super about getting that lock changed immediately. In the meantime, keep the bar lock on when you're home. Someone's likely walking around with a key. There's no sign of forced entry at all and that's not an easy lock to pick."

Julie closed the door behind Drake and slid the bar lock firmly into place. She glanced at her watch. Past eight and she had that entire damn Stanton file to review. It was the last thing she felt like doing. She grabbed an apple out of the fridge—a fine dinner—and looked nervously around the kitchen, half expecting to notice something else had disappeared. Everything seemed to be in place.

Julie unbuttoned her dress as she headed down the hall, mulling over everything Drake had said. He was wrong about Bob. For all that things hadn't worked out between them, Bob would never dream of doing anything like this. He'd been too fond of her to want to frighten her. Too fond... She thought of the letters he'd written when he was away over the Christmas break.

She tossed her dress and slip onto the bed and opened her sweater drawer. Those letters were right here, in the bottom of the drawer. Her hand searched for them under the sweaters. A cold shiver passed through her body when she didn't feel them. She ran her fingers along the entire width of the drawer, began to yank the sweaters out. And then they were a jumbled rainbow on the white carpet and the drawer was empty...and the letters weren't there. Bob! Bob's letters. Could it possibly have been him?

Julie ordered herself to be calm. Her heart ignored the command and continued to pound loudly. She pulled a red sweater over her head, threw the rest of the tangle back into the drawer and tugged on a pair of jeans. Drake's number was sitting on the hall table. She dialed it and left a message for him to call her. How was she going to concentrate on working tonight? Her apartment had been transformed into some theater of the absurd! She grabbed a bottle of glass cleaner and a roll of paper towels from under the kitchen sink and headed back to the bedroom.

There! Staring into the clean mirror made her feel marginally better. Now she'd just have a quick look at the Stanton file, just enough so that she could talk to Rigg in the morning without sounding like a complete idiot. In the den, she switched on her desk lamp and reached for the file that wasn't there.

Fear seized Julie again, wrapping icy fingers tightly around her throat, sending her heart racing. She stared at her desk, knowing she'd left the Stanton file on it the night before. Now its surface was empty except for a small stack of tax regulation updates. Think, she ordered herself; think back through yesterday. She'd come home from work, unpacked her briefcase and put the file right in the center of her desk. She glanced at the crowded bookshelves, realizing the effort was futile. There was no question about where she'd left the file. And there was no question that it was gone now. She sank into the chair behind the desk, overwhelmed by the senselessness of all this. The message, her photograph, a broken clock, love letters and now a partially completed tax audit. She could think of no conceivable relationship between any two of those, let alone all five.

Julie shook her head in frustration, knowing this could get even worse; that there might be other things missing she didn't yet know about. But, at the moment, she had to do something about that file. A burglar stealing a tax audit sounded pretty farfetched. Rigg Stanton would probably think she was a total airhead who'd left it in a taxi.

She forced herself out of the chair. With any luck at all, there'd be backup records at G and K. She'd have to get them. And she'd have to do it tonight if she hoped to manage even a cursory look at everything before calling Rigg in the morning. Julie glanced at her answering machine, checking that it was on, wishing she wasn't going to miss Officer Drake's call. Well, she didn't have any choice. She'd have to get back to him first thing tomorrow. She phoned for a cab, grabbed her gray jacket from the hall closet and headed for the elevators. Mark had always been lax about putting copies of his working papers into the central files. Julie prayed he'd kept the Stanton material up-to-date.

She decided on her plan of action as the taxi headed down Lexington. She'd simply take everything on the Stanton Group that was in Central Records and sort through it for what she needed once she got home. She didn't want to be any longer than absolutely necessary at G and K. The thought of Mark having died, just down the corridor from her own office, made her blood run cold.

Julie flashed her staff ID at the security guard and signed his book. The elevator whisked her to the tenth floor without the stops it generally made during working hours. Its stainless-steel doors swooshed open onto the brass and glass reception area of the G and K offices. Julie glanced about anxiously. Only one panel of lights had been left on and the corridors leading to the offices were in total darkness. She swallowed nervously and flipped on all the light switches beside the receptionist's desk, then headed across the open space and down the short hall leading to Central Records.

The offices were eerily silent. She didn't like being here after hours at the best of times. And this definitely wasn't the best of times. Julie unlocked the door to Central Records, turned on the lights and searched her key chain for the small key that opened the filing cabinets. SN-SZ. She unlocked the drawer and began to check through the green, hanging files. Stabler, Stacey, Stainer, Stanton.

Stanton. Julie swore silently, seeing how skinny the file was, how lightly it hung on the rods. She pulled it open, peered inside and swore again. There was a lone piece of paper on G and K letterhead...the audit agreement signed by her boss and Rigg Stanton. And that was it. Mark had filed no copies of his work! Julie gazed into the empty folder, willing more paper to materialize inside. She ran her hand along the bottom of the file, knowing, even as she did so, that her eyes weren't playing tricks. Except for that single sheet, the file was empty.

And then her fingers slid over the small, flat, smooth object in the crease of the bottom. She traced its outline...a key. She couldn't get it out, yanked the file itself from the rods and opened it flat. A strip of Scotch tape secured the key to the file. Julie slipped her fingernail under the tape, freed the key and inspected it. It was new and shiny, stamped with the number 411. It looked like a filing cabinet key. But the keys to these cabinets were stamped S-100. This 411 must be a key to files at the Stanton offices. Why wouldn't Mark simply have kept it with him? Puzzled, Julie slipped the key into the pocket of her jeans and replaced the file. She shoved the drawer closed, moved her hand to click the lock back in and her arm froze in midair at the sound of the elevator doors sliding open in the reception area.

She stopped breathing, heard the doors close again... then nothing. But her own steps, earlier, had been silent on the plush carpeting. Heart pounding, she moved stealthily toward the door.

"Everything all right in here, miss?"

Julie's hand leaped to her throat at the sound of the man's voice. Then her breath escaped loudly in relief. It was merely the night watchman on his rounds.

"I'm sorry, miss. I didn't mean to startle you. Just on my regular patrol, but I have to check when I see lights on."

Julie nodded, trying to breathe normally. "It's all right. I just wasn't expecting anyone to be here. I guess you weren't, either." She smiled nervously at the man. "I won't be much longer. I have a phone call to make but I'll come back to the reception area with you now."

Julie sat at the reception desk, her fingers nervously tapping her boss's home phone number on the staff directory, knowing she had no choice but to call Ray. Mark hadn't gotten around to making copies. And that meant she'd lost the only copy of the Stanton audit that existed. She felt about two inches tall.

Ray Brent listened in silence while she told him about the break-in and the missing file. "You sound awfully upset, Julie," he said quietly when she finished.

"I am, Ray. What happened in my apartment was crazy and I feel absolutely terrible about the file."

"It couldn't be helped. And, so far as there being no backup goes, that's certainly not your fault. I should have checked Central Records before I distributed the material from Mark's office. But unless the police recover your things right away, we'll have no choice but to do the audit over again. It's going to be a little tight, time-wise."

"I can put in some time on the weekend, Ray. If I start on it tomorrow, I'll have a good idea how things stand by Tuesday."

"I appreciate that, Julie. If it wasn't so hectic right now, it wouldn't be necessary, but, as it is . . ."

"I really don't mind."

"All right. Would you like me to phone Stanton and explain what happened?"

"Thanks, Ray, but I might as well take whatever heat there is myself. I'll have to make arrangements to work in Rigg's offices tomorrow, anyway. It's getting a little late. I'd better try him right now, before I leave here."

The switchboard operator at the Plaza put her call through. Julie bit her lip as Rigg's phone began to ring, hoping he was even half as understanding as Ray had been. He answered the phone and she took a deep breath. "Rigg, it's Julie Lind."

"Julie. I wasn't expecting you to call until the morning. I'm glad to hear from you."

"You won't be in a few minutes," she told him ruefully. Julie gave Rigg a bare-bones account of what had happened and waited anxiously for his reaction. It surprised her.

"You must feel terrible about the break-in, Julie. You're still at G and K?"

"Yes."

"I'll pick you up. I'll be there in fifteen minutes; twenty minutes tops. Wait inside the front door for me."

"No, Rigg, really..." There wasn't any point in continuing her protest. The line was dead. Thoughtfully, Julie replaced the receiver. Why was Rigg Stanton rushing to her rescue like some gallant knight on a white charger or, as the case might be, in a silver Mercedes? Because he was alone in New York and his wife was back home on that ranch they had outside Houston? She hoped that wasn't it, but no other reasonable alternative came to mind. He certainly couldn't want to talk about the audit at ten-thirty at night. Julie sighed apprehensively. If Rigg Stanton turned out to be an octopus, on the loose from Mrs. Octopus, it could make for an awfully difficult and long, long weekend.

RIGG STRODE PURPOSEFULLY along the street toward the office building. The perfectly tailored, charcoal-gray suit he'd worn earlier had been exchanged for a dark pair of casual pants and a creamy fisherman-knit sweater, but he still looked as if he belonged in a Saks display window. Julie glanced down ruefully at her own old jeans and sneakers. Rigg neared the entrance and she opened the glass door into the cool darkness. "Thanks for coming,

Rigg. It was nice of you . . . but, you know, I'm quite used to simply calling a cab."

He shrugged. "You shouldn't be here alone in the middle of the night, Julie. My car's parked just behind that." He gestured to the long furniture van standing in front of the building. They walked, without speaking, toward the Mercedes. A man, huddled on the curb beside the van, toasted Julie with a brown paper bag and Rigg muttered something unintelligible, but clearly uncomplimentary, about the sidewalks of New York.

Rigg started the car and broke the silence. "Was there much damage in your apartment?"

"No . . . In fact, nothing was disturbed at all. It wasn't even obvious, at first, what they'd taken. The whole incident was like one of the weirder scenes from a Pinter play." Briefly, she filled Rigg in on the details, surprised that he didn't seem more concerned that the entire audit would have to be redone.

"So the detective figures it was your ex-boyfriend—this Cramer guy?"

Julie laughed nervously. "Drake isn't a detective, just a uniformed cop who looks so young he makes me feel old. Obviously, my break-in didn't fall into a serious enough crime category to rate a detective. But yes, he did suggest it was Bob. He said ex-boyfriends are likely suspects. I'm sure he's wrong, though. I wouldn't have even considered Bob a possibility except for the coincidence of his calling me today and those letters disappearing. But I really can't believe it was him. Nothing else that was taken made any sense. Why should the letters?"

Rigg nodded. "So you've ruled out the ex-boyfriend. What about your current one?"

Julie glanced at Rigg quickly, his question personal enough to make her a little edgy about its purpose. He was looking straight ahead, no particular expression discernible. "There isn't one," she said simply.

Rigg turned onto East Sixty-ninth, pulled up in front of Julie's building and turned off the ignition. "I'll see you in."

"No. Thanks, but I'll be fine. What time's good for you in the morning?"

"Don't be ridiculous, Julie." Rigg's tone was annoyed; he ignored her question. "You've just been burgled, Drake tells you someone's walking around with a key to your apartment and you expect me to dump you on the sidewalk?"

Julie hesitated, trying to think of a way of saying what she wanted to say without sounding like a fool. "Look, Rigg. I do appreciate your picking me up tonight. And I'm awfully relieved that you're taking this mess with the audit so well. And I would feel better if you came up with me for a minute." She paused, having reached the really sticky part. The last thing she wanted tonight was a wrestling match; she plunged ahead. "Rigg, I'm sure you have nothing on your mind except making certain there's no bogeyman in my apartment, but just in case you do, I don't want you to have the wrong impression. I don't get involved with married men." Well, so much for not sounding like a fool. Julie could feel her face getting warm and was grateful for the dimness of the light. She looked across the small space between them in the little car and saw Rigg was grinning broadly at her.

"Julie, I don't get involved with married men, either. I don't even get involved with unmarried men. But what's your point?"

Julie just stared at him, her face getting hotter by the second. She was already embarrassed as hell and he was teasing her.

His grin subsided a little. "You obviously assume I'm married. Why?"

"Aren't you?"

"No. I'm not. And don't answer a question with a question. I'm curious. What made you think I was?"

Julie shrugged, wanting to be anywhere in the world but here. "When you told me you lived on a ranch, you said *we* have a ranch."

Rigg laughed heartily. "The *we* is my father and I. The ranch is large and he's glad of a hand whenever I'm around. *We* live there. I hope," he went on, still grinning, "that your audits are more accurate than your assumptions or I'll be in big trouble."

Julie buried her burning face in her hands, wishing she were invisible. Finally, she peeked through her fingers at Rigg. "Do you have any idea how stupid I feel?"

Rigg stopped grinning, reached across, took Julie's hands in his own and pulled them away from her face. His touch was surprisingly gentle and alarmingly arousing.

"Don't feel stupid," he said softly. "I have it on the best authority that you were top of your class at NYU."

Julie shook her head. "I wasn't. Ray always exaggerates."

"Well, don't feel stupid, anyway. You didn't sound stupid, just direct. And it's nice to know that you're concerned about not getting involved with married men... How about single ones?"

Julie gazed at Rigg thoughtfully, intensely aware of his large hands dwarfing hers, caressing them lightly with his fingertips, sending tingles of desire through her with each slow stroke of his fingers. "With single ones it depends."

"On?"

"Oh, I have a pretty long list of criteria." Julie tried to keep her tone light, tried to ignore her body's reactions to

Rigg's touch. It was impossible. A liquid warmth was pulsating deep inside her. "Most important," she managed to continue evenly, "they have to laugh at my jokes."

Rigg laughed.

"Did you think that was a joke?" she teased quietly.

"I wouldn't want to take any chances on not meeting your most important criterion, Julie," he said softly. "Let's go in."

The elevator was waiting for them at lobby level. Julie glanced surreptitiously at Rigg as they rode up. Suddenly, the thought of spending her long weekend at the Stanton offices didn't seem like such a terrible fate. Rigg took her arm lightly as they approached her apartment and Julie realized just how nervous she was about going inside. She turned the key in her lock and looked at the doorknob anxiously. "I'm almost afraid to open the door."

Rigg opened the door, preceded her in and walked ahead to the living room. "Very nice," he commented, looking about. "I like Wedgwood blue. And everything seems fine."

"Everything seemed fine this afternoon, too. Want a tour? I could use the company while I check the other rooms." Julie turned lights on as they walked. Asset meowed loudly when the bedroom light flashed on and blinked sleepily at them from the center of the bed. "Sorry, Asset. Go back to sleep." Julie glanced anxiously at the bedroom mirror and saw, with relief, that it was still clean.

Rigg was laughing. "Your cat's name is Asset?"

Julie grinned at him. "You're doing well, Rigg. Two jokes, two laughs. Asset was a graduation gift when I got my C.P.A. I could hardly have named her Liability." Julie turned out the light and led the way to the den. Her answering machine was signaling a message. "Mind if I check that? I had a call in for Drake. He doesn't know about the letters or the file yet.''

Rigg nodded. "Go ahead. Maybe he's found your burglar.''

The first message was indeed from Drake, returning Julie's call. The second was Bob Cramer, sounding upset, asking her to phone him as soon as she got home.

"That the boyfriend?" Rigg asked.

"Ex." Julie grimaced and shrugged at him. The third voice belonged to an older man. His tone was so anxious that, until he said his name, Julie didn't realize it was her stepfather.

"Julie, I hate this damn machine...! Darling, it's Henry. Call us the instant you get in. Something awful has happened! No wait...I don't mean to frighten you. Your mother's fine; nothing's wrong. But call right away, dear. We have to talk to you!"

A cold ring of fear encircled Julie's heart. "My mother," she told Rigg, her voice a mere whisper. "That was her husband. Something's happened to my mother."

Rigg took a step toward her then hesitated. "I'll just be in the living room while you call."

"No! Wait...please wait."

Rigg stepped a little closer, gesturing at the answering machine with obvious disdain. "Your Henry fellow was right, Julie. I hate those damn machines, too. Look how that message upset you and it's probably nothing serious at all. He said your mother was fine. Call her."

Julie nodded, grateful for the comfort of Rigg's logic. Anxiously, she pushed the phone buttons, wanting but not wanting to hear what was wrong in Phoenix. Her mother answered on the first ring. "It's me, Mom." Julie's voice quavered. Rigg shot her a quick, reassuring smile.

"Julie! You're all right?" Her mother's voice was frantic.

"Yes of course. What's the matter? What happened?"

"Nothing's happened here, Julie. But what's going on there. I had the most terrible phone call, darling! Julie . . . he said you were dead!"

Julie's throat went dry.

"What's wrong?" Rigg demanded. "Julie, what is it?"

She tried to speak, felt her lips moving but no sound came out. Her throat was tight with fear. Who had called her mother? What had he said? Why? So many questions and she couldn't force out a single word. She shook her head silently at Rigg.

He stared at Julie's ashen face, distress and confusion written plainly across it, and felt his protective instinct shift into high gear. Tentatively, he put one arm around her shoulder. Her body was tense. The receiver rested limply in her hand but he could hear her mother was speaking again. He took the receiver. "This is Rigg Stanton. I'm a friend of your daughter's. What's happened? Can I help?"

A man's voice was audible in the background, trying to calm Julie's mother. After a moment, the man came on the line.

"Julie?"

"No. Rigg Stanton. I'm a friend of Julie's. What's going on?"

The man exhaled loudly at the other end. "Well thank heavens she has someone there with her. I'm Henry Schaeffer, Julie's stepfather. Grace had a call about half an hour ago from a man who told her Julie was dead."

"What?" Rigg demanded incredulously.

"Said he was someone who worked with Julie and that he'd been asked to call and tell us Julie had been killed in a traffic accident this afternoon. Grace was hysterical...couldn't talk coherently enough to give me any clear details of what he'd said. Something about a black van jumping the curb and knocking Julie down on the sidewalk. Well, we'd met Julie's boss when we were in New York last fall, so I called him to try and find out what had happened... figured if this fellow from her office knew about it, Ray would too. Ray said he'd spoken to Julie on the phone less than an hour ago and that her apartment had been broken into but she was absolutely fine. There'd definitely been no accident this afternoon. That's when I called her apartment and left the message.''

Rigg's mind was reeling. "Everything's all right, Julie," he whispered, stroking her back. "It's all right." He tried to make sense out of this cruel hoax. "She is fine," he spoke into the phone again. "Just upset."

"Well, that's not a surprise. Here, Grace wants to talk to her."

Rigg held the receiver to Julie's ear.

"I am all right, Mom," Julie whispered after a moment. "Yes, I did call the police. I will call them again.... No... I'll phone you in the morning. Mom...did the man who called you give his name?"

Julie's face turned paler than Rigg would have thought possible. She stared up at him, wide-eyed, looking every bit a vulnerable child. "Rigg," she whispered hoarsely, "he told her he was Mark Thompson!"

Chapter Three

SATURDAY MORNING, 2:00 a.m.

Detective Wilcott tapped his pen absently on his note-book and glanced slowly about Julie's living room once more. His jowled face was void of expression but Julie doubted his pale, blue eyes were missing a thing. She wasn't certain if she should be relieved or concerned that her problems now rated a detective instead of a uniform, but at least Wilcott looked as if he'd had twenty-five or so years of experience.

She was still keenly aware of the nervous tension in her muscles, the churning anxiety in her stomach, but Wilcott's somber presence was reassuring...as was Rigg's. Julie glanced at him, on the couch beside her, and he reached over to give her hand a quick, comforting squeeze. She smiled a little, grateful he'd insisted on staying with her until Wilcott finally arrived. She jumped when the detective broke the silence.

"And you've discovered nothing else missing."

Julie shook her head. Wilcott had, she'd noted, a knack of asking questions in the form of statements. "Only the things in Officer Drake's report—and then the letters and the file."

The detective looked down at the initial report again. "Drake talked to this Cramer fellow before he went off duty tonight. He get back to you since then?"

"There was a message on my machine—messages from both of them, in fact—but I didn't return either of the calls."

"Well, Cramer's not a viable suspect. At least, he couldn't have been here in person. When he phoned you earlier...around five..." Julie nodded and he continued. "It turns out he was calling from the airport in Tucson. He definitely wasn't in your apartment today."

"Tucson?" Julie shook her head, confused. "He didn't tell me that when he called. I just assumed he was at home. Why wouldn't he have mentioned he was calling long distance?"

Wilcott shrugged. "Does seem a little unusual." He made a quick note. "He was definitely in Tucson, though. According to Drake, he'd been away a couple of days, had hotel and taxi receipts, his plane ticket stub. He didn't land at La Guardia until after seven-thirty tonight."

"I didn't really believe it could have been Bob," Julie said slowly. "But who? Someone who knows me...and knows where my mother lives...even has to know her remarried name to have gotten her phone number. Someone who knew Mark Thompson as well? There just can't be many people."

"You keep an address book by your phone?"

Julie nodded.

"Your mother's number listed under 'Mother'?"

She nodded again, slowly, realizing what the detective was getting at.

"And what about Thompson's name? Would it have been on anything in that file?"

Julie thought. Everything except the initial audit agreement she'd seen tonight would have been in Mark's working file. "Yes. There could have been several things. I'm sure there'd at least have been a letter of direction from my boss to Mark—probably stapled right onto the inside of the cover."

Wilcott looked at her questioningly.

"The senior partners," she explained, "Ray Brent in this case, are responsible for the audits at G and K. But they assign the actual work to someone else. The letter of direction would have assigned the Stanton Group audit to Mark."

Wilcott nodded. "So it wasn't necessarily someone who knew anything about Mark or your mother or even about you. All the names, numbers and places were right here in your apartment. And so was he."

Julie shivered a little.

"Let's get back to this Thompson fellow for a minute," Wilcott continued. "How well did you know him?"

"Just as a work associate. I've been at Grant and Kellog four years. Mark was working there when I started. We were on friendly terms but not close friends. We didn't see each other socially, never even had lunch together. We chatted now and then, but more because our offices are...were...near each other than because of anything else." Julie shook her head. "Someone calling my mother and giving Mark's name doesn't make any sense. This entire day hasn't made any sense."

"But," Wilcott pressed on, "the file that was stolen contained what Thompson was working on at the time he killed himself."

Julie grimaced.

"The suicide upset you?"

"Yes, but..." She caught herself, knowing it was pointless to raise the issue of her doubts.

"But?" Wilcott prodded.

"Well, what upsets me most of all—and I realize it's irrational—is that I haven't been able to shake the feeling it wasn't suicide."

"You told Homicide that?"

Julie nodded.

"And?"

"And apparently the evidence said it was."

"So, what makes you think it was something else?"

Julie could feel tears welling up. She bit her lip, wishing she hadn't started into this again. She'd had enough of it earlier in the week. "His sons," she managed, again picturing the two small boys at the funeral. "Whenever we did chat, he always ended up talking about them. He was so crazy about them...." She swallowed with difficulty. "He just wouldn't have," she concluded lamely.

"And what did Homicide say about that?"

Julie shrugged miserably. "Gave me some Psych 101 theory about never knowing what was going on in someone else's mind."

"That figures. The boys at Homicide aren't big on intuition." Wilcott made a brief note and turned his attention to Rigg. "And this file of Thompson's was about your company. How well did you know him?"

"Not at all. I'd only met him once, just this past Monday, in fact, just the day before he died. The Stanton Group has its own accounting department. G and K is simply our external audit company for reporting and tax purposes. It's the watchdog for our investors and the IRS. Mark was at our offices for most of the past couple of weeks...to make sure we're honest. But he was dealing with my vice president. I spend most of my time in Texas. This is the first week I've been in New York this month.''

Wilcott nodded. ''Your vice president's name?''

''Neil Overbach.''

The detective made a final notation and snapped his book closed. ''You might mention to Overbach that I'll be contacting him.'' He turned back to Julie. ''Well, that's all I need for the moment. I'll call you if we turn something up and you give me a shout if you find anything else is missing or you have any more trouble.'' Wilcott eased his bulky frame out of the chair, glanced down at his arm and paused to pick a few strands of long, white hair off the sleeve of his dark suit.

Julie shrugged in embarrassment. ''Sorry. That's the cat's favorite chair. I've learned to wear a lot of white. But I guess that's not much help so far as men's suits go,'' she added lamely.

Wilcott grinned for the first time since he'd arrived. ''That's all right. I have a dog myself, and my wife insists on brushing off my suit on my way out of the house every day.'' He paused, one hand on the door, dug a card out of his pocket with the other and handed it to Julie. ''Get your locks changed and keep an eye out for the next little while. But with any luck, this'll be the end of your trouble. Your burglar may simply have been some sicko who's into very warped practical jokes. If anything else does happen, call me. I'm out of the precinct a lot of the time but I always check in for messages before I go off duty.''

Julie nodded, thanked Wilcott and closed the door behind him. She turned and shrugged ruefully at Rigg. ''You certainly got a later night than you bargained for.''

Rigg smiled at her. ''What's a little beauty sleep here and there? But what about you, Julie? You going to be able to sleep at all tonight?''

"Like you said, what's a little beauty sleep? Maybe I'll read for a while. I have some tax regulation updates to go over. If anything can put me to sleep they will."

She smiled at Rigg, but it was clearly not a happy smile. She looked tired and frightened and so damn vulnerable he didn't see how he could just walk out the door and leave her here alone. "Want me to stay for a while?" he offered, hoping he sounded more casual about the suggestion than he felt.

Julie hesitated for a moment, then shook her head firmly. "I'll be fine. What time do you want to get started tomorrow?"

What time? Rigg shrugged. Right now, Julie didn't look as if she'd be up to working any time tomorrow. But he wanted to see her. "How about having lunch together and we can go over to the office after that?"

"Well..." The sudden ring of her phone interrupted them. She glanced nervously at the extension in the living room and then at her watch.

"Want me to answer it, Julie?"

"No... The machine will take it after the third ring."

The phone rang a second time. Rigg followed Julie along the hall to the den and stopped in the doorway. She was standing stiffly in front of the answering machine, watching it intently. Rigg felt the tension in his own stomach as they stood, waiting for it to activate. He knew Julie's anxiety level had to be sky-high. The machine clicked on, gave her prerecorded message and beeped. Rigg recognized Bob Cramer's voice from his previous message.

"Julie, I know it's late but I've been waiting for hours for you to return my call. The police were here to see me earlier. I'm sorry you've been having problems. But that makes what I have to talk to you about even more important. Please call me in the morning. Don't forget we have a date for dinner.''

Julie's body sagged with obvious relief.

"I thought he was an ex," Rigg said quietly, wondering just how this woman defined ex-boyfriends.

"He is. When I talked with him before, he insisted he had to discuss something important.'' She shrugged and glanced back at the answering machine. "I hope that's the last message for the night. My imagination's running away on me.''

Rigg hesitated, not wanting to sound totally inappropriate, but not wanting to go. "Julie," he said finally, "I don't feel right about you staying here alone tonight. You just about climbed the wall when that phone rang. What's going to happen if it rings again?''

Julie paused for a moment. "I guess I'll get nervous... or maybe I'll unplug the phones. It's almost 3:00 a.m. The middle of the night's a little late to start thinking about calling up a friend to stay over.''

"There's me. I'm here already.''

She smiled wanly. "Rigg, I'm not some abandoned puppy you picked up on the street and have to feel responsible for. I'm a grown woman and you've done more than enough for me tonight. Really, I'll be fine.''

Rigg read an entirely different message in her worried expression. "Look, Julie, let's just think about this from my selfish point of view. If I leave, all I'll do is spend the rest of the night worrying about you. For whatever reason, I do feel responsible. It was my file that disappeared. It's as likely your break-in had something to do with that as with anything else that was taken. Look," he rushed on, seeing she was about to object again, "I won't stay very long, only as long as you want me to—only until you're tired enough to sleep.''

Julie hesitated. This situation was getting crazier by the minute. She'd known Rigg Stanton for less than twelve hours. And he was a client, which made his even being here now totally inappropriate. And . . . and the last thing she wanted in the world was to stay here alone tonight. "How are you at Scrabble, Rigg?"

He shrugged nonchalantly. "You don't play poker?"

"Accountants don't gamble. We're too conservative."

Rigg nodded. "Get the Scrabble board. It'll take me back to the innocence of my youth."

JULIE WOKE WITH A START. The fabric against her face wasn't soft percale, it was the tightly woven, blue-and-white tapestry of her couch. She shaded her eyes against the bright sunlight that streamed through the living room windows and looked across the coffee table at Rigg, slouched, asleep, in the overstuffed armchair, his long legs stretching in front of him. The Scrabble board on the table between them was covered with words.

The horrors of yesterday came streaming back into Julie's consciousness. She forced them into the recesses of her mind and focused on Rigg. He hadn't been a dream after all. He had actually been here, watching over her during the night like some self-appointed guardian angel.

His discarded sweater lay in a heap on the floor and the brushed cotton shirt he'd worn beneath it stretched tightly against his body, delineating the firm muscularity of his chest and shoulders. Tousled hair covered his forehead; the stubble of his beard had darkened his face. And still, Rigg Stanton was heartbreakingly handsome. He was simply too good to be true. Remember, the cynical voice of experience whispered in Julie's ear, when a man seems too good to be true, he usually is.

She started coffee and peeked back into the living room. Rigg was awake, rubbing his neck gingerly. She grinned at him from the doorway. "Looks like you're going to pay for falling asleep in the chair."

"It was that damn game." He nodded at the board. "I knew we should have played poker. Scrabble's boring enough to put anyone to sleep."

Julie laughed. "Someday you can teach me poker."

"You're on. How about the next time I sleep over?"

"Your assumptions seem to be getting a little questionable," Julie pointed out with a quiet smile.

Rigg picked the cream-colored fisherman-knit sweater off the floor and inspected it. "Oh, I don't know about that. There's not a single cat hair visible on this. Even my wardrobe fits in here."

Julie shook her head and grinned. "You haven't gotten around to checking those dark pants yet. But don't criticize my housekeeping; I'm well aware of my failings. At least I can cook, though. I have coffee on. Want something to eat with it?"

Rigg's amused look admonished her for switching subjects, but he let it pass. "Thanks, but all I want is a cup of coffee. Then I'll head on back to the Plaza for a shower and shave. As far as eating goes, it's practically lunchtime. I've always heard you New Yorkers were go-go-go. But if you're any example, it's all been lies. The truth seems to be that you're a slothful bunch."

"I woke up before you," Julie teased. "Besides, I think entertaining a police detective for half the night entitles even a New Yorker to sleep late."

"Well, keep in mind it's an hour earlier in Texas." Rigg protested. "That's got to count for something in my favor. Anyway, how about catching lunch someplace in an hour or two?"

"Sounds good. And then we can go to your office so that slothful old me can get started on the audit."

Rigg hesitated. That wasn't quite what he'd had in mind. Julie Lind had dropped into his life out of the blue yesterday, a totally unexpected windfall, and his backlog of work in New York had suddenly faded to insignificance. He'd been contemplating a more pleasant day, today, than working. "Julie, let's take the day off. Maybe you can have a look at things tomorrow but, after yesterday, I think you deserve a break."

"No, I'm fine, Rigg. Really. New Yorkers may be slothful but we're resilient. And Wilcott probably hit the nail bang on—my visitor was just some sicko I'll never hear from again. At any rate, I told Ray I'd get going on your audit first thing today." She smiled ruefully. "That makes me a liar already, doesn't it? But if we're going to get it completed before your reporting deadline, I just can't afford to waste any more time."

Rigg didn't give a damn, at the moment, about any deadline. If the tax return was filed late, he'd simply pay the fine. But Julie clearly didn't see the situation in the same light. She'd been given a job to do and was obviously determined to do it properly. He wondered how stubborn she was about other things. "All right. If you're going to insist on working, why don't we just have lunch in the Oyster Bar. At least in the Plaza we're sure of getting good service."

"The Oyster Bar it is then."

"Fine. I'll be back to pick you up in an hour."

Julie laughed that tinkling laugh that made him smile every time he heard it. "On a day like this?" She shook her head. "I'll walk."

"No problem. I don't mind coming back." Rigg smiled, not wanting Julie to sense his concern. He didn't relish letting her out of his sight at all, at least not until they were certain today wouldn't be a replay of yesterday.

"Thanks, Rigg, but I'd prefer to walk. I walk everywhere. I'm not into fitness clubs so it's the only exercise I get. It's just ten blocks. Tell you what. Take my briefcase with you in the car and I'll meet you outside the Oyster Bar at noon."

And that, Rigg realized, answered his question about how stubborn Julie was. She didn't come on as aggressive, but she certainly wasn't going to be pushed around.

Julie slid the bar lock behind Rigg. She probably shouldn't be having lunch with him. She should be grabbing something at a deli and starting work. Well, she rationalized, lunch at the Plaza was difficult to resist. She grinned to herself. Who was she kidding? It was Rigg Stanton who was difficult to resist. The annoying little voice in her ear spoke up again. *The Stanton Group,* it reminded her, *is the subject of your audit, which makes socializing with its president more than a little dicey. And, if that isn't enough, remember he lives in Texas, not in New York; he'll be gone again in a day or two. Don't get any foolish ideas, Julie Lind,* the little voice concluded.

She hated that little voice of common sense. It was such a spoilsport...and it was almost always right. Julie grabbed some clean lingerie and headed for the shower. She was barely dressed again when there was a tap on her door. She swallowed anxiously. People didn't wander freely in and out of the apartment house, and no one had buzzed to be let in the front door. And, she reminded herself nervously, it wasn't likely anyone had been buzzed in yesterday, before they'd done their number on her apartment.

She walked quietly along the hall and peered out through the peephole in the door. With a sigh of relief, she slid the bar lock and opened the door to Charlie Thomas.

The super grinned his toothy grin at her. "Just wanted to let you know someone will be changing your locks today. Will you be home this afternoon?"

Julie shook her head. "I'm just on my way out. I won't likely be back until five or so."

"Well, don't worry, Miss Lind. I can look after everything for you. Just stop by my place when you get back and pick up your new keys." Charlie hesitated. "What did the police officer have to say yesterday?" he finally asked. "Could he tell how the guy got into your apartment?"

"He said there was no sign of forced entry, that someone must have had a key. I suppose it's possible. The same lock's been on this door for years. I guess somewhere along the way I was careless, or my mother was. Anyway, I'll feel a lot better once you've had it changed."

Charlie nodded. "So will I. I feel really badly about what happened here. Wouldn't want anyone to think I wasn't doing my job."

Julie smiled encouragingly. "I can't imagine anyone would think that, Charlie. We'll just get the lock changed and forget about it."

The super appeared extremely relieved and Julie closed the door, wishing she felt half as reassured as Charlie Thomas had looked.

RIGG CHECKED HIS WATCH for the nineteenth time in the past ten minutes, looked up, and saw with relief that Julie was heading across the elegant lobby of the Plaza toward him. She was wearing a white dress that swirled around her legs with each step like some cotton cloud. Her pale hair was pulled back into a braid and her bangs had been tossed by the wind into a jumble of corn silk. She saw him, flashed him an impossibly white smile and brushed her bangs more or less into place with one hand.

Rigg gestured at her white dress as she reached him. "I see you're wearing an Asset special."

Julie grinned wryly in reply. "If I ever have another cat, it's going to be a bald one." She smiled across the table at Rigg once the maître d' had completed his flourishing. "You looked as if you'd decided I wasn't going to show. I was barely ten minutes late. Accountants don't have to be totally obsessional, you know."

"I guess I jumped the gun a little on worrying. Maybe yesterday is still bothering me, but I'd have felt better picking you up. There seems to be a loony on every street corner in this town."

"I gather," Julie said quietly, "you're not overly fond of my city."

Rigg heard what was definitely a defensive tone in her voice and regretted his sarcasm. But there was no point in lying to her. "Not overly fond," he admitted. "It's the number of people, and the number of crazies. Houston is big, but it sprawls all over. I guess I'm too used to the wide-open spaces of Texas to feel at home in the closed-in spaces of New York.

To his relief, Julie laughed. "Those wide-open spaces would probably give me agoraphobia. In fact, I'm such a city slicker that I might not even recognize an open space if I saw one."

Rigg shook his head. "You mean to tell me I've been saddled with an auditor who has both phobias and perceptual problems?"

"Don't exaggerate, Rigg. I'm one of the few New Yorkers I know who's never been in analysis. And I only admitted to a possible phobia, not phobias. But," she continued more seriously, "if you don't like New York, what made you start up your eastern division here? Why not some other city?"

"It was a simple business decision. Real estate development was booming in Houston until the oil bubble burst. Now, it's redevelopment in Manhattan that's hot. The Stanton Group is basically a syndicate of investors. I decide on the investments, oversee the operations and earn a percentage of the syndicate's profits. If the investors don't make any money I don't make any money. I have to keep everybody happy; that means new projects, new profits."

The waiter, arriving with menus, interrupted them. Julie barely glanced at the menu. "Just Perrier and a Caesar salad . . . extra garlic, please," she told the man.

Rigg nodded that he'd have the same and reached hungrily for a roll. "A person could starve to death eating with you," he complained. "The only thing I approve of is the extra garlic—wards off the werewolves." He was pleased when Julie laughed at his remark.

"Werewolves haven't been much of a problem for New York for years, Rigg. Aside from the odd one lurking in Central Park, they're pretty well extinct here. But I guess you must still get a lot of them in Texas, what with all those wide-open spaces."

Rigg grinned. "Every time there's a full moon, we just quake in our boots."

Julie laughed again. "I don't think there's another full moon until the middle of June. I guess we'll be safe at night for a while yet." Her face clouded over as she finished speaking and Rigg realized she was still every bit as worried as he was about what had happened yesterday.

The arrival of the salads, interrupting their thoughts, was timely.

"Did you remember to call your mother back this morning?" Rigg asked once the waiter had left.

Julie nodded. "That's why I was late. She didn't want to let me hang up. I didn't have time to phone Bob, though. I'll have to call him from your office. I'm supposed to be having dinner with him tonight.

Not if I can help it, Rigg vowed silently. "I phoned our internal accountant after I got back to the Plaza," he said aloud. "She's going to meet us about two; give you a brief run-through of the office files."

"You're dragging some other poor woman in to work on a beautiful day like this? I imagine she was absolutely delighted to hear from you!"

Rigg grinned. "It's all in the line of duty. I figured it would save you some time. And, with Tracy there to show you where everything is, I won't have to be embarrassed over how little I know about the nitty-gritty of the office routines."

Julie smiled at him. "Nitty-gritty isn't what the president gets paid for, is it?"

"Well, anyway, there's no need to feel sorry for Tracy. I'm sure she'll convince Neil she deserves at least three long weekends in June to make up for this imposition. He's doing a great job for us here, but when it comes to Tracy I don't think he can see straight. You don't know her, do you, Julie? Tracy Alders? She'd be about your age; probably did her C.P.A. around the same time."

"I don't recognize her name. But she likely went to school in Timbuktu and Tuktoyaktuk or some other remote place. Sometimes I think I'm one of about eight native New Yorkers in the entire city. Everyone I meet seems to have migrated here from somewhere else." Julie shook her head and turned her attention to the large salad.

Rigg signaled for the bill when they'd finished eating. "What'll it be? The car or another walk?"

"Walk," Julie told him decisively.

They strolled in the dazzling sunlight along Central Park South toward Rigg's offices. The sidewalk teemed with bodies. "I thought you said everyone would be going away for the long weekend," Rigg teased as they stopped to let a horde of children, accompanied by an extremely frazzled-looking woman, rush past.

"Most of them have. There can't be more than seven, maybe seven and a half million people left in all of Manhattan. And, good grief, Rigg, the island's huge—more than twenty-two square miles!"

He shook his head ruefully. "Huge? I was right! You do have perceptual problems. Either that or a definite gift for overstatement. The Dallas-Forth Worth Airport's bigger than this island. My cattle have a whole lot more room per head than New Yorkers have."

Julie made a face at him. "Isn't there some saying about bigger not necessarily being better?"

Rigg grinned. "There's probably some saying about anything you could imagine." Including, he added silently, glancing at the way Julie's hair glistened in the sunshine as they walked, the one about the bigger they are, the harder they fall.

Chapter Four

Julie's gaze drifted across the open expanse of the Stanton Group offices. They comprised the top floor of a recently renovated building near Fifty-sixth and Ninth, and skylights virtually made up the roof, allowing sunshine to splash freely over the heavy, dark wood and leather furniture below. The contrast between the modern, white office space and the traditional furniture was effective. "Your own building?" she asked Rigg.

He nodded. "The company's into collecting rents, not paying them."

Tracy Alders was waiting for them, apparently not the least perturbed about being summoned to the office on a Saturday. Small and very pretty, with shaggy, dark hair and huge hazel eyes, she wore a casual, checked shirt, a short denim skirt and extremely high heels that still left her several inches shorter than Julie.

Rigg introduced the women. "I'll leave the tour up to you, Tracy. I'll be in my office if you need me."

Tracy grinned at Rigg's departing back. "He's quite a hunk, isn't he?"

Julie laughed, taken somewhat aback by Tracy's forthright observation. "If I told you I hadn't noticed, you probably wouldn't believe me, would you?"

"Not for a second. I do have eyes. He's a nice guy, too, but he's not my type at all. Men who are better looking than I am make me extremely nervous. My shrink says it's a manifestation of a basic insecurity, something I have to work on...one of several somethings, in fact." Tracy shrugged, as if dismissing whatever the other somethings were as inconsequential. "It's just as well I don't have the hots for Rigg," she continued with a grin. "He's hardly ever in New York. In fact, I was surprised when he arrived at the office Monday morning. We weren't expecting him.

"Rigg told me a bit about your break-in," Tracy went on, switching subjects abruptly, "about how the file had disappeared from your apartment. Must have been awfully upsetting."

"It was. It's the only time anything like that's ever happened to me."

Tracy nodded. "Rigg said it was all pretty weird. The police have any idea why somebody would take the working papers for our audit?"

"I think their best guess is that the burglar has a warped mind." Julie recalled Drake's theory and frowned. "Although the young cop, the one who came initially, figured it was someone who knew me. I certainly hope that was just the voice of inexperience. I'd hate to think anyone I know would do something like that. Did Rigg tell you the guy called my mother later?"

Tracy shook her head; Julie filled her in. Tracy shivered visibly. "I think I'd go with the warped-mind hypothesis. Nobody has friends like that." Tracy hesitated, as if uncertain whether Julie might be about to tell her more. Finally, she pointed in the direction of several canary-yellow filing cabinets. "Where do we have to start?

Did you have a chance to go over Mark's records at all? Can we just pick up some details?"

Julie sighed. "I'm afraid we're right back at square one. I hadn't even opened Mark's file, let alone looked through it."

Tracy nodded. "Square one it is then. You'll find everything's in pretty good shape."

The more Tracy told her about the Stanton Group systems the more relieved Julie felt. Tracy obviously knew what she was doing. The accounting principles she'd based procedures on were appropriate for a real estate development company and the receivables appeared to be completely up-to-date. Tracy concluded her briefing and Julie smiled at her gratefully. "I feel a lot better than I did when Ray Brent first handed this over to me, Tracy, and a whole world better than I did when I found out that file was missing. I hope Rigg and Neil appreciate what you do for them."

Tracy laughed. "If they do you'd never know it! I'm overworked, underpaid and neither of them is about to admit that this entire office would grind to a halt if I didn't show up one day. But if that day came, Rigg would be in Houston, Neil would be out scouting new acquisitions and our office staff would be sitting here filing their fingernails because I wasn't here telling them what to do."

She shook her head and grinned. "Actually, I'm exaggerating—another of my 'somethings' that I'm working on. The truth is, Neil knew what I could do before I ever started here. He's been involved in Manhattan real estate for years and I worked for a company that operates much like the Stanton Group. Neil lured me away from it.

"He wanted someone he could depend on to look after the day-to-day details. I have the financial background but Neil has the street smarts and he spends most of his time away from the office inspecting potential properties, troubleshooting with contractors and suppliers, that type of thing. He needed someone who could handle the office end of the operation. He hired me for my brains and my knowledge of the real estate business. He's sort of gotten the rest of me as a bonus." She glanced knowingly at Julie. "He's no Rigg Stanton as far as looks go, but I'm crazy about him."

Julie tried not to reveal her surprise. Neil Overbach hadn't struck her as anybody's romantic ideal, let alone someone as attractive as Tracy. "Well, if you're the one with the office brains, I'm glad it was Neil who went away this weekend, not you."

Tracy grinned an infectious grin. "Rigg's lucky I was at loose ends. Otherwise, I'd be snarling at the two of you. But Neil's folks retired to Florida last year and he's on his first duty visit this weekend. And he isn't quite ready yet to do the introduce-her-to-the-parents routine." Tracy laughed. "I'm working on it, though; I'd say by Thanksgiving, at the latest."

"Well, to a happy Thanksgiving, then." Julie smiled, miming a toast. "I guess now that Rigg's dragged you in here, we'd better get started."

An hour later, Tracy placed a list of company names on the desk Julie was using. "These are our major payables and receivables." She tapped her finger on the first name. "Craig Howarth is the general contractor we use for the majority of our renovation work. He direct-orders most of the material he needs and forwards the various suppliers' invoices to us. He tends to use the same suppliers all the time so you'll definitely want to do verifications with some of them. I've indicated the most important ones."

Julie glanced at the list and nodded. "That's great. You've given me more than enough to keep me going. I can get the verification letters ready to go out when the city revs up for business Tuesday morning. We'll use a courier both ways, and with any luck the replies will start coming back before the end of the week. In the meantime, why don't you get going now, while there's still some of the day left to enjoy?''

"You're sure there's nothing else you'll be needing before Tuesday?''

"Tracy, I'll be thrilled if I get through all of this. I'm feeling more than a little overwhelmed at the moment.''

"Okay. I'll see you on Tuesday then. Have a good weekend." Tracy nodded meaningfully toward Rigg's office.

Julie laughed, rising to walk with Tracy to the elevator. "It's a purely professional relationship.''

"Whatever you say, Julie." Tracy glanced back at Rigg's half-open door. "Bye, Rigg,'' she called. "See you next time you're in town.''

Rigg appeared in the doorway and Julie noticed he'd removed his suit jacket and loosened his tie since they'd arrived. Tracy was right. He was quite a hunk...and a nice guy. But, if he really wasn't Tracy's type, she certainly differed from Julie there. Rigg Stanton was very definitely her type. It was unfortunate he was also a client. Otherwise...

Rigg strode across the office to join them. "Thanks again for coming in, Tracy.''

She tossed her head. "No big deal. Don't work Julie too hard." The elevator door opened; she grinned at the two of them and disappeared inside.

Rigg glanced back at the files spread across the desk. "Looks like you've made a good start, and I'm at a good point for a break. How about playing hooky for the rest of the day, Julie? You could give me a tour of the wide-open spaces of Central Park and then I'll buy you dinner."

"Oh Lord, Rigg! I forgot all about calling Bob. Thanks for the offer but I've got that date with him tonight. Would you mind if I phone him now? He'll be wondering why I haven't called back."

"Sure. Call him. But Julie, before you do...you did say he was an 'ex.' And he lives in New York whereas I'm only here for a few days. I don't mean to sound pushy, but could you break your date? Have dinner with me instead? I really do enjoy your company."

Rigg's dark eyes caught Julie's. He gazed at her steadily and she hesitated. Spending more time with Rigg Stanton was something she'd like, something she'd like very much. But it wasn't a wise idea under the circumstances. She shook her head. "Thanks, but I really can't."

He nodded slowly. "Julie, before you call Bob..."

Rigg touched Julie's cheek softly with his fingertips and an electric current of anticipation raced through her body. He tilted her face slightly and bent to kiss her. His mouth felt amazingly soft and warm against hers and his musky, masculine scent enveloped her. His lips moved slowly and gently against Julie's and his mouth began to play, teasingly, with her bottom lip so that his tongue could slip easily inside her mouth. It probed tantalizingly against her sensitive skin, making tiny circles on the inner surfaces of her lips, making her shiver with delight, making her want him to go on kissing her forever.

Tentatively, Julie rested her palms against Rigg's chest. She could feel his heart beating as rapidly as her own. His body felt warm and wonderful to her touch. She slid her hands across the fine smoothness of his shirt, her fingers tracing the firm muscles beneath it. Rigg captured her fingers with one hand and his tongue continued the lazy circles of his kiss. Her entire body began to tingle. Instinctively, Julie moved closer so that the length of their bodies were touching and the tingling within her became a steady throbbing.

Rigg's hand shifted from Julie's cheek to softly caress the side of her neck. His other hand released hers and trailed slowly down her back, pulling her body tightly to his own, crushing her breasts against his chest. His hand drifted lower, drawing Julie's entire body even closer, pressing his hips against hers, not attempting to conceal his hard arousal. The heavy, throbbing response deep inside her became a rhythmic ache of desire.

Julie ran her hands across Rigg's back, massaging the firmness of his body. Her fingers wound themselves around the hair that curled down onto his shirt collar and her tongue played a lover's game with his.

Finally, Rigg released her from his kiss, but he continued to embrace her tightly, whispering softly against her ear, his breath warm and tantalizing on her bare neck. "Julie, I've wanted to hold you like this since the first moment I saw you. And it feels even better than I'd imagined. I don't want to let you go for a single minute. I certainly don't want to let you go off to spend the evening with some other man!"

Rigg brushed Julie's bangs aside and kissed her forehead tenderly. His fingers began to caress the side of her neck once more, making it impossible for her to think of any alternative but breaking her date and spending the evening with Rigg. She pushed gently against his chest and he loosened his hold slightly. "Just let me sit down for a minute, Rigg."

Rigg sat beside Julie on one of the leather couches, reached for her hands and began to stroke them slowly. Julie stared at her hands in his, wishing she wanted him to stop caressing them. "Look, Rigg," she said, gazing at him evenly, "it isn't that I'm trying to play hard to get, but you're putting me in a very compromising position. I'm auditing your company's records. It simply isn't ethical for me to be spending time with you aside from that. And certainly not this kind of time." She glanced meaningfully at his hand, holding hers.

"But you'd like to?"

"Of course I'd like to. If you hadn't realized that earlier, it became pretty obvious a few minutes ago, didn't it? But that isn't the point. The point is, I shouldn't be socializing, for lack of a better word, with you while I'm auditing the Stanton Group."

Rigg gazed at her for a moment, then exhaled slowly. "You're right. I wasn't thinking of you as an auditor just then. Sorry. I guess, ethically, I should be every bit as concerned about keeping things kosher as you are. And I don't imagine there's any way of suggesting to Ray that he have someone else take over the audit."

Julie shook her head. "You can't do that. Things are crazy at G and K right now. Everyone's overloaded with work and I've already got a start made on this. Ray's counting on me to get it done."

"Well then, why don't we simply put the Stanton Group and G and K out of our minds for the rest of the day. Who's to know if we socialize? It's a big city. We aren't very likely to run into Ray Brent in Central Park, are we?"

"Rigg, it isn't only Ray," Julie protested firmly. "There simply shouldn't be anything for anybody to know. And Tracy already made a couple of remarks after seeing us together for about three seconds. We must have been emitting sparks or something."

Rigg grasped Julie's hands even more firmly in his. "Doesn't that tell you something then, Julie? I don't know about you, but I haven't emitted many sparks in my life. If that's what being near you does to me, then near you is where I want to be. Julie, I have to go back to Texas on Monday. By the time I'm here again the audit will probably be finished and my seeing you won't be a problem. But let's not miss out on whatever time we can spend together now. I don't want to miss any possible moment." He gazed at her steadily. "Cancel your date?"

Julie hesitated, a battle raging between her common sense and her heart. She drew her hands free, allowing her common sense a little more advantage. "Look Rigg," she said slowly, "the next time you're in New York, if you're still interested, I'd enjoy seeing you ... very much. But for the couple of weeks that I'll be working here, I don't want to feel uncomfortable every time Tracy or Neil looks at me, or every time I have to talk to Ray about something. And I know the state licensing board, even more than Ray, would view my seeing you socially in a very dim light."

Rigg shook his head slowly, the merest trace of a smile on his lips. "Julie, first you tell me you don't want me in your apartment because you don't get involved with married men. I assure you I'm not married, and the next thing I know you're saying you can't have dinner with me because I'm a client. If I wasn't so certain that you have excellent taste, I'd be worried that you just don't want anything to do with me, period. What do I have to do? Find myself a new accounting firm just so you'll go out with me?"

Julie laughed. "I also wouldn't have anything to do with a man who got me into trouble with my boss. And I guarantee that Ray wouldn't be at all pleased if G and K lost your account." She paused, then continued more seriously. "Wait until after the audit's done, Rigg. I promise I won't come up with any more objections then."

"You promise?"

Julie nodded.

"And, in the meantime, we can be friends?"

"Of course."

"Then, Julie, suppose you have this friend—that's all he is—just a friend who's in town for a couple of days and is desperate for a walk in Central Park and someone to have dinner with. Couldn't you see your way clear to spend a little time with this friend? Couldn't you explain the situation to Bob?"

Julie started to say no, but Rigg touched her lips gently with his fingertips, sending a warm shiver through her. "Just friends, Julie," he assured her softly. "Not even one more kiss until you've finished the damn audit. I give you my word." He grinned at her. "And you know, ma'am, Texans have a code of honor when it comes to women and horses."

Julie couldn't help laughing and Rigg rushed on, seizing his advantage. "Julie, I promise I'll be the soul of circumspection if we run into anyone who knows you. I'll even promise to talk business over dinner if it'll make you feel better."

Julie sighed. Bob was one of the last people she wanted to see tonight. And Rigg Stanton was very, very far from last. "Okay," she agreed hesitantly, "but I want it on record that this is against my better judgment."

Rigg grinned. "Thanks, friend. I'll get my jacket while you call Bob."

Julie dialed reluctantly and breathed a sigh of relief when Bob's answering machine took her call. Leaving a message would be much easier than feeling obliged to explain herself to him. The beep sounded and she took a deep breath. "Bob, I apologize but I have to cancel out tonight. Something's come up with one of my accounts.

We'll have to get together another time. Call me." She hung up the receiver as Rigg strode back out of his office. "I feel guilty."

"Don't. The New York City Chamber of Commerce would be proud of you for taking pity on a lonely out-of-towner. Where do you want to head first? Directly to Central Park?"

"That's definitely the closest thing we've got to wide-open spaces. Are my briefcase and these files safe here till tomorrow?"

"Yes, they'll be fine." Rigg locked the main door and pushed the elevator button.

"How do the financial records look?" he asked as they waited.

"They look terrific from what I've seen so far. Tracy seems to have everything well under control. If the accounts are in as good shape as they appear to be, I shouldn't have to put in very many hours here at all. The only part that'll take time will be getting my letters of verification back from the various companies. I just hope I don't choose any of the same ones to sample as Mark did. They'd think two queries about the Stanton Group in a matter of weeks was a little unusual."

Rigg nodded slowly. "I'm relieved to hear everything looks okay. Frankly, I was getting a bit worried that Mark was taking so long, was starting to wonder if there might be some problems. If everything's under control, why wouldn't he have just whipped right through the process?"

"I don't imagine your audit was getting Mark's complete attention the past couple of weeks," Julie pointed out quietly.

"You're probably right." Rigg shook his head. "That was an unfortunate business, wasn't it, Julie? It's hard to figure what would drive a man like Mark to take his own life."

Julie simply nodded, hoping Rigg would take the hint. She'd had enough discussion of Mark Thompson's death to last forever.

Rigg cleared his throat. "Julie...I realize you don't like talking about Mark, but something you said to Wilcott has been bothering me. Just let me ask you about it and then I'll drop the subject permanently. You said you had a feeling his death wasn't a suicide. Well, there certainly aren't many alternatives. Do you know anything more about it, Julie? Something you haven't told anyone? Something that could be at the root of your trouble yesterday?"

Julie sighed wearily, wishing she'd kept her thoughts to herself from the beginning. "You're right, Rigg. I don't like talking about this. And no, I don't know anything. It was just a feeling, just intuition. And obviously, in this case, my intuition got its wires crossed. I had a feeling Mark wouldn't have—didn't—commit suicide, and the police had a whole lot of evidence that said he did. My intuition's no match for the NYPD." She smiled weakly. "Maybe for the Keystone Cops, but not for the homicide division of the largest city in the country." The elevator arrived and Julie exhaled quietly with relief. "So, can we drop the topic now and enjoy playing hooky?"

"Consider it dropped," Rigg assured her.

The elevator door opened on the ground floor and Rigg grinned over at Julie. "Am I allowed to hold your hand while we walk? Just a friendly gesture, mind you—just so I won't get lost in the crowds."

"Well, I don't know about that. I haven't read the chamber of commerce guidebook on being kind to lonely out-of-towners. How kind am I supposed to be?"

"Extremely." Rigg took her hand firmly in his. "Come on. Let's live dangerously. What are the odds that we'll run into Ray Brent?"

Julie laughed. "I'm an accountant, not a statistician. But, with all those people out of town, they're not as good as they could be. They might even be as small as one in seven million."

Rigg nodded, managing to look extremely serious. "Even so, let's risk it. I like holding hands with you."

Julie glanced over at Rigg as they walked up Ninth Avenue, against the flow of traffic on the one-way street. He was grinning like an idiot. She bit her lip, trying to erase the grin she knew was on her own face. This was crazy! She'd be hard-pressed to keep things platonic with this man, even for a short while. She should never have gone along with his friendship ploy. He was simply too difficult to resist.

Rigg looked down at her and squeezed her hand. "Do you believe in fate, Julie?"

"I've never really given it a lot of thought. Why?"

Rigg shrugged. "I was just thinking how unlikely it is that we would ever meet. Here we are, two people from two of the biggest cities in the country, with—how many—five or six states between Houston and New York. I haven't forgotten you're not a statistician," he told her teasingly, "but the odds on us having met have got to be astronomically high. Seems to me that fate is the only logical explanation."

Fatalism, Julie mused, had suddenly become an appealing philosophy.

Rigg glanced along the street ahead of them. They were almost at Fifty-eighth, only a couple of blocks away from the park, but there were nowhere near as many people out walking as there'd been earlier in the day. The sun had progressed westward and the buildings lining the sidewalk threw their dark shadows out into the street. The traffic heading down Ninth wasn't as heavy as usual. Julie must be right, he realized. A lot of New Yorkers had left town. He looked back over at her. Being here, with her beside him, holding his hand, seemed like some sort of dream. Perhaps he'd been misjudging New York a little. If a woman like Julie had been raised here, the city couldn't be all bad. And then his gaze wandered back out to the street and the dream vanished.

The dark van was in the curb lane, rushing toward them, its driver merely a shadow behind the heavily tinted glass. And Rigg knew, with sudden, horrible certainty, that something wasn't right. His brain wasn't working fast enough to tell him how he knew that or what to expect but it told him something was terribly wrong. He froze in midstride, felt Julie's arm jerk his own as she continued to walk. And then, in slow motion, she turned back to him, her bangs blowing in the breeze as she turned, the puzzled smile on her face asking why he'd stopped. And the van jumped the curb and headed for them.

Rigg dived at Julie, knocking her off her feet with the impact of his body, driving her against a building, spinning her into its doorway, shielding her from the sidewalk. He heard a woman scream, a man shout. Then he heard the throaty motor, felt air moving against the back of his neck. He knew it wasn't the wind. It was the motion of the van passing the doorway. Rigg whirled back into the street. The van was already bouncing away, over the curb, metal shrieking against concrete. Then it was off the sidewalk, continuing its race down Ninth Avenue, into the distance, dragging the remains of a bag of garbage behind it. And the the van was engulfed by the traffic and vanished. The curb was now littered with the contents of the bag; a single soup can rattled slowly into the gutter.

Rigg looked around frantically. A handful of people was watching. No one seemed to have been hurt. "Did anyone get the license number?" he demanded.

The onlookers mumbled and began to disperse. One man paused. "I tried to get it but the license plate was too dirty." He shrugged and moved off.

Rigg swore and turned his attention back to Julie. She was still in the doorway, her back pressed against the wall, staring at him as if he were a madman.

"Rigg," she whispered, "what happened?"

"Didn't you see it?"

She shook her head. "See what? I didn't see anything except you trying to drive me through this building. What on earth is going on?"

"Julie, are you all right?" He grabbed her by the shoulders. "I didn't mean to hurt you but there wasn't a lot of choice. Didn't you see the van?"

She merely shook her head again.

"There was a van, Julie, a black van. It jumped the curb and— Oh my God!"

"What, Rigg? What is it?" His face had turned so pale Julie though he might faint. She took a step toward him and realized it would more likely be she who fainted. Her body suddenly felt as if it was one massive bruise. She leaned back against the building for support. "Rigg, what is it?"

"The black van," he said hoarsely. "The black van that whoever called your mother said had hit you yesterday."

"What black van?" she demanded, not comprehending, wondering if this man had suddenly gone insane.

He ran his fingers through his hair. "I didn't tell you. It was nothing, just a detail that Henry mentioned on the phone last night. Whoever called your mother told her it was a black van jumping the curb that had killed you."

Julie closed her eyes, her body trembling. This couldn't be happening to her. She felt Rigg's hand on her arm, felt his other arm around her shoulder. "Let's get out of here, Julie," he said firmly.

She opened her eyes. Bits of the garbage were blowing down the street now. There was no doubt something *was* happening to her. She looked at Rigg and shook her head slowly. Her voice, when she spoke, was a terrified whisper. "Welcome to my nightmare, Rigg."

Chapter Five

Wilcott glanced up from his notebook. His gaze moved briefly over the full Scrabble board still sitting on Julie's coffee table. He leaned forward, picked up an *H* tile and fingered it briefly before replacing it. "Homicide." He read the word tonelessly. "Not exactly an accounting term, is it?"

"Actually, it was one of Rigg's words."

The detective merely nodded and focused his attention back to Julie. "So you didn't see this van at all."

She shook her head, wondering how many more times he intended to rehash the incident. "Will we be much longer?"

"No. But I do want a few words with Mr. Stanton. You said he'll be here shortly?"

"I think so. He just went back to the Plaza briefly—and to a deli. We didn't know how long it would be before you got here."

"Fine. Then let's get back to my question. You didn't see the van at all?"

"Not really. Everything happened in a flash. Suddenly Rigg was slamming me into a wall and the next thing I remember is him telling me about the van."

"All right. Let's continue on the assumption Mr. Stanton did see it."

Julie glanced at him sharply. She was tired, frightened, totally confused and her entire body ached. And his questions were only making her feel worse.

"Why do you keep implying that this incident was all some figment of Rigg's imagination?"

Wilcott looked at her evenly. "I'm not saying he imagined it. I'm merely keeping in mind that the power of suggestion can be a pretty strong influence. That, and the fact there were no witnesses."

"There were witnesses. I told you. They all disappeared as soon as the excitement was over."

"Fine. Then if there was a van and it was related to your break-in and the phone call to your mother, our questions become 'who's behind all of this?' and 'what is he trying to do?' Get something you have? Scare you? Harm you?"

Julie merely shook her head. "I haven't got the foggiest idea of who or what or why. I'm beginning to feel as if some omnipotent being decided to get his jollies by dropping me into the middle of an Alfred Hitchcock movie. And I didn't even get to read the script."

Wilcott almost smiled. "Let's go back to yesterday and try again to make some sense out of things." He flipped over a few pages in his book, rubbing his jaw slowly as he reviewed his notes. "The clock I can't figure at all," he said finally. "And I don't see that either the picture or the message would be significant. That leaves us with the letters and the file. Start with the letters. They disappear and Cramer calls you that same day—for the first time in months. Quite a coincidence. Why might he have wanted those letters? When did he write them?" He pressed when Julie hesitated.

"He went skiing over the Christmas break last winter. He wrote them then."

"Were they love letters?"

Julie felt her face flush. "I guess you'd have to call them that."

"But then you broke up shortly after Christmas?"

Julie nodded.

"Why?"

She sighed wearily. Bob had been in Tuscon when the letters were stolen. Wilcott had told her that himself. And that made all of this irrelevant. But she was simply too tired to protest anymore; it was easier just to answer the questions. "We broke up because I didn't want to marry him. I hadn't realized quite how serious he was but those letters made it only too clear. And right now I wish I'd thrown the damn things out. I don't know why I didn't. I just put them in the drawer and forgot about them, really. At any rate, Bob likely didn't even realize I'd kept them until Officer Drake appeared at his door to question him."

Wilcott nodded slowly. "You're probably right. From everything you've told me about him, Cramer doesn't sound like a very plausible suspect. But I'll have to talk to himself myself, double-check on those receipts from Tucson that Drake's report says he has. Have any idea what he'd be doing in Arizona?"

"None. I hadn't talked to him since January."

"Until yesterday, just before you were dropped into the Hitchcock movie." The detective paused, his expression telling Julie he was still trying to figure out if there was anything more than coincidence to that timing. He shook his head and spoke again. "Let's talk about the missing file. Thompson kills himself, you end up with the working papers on the Stanton Group and they're stolen before you have a chance to look through them."

Julie nodded.

"By the way," Wilcott continued, "I checked with the boys at Homicide who investigated Thompson's death. They're content it was a suicide. The facts added up. His wife told them he'd been very upset recently but wouldn't talk about what was bothering him. And the gun was his own—he'd bought it just a few days before he used it."

"The detectives told me all that. But I still had this feeling..." Julie sighed in resignation. "I guess women's intuition isn't always what it's cracked up to be."

"All right then, back to the file. If the thief was after the papers on this audit he was someone who knew they'd been given to you. Who could that be?"

"Only people at G and K or at the Stanton Group. But no one at G and K would have had to break into my apartment for the file. Mark's papers were all moved into an empty office and just sat there from Tuesday until Thursday. Anyone could have looked at them or even taken them during that time."

"But people at the Stanton Group knew you had them."

Julie nodded. "I was in Ray's office when he called Rigg on Thursday to let him know I'd be the one completing the audit. He mentioned that I was taking the papers home with me that night. So Rigg knew where the file was. I met Neil Overbach at the funeral and he'd obviously been told."

Wilcott was writing furiously. He finished, looked up and gazed evenly at Julie. "Miss Lind, what if the Stanton Group isn't exactly on the up-and-up...and Thompson had found out? What would he have done?"

"You mean if he'd found irregularities?"

"Irregularities?"

"Intentional errors," Julie explained.

"What sort of intentional errors?"

"Some form of fraud, some sort of theft by insiders."

Wilcott leaned forward heavily in the chair, his stomach bulging over his belt, his round face radiating interest. "I'm not an expert on white-collar crime. Give me an example of what you mean."

"Well, for example, if a company deposits paychecks directly into employees' bank accounts, a common scam is to put a 'horse' on the payroll—pay a nonexistent employee."

"But that couldn't have happened in this case. There are only a few staff. Someone would have noticed."

"That was just an example. There are a lot of ways of skimming money from the top. Most of them are relatively simple to set up and difficult to discover."

Wilcott nodded slowly. "And who generally engages in this sort of fraud?"

Julie shrugged. "It can be virtually anyone from the president on down."

"All right. Let's get back to my original question. Say Thompson had turned up irregularities. What would he have done?"

"Well, first he'd have discussed them with the senior partner in charge, Ray Brent. And then the Stanton Group's management would have been advised."

"And that's all?"

"Yes. In the short term, at least. We work for the client, not the FBI or the IRS. We tell the client what problem we've discovered and expect him to rectify it so that we can give an unqualified audit report. But in this case Mark couldn't have found anything. At least he hadn't mentioned anything to Ray, or I'd have been told about it."

Wilcott tapped the arm of the chair thoughtfully with his stubby fingers. "All right...maybe Thompson hadn't talked with your boss yet but let's suppose he had found something, had information about it in his file. But then he kills himself and suddenly, whoever is playing games gets a second chance. The papers disappear from your apartment and you have to start from scratch again. Maybe you don't find what Thompson found. Maybe the evidence of fraud has disappeared from the records by now. That possible?"

"Yes, it's possible."

Julie's buzzer sounded, announcing Rigg's return. She buzzed the front door open and waited anxiously; Wilcott's inferences were making her extremely uneasy.

"I won't be much longer," Wilcott assured them once Rigg was settled on the couch. "I just wanted to catch you, Mr. Stanton, ask you a couple of questions about this van. You're certain it was trying to run you down, that it really did leave the street, that it was coming at you, momentarily."

"It was one hell of a lot longer than momentarily! It crossed the entire sidewalk, practically crashed into the building."

The detective looked down at his book, flipped back a page. "But according to Miss Lind's story, you must have been facing into the building by that point. You couldn't actually have seen how close it came."

"Look, Sergeant . . ."

Rigg's tone, Julie realized, was distinctly annoyed.

"I didn't see it pass us," Rigg continued tersely, "but it came so damn close I felt the breeze as it shot by."

Wilcott nodded slowly. "And you told Miss Lind the van was black. Did you see the license plate or the driver?"

"No. The windows were smoked glass and I didn't see the license at all."

"The van itself then. What make? Chevy? Ford? Dodge? Import?"

"I haven't any idea. For Pete's sake! I was trying to keep us from getting killed, not playing name that auto-maker!" Rigg stood up and glared down at Wilcott. "Look! I saw the van jump the curb. It was coming directly at us. Do you really believe it's a coincidence that Julie's mother gets a call yesterday telling her a black van killed her daughter, and today one practically does?"

Wilcott exhaled loudly. "Let's move on from the van. Miss Lind and I were discussing the possibility that her burglar was after Thompson's file, that it was taken because he'd uncovered something unusual going on at the Stanton Group—what Miss Lind refers to as an irregularity. You or I would call it fraud." Wilcott stared evenly at Rigg as he spoke.

Julie glanced over anxiously, wanting to see Rigg's reaction to the suggestion.

He was eyeing the detective coldly. "If I'd learned about any fraud, it wouldn't have continued for two minutes. And whoever was responsible would be either looking for a new job or in jail. I assume if Thompson had uncovered anything unusual, he'd had told me about it at our meeting on Monday."

"The day before he killed himself," Wilcott commented dryly.

"Are you inferring something by that remark?"

"I'm merely suggesting," Wilcott continued evenly, "that if Thompson was contemplating killing himself the next morning, problems in your company wouldn't have been very important to him. Who was present at this meeting on Monday?"

Rigg exhaled deeply, suddenly looking more concerned than angry. "Only Thompson, Overbach and myself. We basically just got together because I hadn't met Mark. We talked about the audit a little and Thompson said he hoped to have things wrapped up shortly."

Julie listened with barely half her attention, trying to decide exactly what Mark would have done if he had, in fact, uncovered something. How soon would he have approached Ray about it? Who in the Stanton Group might he have suspected—Neil, Tracy, one of the support staff she hadn't met?

Wilcott rubbed his jaw. "Give me a rundown on your company, Mr. Stanton. How does it operate?"

Rigg shrugged. "It's pretty simple, really. Neil checks out potential properties, possible deals. I review his plans and projections, assess the risks and potential profits as I see them and we decide which ventures are goes—where we'll put our money. The actual renovation or development work, we contract out. Neil oversees that as it progresses."

"And," Wilcott asked slowly, "Overbach is responsible for finances on the projects?"

"Yes. Ultimately, he is. Our accountant, Tracy Alders, handles most of the details but Neil has final approval on expenditures. The division's checks require his signature."

"And what about you, Mr. Stanton? Are you involved with everyday expenditures in New York?"

"Not very often. Occasionally I sign for expenses directly, mostly related to management details that Neil hasn't been involved with. But normally I just approve a global budget for each project. As long as it comes in within budget, I figure Neil and Tracy are doing their jobs."

Wilcott made a final note and pushed himself heavily out of the chair. "One more thing. Ray Brent called you on Thursday to tell you that Miss Lind would be taking over from Thompson, that she'd have your file at home with her. Who did you tell about that? Who would have known to come here after Thompson's file?"

Rigg looked anxious. "I got off the phone from talking with Ray and went to tell Neil about the conversation. He was out in the general area, not in his own office. Anyone in earshot could have heard me, anyone on staff—Tracy and the other two women who work in the office. The fact that we had a new auditor, what her name was and that she'd be getting to work on things over the weekend wasn't exactly classified information. At least," he added slowly, "I had no reason to think it was at the time."

Wilcott merely nodded and turned to Julie. "You've had the locks changed here?"

"Yes, the super looked after that today."

"Good. Be careful for the next little while but keep in mind that we've been talking theories, not facts. If that black van was merely a coincidence, then your burglar could still just be some weirdo who's long gone. I'll be off duty from now until Tuesday but don't hesitate to call the precinct if anything bothers you."

Julie locked the door behind Wilcott and glanced back at Rigg. His face wore a scowl.

"Wilcott doesn't believe there was a van," he muttered angrily, jamming his hands into his pockets. "Damn it, Julie, I know what I saw!"

"I wish I'd seen it too, Rigg."

Rigg glanced at her sharply. "You think I'm imagining things as well?"

"No, Rigg. I'm sure you saw a van, and that you believed it was trying to hit us. I just wish I'd seen it too, that's all. Mostly," she added ruefully, "I just wish I knew what the hell is going on."

Rigg nodded, his expression still black. "What did Wilcott have to say before I arrived?"

"Not much, really. He was still trying to figure out what the thief was actually after."

"He come to any conclusions, other than the possibility that someone on my staff is a crook?"

Julie hesitated. "He pretty well ruled out everything except the file," she finally admitted.

"I see." Rigg ran his fingers slowly through his hair. "So, the bottom line is that he does figure Mark found something wrong during the audit—that there's something fishy going on in my company."

"Rigg, you just heard him say that's only a theory. And I certainly didn't notice anything suspicious about the accounts this afternoon."

Rigg slumped down onto the couch beside Julie. "Look," he said wearily, ignoring her attempt at reassurance, "if there is something going on, I have to know about it, have to figure out who's behind it." He exhaled slowly. "If you do turn anything up, I want you to tell me first, before you say anything to Wilcott. He might let something slip that would give whoever it is a chance to cover up."

Julie nodded slowly, feeling more uncomfortable by the moment. Her obligation, as an auditor, was to tell Rigg. But, now that she was in the middle of a police investigation, maybe that changed all the rules. She simply didn't know.

Rigg was gazing steadily at her with those warm, brown eyes, looking extremely concerned about what her response was going to be. He fumbled in his wallet, pulled out a business card and wrote a couple of telephone numbers on the back.

"Julie, I know I can trust you. If there's anything wrong, maybe you'll discover it tomorrow. But look. My office numbers are both on here and I've added my numbers at the Plaza and the ranch. Call me right away if you turn up something, before or after I've gone. If I'm in Houston, I'll take the next plane back so we can go over what you've found."

Julie glanced at his card, uncertain what to say. She'd have to think this situation through very carefully once Rigg had left, once he wasn't here, watching her so compellingly. "All right, Rigg," she finally told him hesitantly. "If I do find anything, I won't talk to Wilcott before I call you."

Rigg beamed at her and she breathed a silent sigh of relief that he hadn't asked her not to tell Ray. She couldn't have promised that much.

"Why don't we have dinner, such as it is?" Rigg suggested. "A takeout from Cleo's wasn't exactly what I had in mind when I offered to buy you dinner tonight."

They ate in silence, Julie lost in thought. Something was going on at the Stanton Group. The more often she turned that possibility over in her mind, the more certain she felt it was true. Something was going on at the Stanton Group and someone in Rigg's company was behind whatever it was.

Rigg interrupted her thoughts. "Do I get to teach you poker tonight, Julie?" He smiled a lazy smile at her.

Julie did her best to ignore the rush that smile caused and shook her head. She had to be alone, had to think about things. "Not tonight, Rigg. We were up so late last night, I'd just like to get some sleep. I'll meet you at your office in the morning—about ten?"

"Look, Julie, I really don't like leaving you—"

"I'll be fine, Rigg," she cut him off. Despite his promise about being just friends, spending another night alone with Rigg Stanton would be pushing her own resolve a little far. "I'm perfectly safe. Not only do I have a brand-new lock on the door but someone would need a blowtorch to get through that bar lock. There's absolutely nothing to worry about. I'll probably fall asleep the instant my head hits the pillow. I'll see you in the morning," she concluded firmly.

"Julie." Rigg started to reach his hand out to touch her and then stopped. "Look," he said slowly, "I know I promised to cool it until after this audit was done but that was before the van almost nailed us. I can't help what I feel, Julie, and what I feel at the moment is worried sick about your safety. Wilcott was right about one thing. We have nothing but theories. We don't know who was in here yesterday or who called your mother or who was driving that van today. But whoever's behind all this is definitely not a sane individual, and the thought that he's out there on the loose scares the hell out of me.

"Julie," he continued more softly, "I realize we've barely met and that you're concerned about a conflict of interest as far as the audit goes, but the thought that there might be some crazy out there who's after you..."

"Don't say that!" Julie shivered. "Maybe the van today *was* just a coincidence. Maybe we're getting all worked up over nothing."

"And maybe pigs fly!" Rigg snapped. "That van was no coincidence! Julie, maybe my file has nothing to do with all this—and I hope to hell it doesn't! But maybe it does. It seems as if I walked into your life and from that moment on it turned into...what did you call it earlier? A nightmare! How do you think that makes me feel? Julie, all I want to do is be with you to make certain things don't get worse for you than they already have!''

Julie simply stared at him. He was right. Her life had been perfectly normal until yesterday afternoon. Then she'd gotten out of his car and walked into the twilight zone. How could this Mr. Wonderful have shown up in her life just as it began to disintegrate into lunacy?

She wanted to be alone, to think things through without the distraction of Rigg sitting beside her, chauvinistically implying that he had to stay here to protect her, insinuating she couldn't take care of herself. She'd been on her own for five years; she could probably manage to get herself through one night. As attracted as she was to Rigg Stanton, she certainly wasn't about to turn into Little Miss Meek for his benefit.

She stood up and began to collect the remnants of dinner. "Rigg, let's talk about this again tomorrow when neither of us is so upset. It's been a long day. I really would like to get some sleep."

Rigg nodded slowly. "You're a stubborn woman, Julie. But I guess I can't force my company on you." He picked up his business card from beside the Scrabble board. "Put this by the phone and if anything at all makes you nervous, call me right away."

Rigg lingered at the door, obviously reluctant to leave. For an instant, Julie thought he was going to kiss her. She felt a curious mixture of relief and disappointment when he didn't. He merely gave her a weary half smile and turned down the hall. She wandered slowly back to the living room and sank into the wing chair. Asset instantly materialized from hiding, to settle with a contented purr in her lap.

Absently, Julie stroked the cat. If there were irregularities at the Stanton Group she had to find them. If someone had set up a scam, she mused, who was the most likely suspect? She shook her head ruefully. She'd spent an hour with Tracy today, a few minutes with Neil yesterday, and hadn't even met the other two women Rigg had mentioned. The only one of the five she knew at all was Rigg.

She smiled to herself, recalling she'd told Wilcott that a fraud could be perpetrated by anyone from the president on down. But in this case it certainly wouldn't be the president. Rigg obviously wasn't short of money. A Mercedes, the Plaza, expensive clothes—he clearly could afford the best, clearly liked the best. And—she smiled a little more—he clearly liked her. He might be coming on a little strong, and under the facade of those custom-tailored clothes he was undoubtedly more the Marlboro Man than Cary Grant, but she felt a happy bubbling inside at the thought of how concerned he was about her. His attraction to her had been so immediate, so apparent, that it seemed incredible, almost too good to be true.

The caustic phrase that had run through her mind this morning returned to lodge there like a somber cloud. *When a man seems too good to be true, he usually is.* Don't *look* for problems, Julie ordered herself sternly. Rigg Stanton was undeniably a bit macho for her taste, but in twenty-eight years she'd never found any man who excited her even half as much as this one did. And, as soon as she'd finished the audit, she intended to see him every time he was in New York, every time she could.

As soon as she'd finished the audit...the audit that she'd been assigned because Mark Thompson had killed himself...or been killed. That nagging suspicion simply wouldn't leave her alone. Who did she think she was? Nancy Drew? But what if Mark had been murdered? She couldn't switch her mind away from that thought. And then there was the missing file. Wilcott had obviously decided it was the only potential clue to her break-in. What if Mark had uncovered something during his audit? What if there had been evidence about it in that file? What if someone had murdered Mark because of what he'd found, stolen the file so she wouldn't find it? What if . . .

Stop this! Julie ordered herself. *You're being ludicrous!* Was she? Could anyone in the Stanton Group have killed Mark, made it seem like suicide? No, the idea was absurd! Mark had been at least six feet tall and athletic, certainly more than a match for someone as obviously out-of-shape as Neil, for a five-feet-tall woman like Tracy, probably for almost any woman. And those were the only people at the Stanton Group . . . except for Rigg. Julie shook her head. She was going from absurd to absurder!

She recalled the force of Rigg's body hurtling hers against that building. He was a powerful man. So what? And so what if Neil was out of shape? Murderers were hired killers, not real estate developers. Then that damn little voice in her head spoke up again, reminding her that Rigg had arrived in New York unexpectedly on Monday and had met with Mark. They had talked about the audit . . . and Mark had died the next morning. And then the audit papers had disappeared, and Rigg was one of a very few people who'd known Julie had that file.

Julie's thoughts began to whirl crazily. What if Rigg's appreciation of the best was *too* costly, even for him. A senior executive skimming a little, or more than a little, off the top, certainly wasn't unheard of. And what about those management-related expenses he approved now and then?

Stop! she ordered herself again. None of this made any sense, it was simply her New Yorker's ingrained suspicion working overtime. Rigg Stanton was the most fascinating male she'd met in an awfully long time. He was an absolutely charming man.

A slight shiver seized her as she realized he might have some special reason for being charming to her. And, charming he'd certainly been. He'd virtually swept her off her feet, had stuck to her like glue since he'd picked her up at G and K last night. Why? Because he'd fallen for her like the proverbial ton of bricks? Or because she was his company's new auditor? Because he wanted to know what she might be finding out? And why was he so concerned that, if she did find anything, she tell him . . . only him? A second, colder, stronger shiver raced through her body.

Julie forced herself up, dumping Asset unceremoniously onto the carpet in her haste. She was being ridiculous! She'd make a cup of tea and try to calm down. Of course Rigg Stanton wasn't involved in anything illegal. No fraud, and certainly no murder. What was the matter with her? She'd simply had a couple of nerve-racking days; that was all it was. Her mind had gone into overload, taking two plus two and adding them up to three hundred and seven.

Right now, she'd have some tea and get to bed. And in the morning she'd meet Rigg Stanton at his office. She didn't have a lot of choice about that. She'd left all her papers there this afternoon. And whose idea had that been? Her own? Rigg's? She couldn't recall. Damn! She'd be walking into Rigg Stanton's office in the morning . . . alone. She'd be walking into his territory and he'd be right there. She only hoped she wouldn't be walking into something she couldn't handle.

Chapter Six

SUNDAY MORNING

Julie glanced up from the stack of canceled checks she'd been systematically flipping through, not surprised to catch Rigg watching her again. He'd barely said a word since she'd arrived but he'd made a point of bringing work out of his office and spreading it on the desk across from the one she was using. Why? Was he so concerned about what she might find that he wanted to watch her every move?

Each time she looked over, Rigg's dark eyes were gazing at her. His presence was so disturbing that she might as well not be here for all she was getting done. And, she realized, there was nothing that she couldn't work on just as well at home. "You know, Rigg, if I take these accounts back to my apartment I can do the work there and you won't be stuck in the office to lock up after me."

"Julie, that's not why I'm here. I have work of my own to do, and frankly," he added slowly, "I feel a lot better with you here, where I know you're safe. Unless," he suggested with a lazy smile, "you'd like me to come back to your apartment with you."

Julie shook her head. "I work much better when I'm on my own." The words came out far more abruptly than she'd intended and she shot Rigg a smile, immediately suspecting it looked insincere. His frown confirmed that it had.

"Look, Julie, I know you're upset. And you have good reason to be. But why do I get the distinct impression that you're upset with me as well as about this whole damn mystery we're in the middle of? We're friends, remember? We're in this together... so why are you acting as if I have some horribly contagious disease?"

Julie shrugged, thankful she'd been born with an aptitude for numbers. She'd obviously never have made it as an actress. At the moment, she couldn't even improvise a decent line to answer Rigg's question. He was a client, after all. She had to be careful what she said to him. And, she told herself for the hundredth time since she'd woken up this morning, her suspicions were probably ridiculous.

"I hadn't noticed any sign of a contagious disease." She tried another smile. "I guess you're just distracting me from working."

Rigg shook his head slowly. "Unfortunately, I don't seem to be distracting you in the way I'd like to be."

Julie gazed at him evenly. "Just friends. Remember? We agreed it would be that way until the audit's done." And at least by then, she thought ruefully, she'd know how things stood, whether there was any basis for her fears. "I'd really like to get on with this, Rigg, and I think I'd be a lot further ahead working at home. That is, unless you mind me taking these files out of the office."

He hesitated before replying. "No, of course not. It's not the files I'm concerned about, Julie. It's you. I'm worried about your safety after everything that's been happening to you. And I'd thought we might have lunch together."

"Sorry, but I have plans for the evening," Julie lied, "so I really can't take any more time out of the day." She be-

gan to gather up the papers she needed, aware that Rigg
was watching her closely. She was determined not to let
him catch her eye.

"I see," he said finally, his tone laced with sarcasm.
"And will you be spending any time with me tomorrow,
before I leave for Houston, or can't you take any time out
of that day, either?"

"I'm pretty busy, Rigg." Julie realized her reply
sounded sharp, but she no longer cared. She just wanted
to get away, to get home, to stay away from Rigg Stanton
until she was certain he wasn't involved in anything he
shouldn't be. She stuffed the last of what she needed into
her briefcase. "That's it then."

She walked to the elevator and pressed the button.

Rigg eyed her for a moment before he spoke. "I don't
suppose you'd like me to drive you home, would you?"

"I'll walk or grab a cab."

The elevator door opened. Julie flashed what Rigg
imagined was supposed to be a smile in his general direction and disappeared. He ran his fingers slowly through his
hair, trying to figure out what on earth he'd done to deserve the cold shoulder. Cold? Hell, icy wouldn't be any
exaggeration! Sure Julie was upset; anyone would be under the circumstances. He was pretty damn upset himself.
But why had she cut him off as if he were some utter nerd
she couldn't bear to be around? That certainly hadn't been
her reaction yesterday. Yesterday afternoon he'd been
certain she was every bit as attracted to him as he was to
her. But today, he might as well have been the Elephant
Man.

Slowly, Rigg gathered up his own work and took it back
into his office, hoping he'd be able to concentrate, that his
mind wouldn't be diverted by thoughts of Julie Lind,
whom he didn't want to let out of his sight for a moment

and who obviously didn't want to be in his sight for one second longer than she was forced to be.

JULIE HAD BARELY GOTTEN the audit papers spread out on the desk in her den when the phone rang. A current of excitement raced through her body. It was Rigg calling! She simply knew it was! But why was that thought so exhilarating? She'd come home because she didn't want to be with him, was afraid to be with him. So why was the mere thought of him calling enough to send her pulse racing? She grabbed the receiver. "Hello? she answered breathlessly.

"Hello, Julie. It's Bob."

Julie sank back into her chair, spirits plummeting. "Hello, Bob," she managed.

He chuckled a little. "I'm glad to have finally gotten hold of you in person. I was starting to think our answering machines had taken over our entire relationship."

Julie forced a laugh, wishing Bob wouldn't use words like *relationship*, particularly when they no longer had one.

"Are you all right, Julie? I've been awfully worried about you since that Drake fellow came by to see me."

"I'm fine, Bob. And I'm sorry the police bothered you. I told them you couldn't have been involved but they insisted on talking to you."

"That's okay. I just wish I could do something to help. Well...maybe I can. How about dinner tonight? I still have to talk to you about something. It's important," he pressed when Julie hesitated.

She sighed quietly. Bob was obviously going to keep at her until they talked about whatever was on his mind. Much as she didn't want to see him, she might as well get it over with. At least he was safe, she reminded herself.

He'd been in Tucson when her burglary happened. "To-night would be good, Bob."

"Great! I'll pick you up about seven. Is Luigi's all right? I can never remember which other restaurants are open on Sundays."

"Luigi's is fine . . . but don't pick me up. I'll meet you there. Say at seven-thirty?"

"I don't mind coming by, Julie."

"No," she told him firmly, surprised that the idea of Bob coming to her apartment, the thought of being alone with him, made her so nervous. Everything and everyone seemed to be making her anxious today. "I have something to do before dinner, Bob. I'll meet you there." Julie hung up pensively, wondering how practically overnight, she'd become such a proficient liar.

She tried to force her attention back to the papers on her desk but the effort was futile. Thoughts of Rigg kept interfering with her concentration. He couldn't possibly have anything to do with any fraud . . . or with Mark's death. Her intuition about people wasn't that far off base. All her crazy ideas were just a result of her imagination working overtime. That had to be it, simply *had* to be. Because, she admitted to herself, Rigg Stanton made every other man she'd ever met totally forgetable.

BOB BEAMED AT JULIE from a corner table in Luigi's and rose to greet her. He leaned over and brushed her cheek lightly with a kiss, making her feel extremely uncomfortable. "It's awfully good to see you again, Julie."

Julie nodded, trying to seem even half as pleased as Bob apparently was. He looked exactly as he always did, more like a basketball player than an archaeology professor, his clothes hanging loosely on his long, lanky frame as if he'd lost weight since he bought them. She glanced at the dark green bottle nestled in a silver wine bucket beside the table. "Champagne? Are we celebrating something?"

Bob grinned and nodded, brushing a stray lock of straight, brown hair up off his forehead—a gesture, Julie recalled, that indicated he was nervous. He motioned the waiter to uncork the champagne.

"Well?" Julie asked with genuine curiosity. Bob had never been one to splurge. "What's the big secret?"

"I've been offered a new position, Julie, in Tucson—a full professorship at the University of Arizona. I'll be starting there in the fall."

"That's marvelous, Bob! You'd have waited years for a full professorship at Columbia! To your new position, then," Julie toasted, realizing his news answered the question about what he'd been doing out of town. The champagne bubbled a spicy tickle down her throat.

Bob smiled warmly at her. "I'm pretty excited about it. I could hardly keep from telling you all about it when I called you from Tucson. But I wanted to keep the whole thing a surprise, see your expression when I told you." He reached across the table and covered Julie's hand intimately with his own.

She merely looked at it, feeling nothing but uneasiness at his touch, and the silence grew awkward before he spoke again.

"You know, Julie, I kept thinking about you the whole time I was in Tucson. It isn't very far from Phoenix—just a little southeast. I'll be living pretty close to your mother." He paused, obviously finding it difficult to say what was on his mind. "Julie, I've missed you since we broke up. I thought if I left you alone for a while you'd miss me, too. Have you?"

This conversation, Julie realized, was rapidly deteriorating into one she didn't in the least want to have. "Of course I've missed you, Bob. But," she continued as gently as she could, "my feelings for you haven't changed. I like you, Bob, I like you a lot, but I don't love you. I'm sorry," she added lamely, wishing the waiter would reappear.

"I got to thinking about that," Bob continued, "about how maybe we just never gave things enough time. Love doesn't always happen overnight. Maybe I didn't give you long enough ; maybe I pushed too hard; maybe you just weren't ready." Bob's words were beginning to tumble out. "Look, Julie, I'd do almost anything to convince you to think about us getting together again. I'll be going back to Tucson in a week or so to apartment-hunt. I thought you might consider coming with me, look around, see how you like Tucson, see if you think there'd be any chance..."

His voice trailed off as Julie shook her head. "My life's here, Bob. New York is my home. There really wouldn't be any point," she added firmly, fervently hoping he'd let the discussion drop. She slid her hand from under Bob's, picked up her glass and took a second sip of champagne. This time the bubbles tasted flat and sour.

Bob surveyed her with studied casualness. "Why don't you just come along for a few days' vacation, then," he persisted. "Tucson's a beautiful city. And we could go to Phoenix for a day or two to visit your mother."

Julie shook her head even more firmly. This had gone far too far already. "Bob, I'm sorry, but no, definitely no."

Bob tapped the table nervously. "I thought you might have changed your mind, and I didn't want to leave the city without making sure. Then, after the police talked to me, Julie, after I heard what had happened, I thought you might want to get out of New York, might think about giving Tucson a try, about getting away from the rat race here."

Julie stared across the table at Bob, barely hearing his last few words, her mind fixated on his earlier phrase. He thought she might want to "get out of New York." And the message on her mirror had read: GET OUT OF NEW YORK BITCH! No! Bob couldn't have had anything to do with that. There was nothing unique about the phrase...his using it had to be simply coincidence. Or maybe Drake had told him about the message and the words had just popped back into his head.

"What did Drake tell you, Bob?" Her voice sounded strained; she hoped Bob hadn't noticed.

"Not much—very little in fact. Only that someone had taken a few things from your apartment, including my letters; that he wanted to talk to me because of them. Once he learned I'd been out of town, that was the end of our discussion."

"He didn't tell you about the message?"

Bob paused, looking uncertain. "What message?"

"On the mirror."

Bob shook his head, his expression puzzled...or guilty. Julie wasn't certain which it was. But one thing was certain. Drake hadn't told Bob about the message. And yet he'd used the precise wording. Julie's chest felt tight, her breathing was suddenly shallow. Bob was speaking again. She forced herself to concentrate on his words.

"...and New York's just too dangerous a place for a woman to live alone, Julie. You had a taste of that on Friday, didn't you? Maybe a break-in is no big deal, but do you want to wait around for something worse to happen?"

Julie's thoughts began reeling. Did Bob intend what he was saying to sound as threatening as it did? Or was her imagination simply running away with her? She had to be overreacting. Bob wasn't a fool. Surely he wouldn't believe that he could frighten her into leaving New York, rushing off to Tucson with him, by setting up some stupid burglary. Never, in a million years, would Bob have arranged for someone to break into her apartment. And, if he had, he'd certainly never have been stupid enough to have his own letters taken, to leave a clue related directly to himself.

Julie realized she was trembling, took a deep breath, glanced back across the table at Bob, sitting there silently, watching. Her thoughts continued to whirl, her mind tried to connect fragments of fact and logic. She had to sort this out; had to determine whether Bob might have been the one . . . whether he was the one.

She watched his face, fixated, where she sat, by her need to know. She wanted to get out of the restaurant, away from Bob. Yet she had to be certain the impossible was, in fact, possible. She had to continue this conversation with some semblance of emotional control. If Bob was the one, then he'd arranged for the black van as well.

"Something else happened to me this weekend, Bob," she said tentatively.

He looked at her with interest.

"Yesterday a van tried to run me down."

"Are you serious, Julie?"

She nodded, watching his expression, trying to read his thoughts. She couldn't.

"What are you telling me? That your break-in wasn't an isolated incident? That someone's trying to kill you?"

Julie, tried to appear far calmer than she felt. "It's starting to look that way."

"Julie, then you're crazy if you don't think over what I've said, if you don't get out of New York! I'm offering you the ideal alternative!"

"I have absolutely no intention of letting anyone frighten me out of the city, Bob," she managed evenly.

"Julie, why would you even want to stay here? I've lived in New York for five years and I'll be happy as hell to get out! You've been here all of your life. Isn't it time to try someplace else? You'd have me, and your mother would be nearby. And you wouldn't need one hundred and seven damn locks on your door! What's the matter with you that you can't see a logical alternative when it's staring you in the face?"

Julie bit back the nasty retort that leaped to her tongue, realizing anger was seizing control over fear. She tried to keep her voice even. "Bob, let's part friends. But that is what we're going to do—part. Because I haven't the slightest intention of moving as far away as Long Island, let alone move to Tucson with you or anybody else!"

Bob shook his head, clearly more upset than she'd ever seen him. "You won't even stop to consider it, will you?" he snarled. "You never consider compromising, do you? That was always one of your major problems, Julie! You can be such a stubborn bitch when you want to be!"

Bitch! There it was! A word Bob almost never used, and certainly not one he'd ever used about her... until when? Now or on Friday? She had to know for sure! "It was you, wasn't it, Bob?" Her words hissed across the table at him.

"It was me what?" he practically shouted at her.

"You had someone break into my apartment, didn't you? You thought you could make me want to go to Tucson with you!"

Bob stared at her as if she were crazy, then shook his head slowly. "You need help, Julie. Living in this city has finally warped your mind if you can believe a thing like that!"

Julie pushed back her chair. Had she really thought he'd admit it? "I think, on that fine compliment, I'll leave, Bob," she snapped. "Good luck in Tucson!" She tore her sweater from the back of the chair and bolted for the door, barely aware of Bob calling after her. A taxi was standing in front of Luigi's. She jerked its door open, gave the driver her address and they roared off.

Julie slumped back against the vinyl car seat, breathing hard. Had it been Bob? For all that it made no sense, was completely out of character, it could well have been. She had to think! What had he said? He'd do almost anything to convince her to think about them getting together again. But could he have planned the break-in, the phone call, the van? Review the details, she ordered herself. What would he have had to know? Have had to do?

The van. Anyone could hire a van. And the break-in...he certainly knew her apartment. But the phone call—he didn't know Mark Thompson. And the man who'd called her mother had given Mark's name. Bob couldn't have been the one who'd phoned her mother.

Unless... Suddenly, a forgotten fact surfaced from her memory. When Bob phoned her from Tucson on Friday he'd mentioned calling earlier, leaving a message that she could ignore. But there'd been no message on her machine Friday afternoon, none until the evening. That could only mean one thing. Bob had left the message at G and K—after the office had closed for the funeral. And the receptionist who'd remained to answer the phones had probably told him where Julie was, why the offices had closed early... because of Mark Thompson's funeral! Julie's breath caught at the thought.

So Bob could have learned Mark's name. And then could have used it to frighten her and her mother half to death. The pieces were all falling into place. And telling her what a great idea it would be to get out of New York! And calling her a bitch, just to ice the cake!

Julie exhaled slowly, uncertain if she was more frightened or angry. Angry, she decided. There was nothing further to be frightened about...not if she had the answer. But how could Bob have thought, even for an instant, that she'd be the least bit interested in going to Tucson with him? And how could he have even dreamed up such a stupid, cruel plan, let alone actually found someone to carry it out?

She realized her fingernails were digging into her palms and concentrated on relaxing her muscles. She'd call Wilcott as soon as she got home. No, he was off duty until Tuesday. Well, it could wait until then. Bob certainly wouldn't bother her again after tonight. But she'd call Rigg and tell him. A surge of relief swept through her. Those crazy suspicions about Rigg had been absurd after all. This whole nightmare must have been Bob's creation. The Stanton Group file had been just one of the things taken as part of his ridiculous scheme. There was undoubtedly no problem within Rigg's company. And no problem with Rigg.

She thought back to the morning, to how abrupt she'd been with him. Damn! How could she have been so stupid? Have thought the things she'd thought? Have been so snotty to Rigg that he probably had no interest in ever seeing her again? She'd have to apologize for her behavior and hope to hell he was the forgiving type.

Julie was still swearing silently about her foolishness when the cab pulled up in front of her building. At least, she reassured herself, waiting for the elevator, she had a perfect excuse to call Rigg. He'd certainly be relieved to hear that this whole, bizarre experience had nothing to do with his file...hadn't been related to any problem with the audit. She just hoped his relief at the good news would make him forget what a bitch she'd been this morning. She grimaced at the thought of that word, at the thought she might be one after all.

Julie fumbled with her keys as she walked down the hall to her apartment. She unlocked the door with anxious anticipation, threw her sweater onto the couch, glanced at Rigg's business card beside the phone and dialed the Plaza. "Mr. Stanton's suite please." She could hear the excitement in her voice. She listened impatiently to the phone ring...and ring...and ring. Finally, a voice came back on the line, asking if she wished to leave a message.

"No. Thank you, but there's no message." She wanted to surprise Rigg with her call, to hear the relief in his voice when she told him the good news.

JULIE'S FINGERS DRUMMED the arm of her couch. She listened once more to the unanswered ringing at the other end of the phone line and glanced wearily at her watch. Eleven thirty-two, precisely three minutes since she'd last checked the time. The ever polite voice at the Plaza interrupted the ringing. "I'm afraid there's still no answer in Mr. Stanton's suite. Would you care to leave a message this time?"

Julie sighed and gave her name and number. She couldn't go on calling him all night. "Please put that it's important he call me." She hung up and leaned back on the couch. Asset meowed, disgruntled by the movement, and rearranged herself in Julie's lap.

Julie slowly stroked the cat's neck. "What did I expect, Asset? That he'd be spending the evening sitting alone in his suite, brooding about not being with me? Well, he obviously isn't, is he?" Julie closed her eyes, trying not to think about where Rigg might be, what he might be doing... who he might be doing it with. The possibilities were endless. And if she hadn't been such an idiot, she'd be the one he was with instead of God only knew who. Maybe Rigg wasn't Tracy Alders's type, but she must be one of a very small minority. There were probably three or four million women in New York City alone who would think Rigg Stanton was very much their type!

Just friends. What a dumb idea that had been! And what a dummy she'd been to insist on it! She'd gotten more than a little carried away by her concern about any conflict of interest. How much could her professional integrity possibly have been compromised if she'd spent more time with Rigg this weekend?

Julie shook her head ruefully. "What do you think, Asset? Is he spending the evening with a blonde or a brunette?" What a terrific state of affairs. Rigg was out somewhere on a red-hot date and she was sitting here talking to a cat!

Well, she'd give him until midnight to call. Then she'd unplug the phones and go to bed. She glanced at her watch one more time. Midnight wasn't very far off. The refrain of an old song drifted into her mind... "goin' to wait till the midnight hour." She hummed the song tunelessly to herself, forcing her mind to go blank, forcing out all thoughts of what Rigg might be doing...of what Bob had done.

The ringing phone jerked her out of semisleep. Eleven forty-eight. Julie smiled sleepily. Rigg had beaten her deadline after all. She picked up the receiver and Bob's voice exploded in her ear.

"I got your message loud and clear at Luigi's, Julie! Sending those letters back in the middle of the night was well into overkill! You're crazy, Julie! Let's make a deal— you don't bother me anymore and I certainly won't bother you!"

Julie stared at the receiver, trying to comprehend what Bob was yelling about. She forced herself to speak. She had to know what was going on.

"Bob...I don't understand."

"Look, Julie. Understand this. I didn't appreciate your scene in the restaurant and I appreciated getting wakened by a taxi driver, delivering those damn letters I wrote, even less! Good night, Julie. And goodbye!"

The slam of Bob's receiver in her ear was followed by the drone of a dial tone. She was barely aware of either. What the hell was going on? Had those letters really turned up at Bob's door? That seemed awfully unlikely. And, even if they had, why would anyone want to send them to him? Who would have had them to send? She couldn't begin to imagine a single who or why.

If Bob was telling the truth, Julie was in bigger trouble than she could even think about. But if Bob was lying, if he'd had the letters all along, it made perfect sense for him to call her and put the final touch on his plan. That must be it. He wanted her to think someone else was guilty. Wanted to scare her right into his waiting arms. Well, Julie thought, let him wait. This was one time when brilliant Bob had overplayed his hand.

Slowly, she replaced the receiver and glanced over at her apartment door. The bar lock was solidly in place. *Don't even think about that,* she told herself. Surely, she'd seen the last of Bob. He wouldn't have the nerve to show up here. Whatever the truth about those letters, his call had convinced her he was behind all this. Maybe some women might consider his motives romantic, but in her books they were the motives of a madman. An angry madman who's plan had backfired badly. She closed her eyes, praying Rigg would call.

JULIE WOKE to Asset's cold, moist nose nuzzling her neck and glanced around the sunlit living room. Falling asleep on her couch was apparently habit-forming. She looked over at the phone—the silent phone. *Don't think about Bob,* she ordered herself, *... not just now. Think about Rigg, the Rigg who hasn't called. What was she going to do about that?*

Julie made coffee and caught herself glancing at the phone as she drank it. If she thought it might be possible to will it to ring she'd try. But Rigg was obviously in no hurry to return her call ... if he intended to return it at all. Perhaps he'd decided to ignore the message, to simply catch his plane back to Houston without calling.

She drained her coffee, poured a second cup and sat back down beside the phone. She could swallow her pride and try Rigg again or she could wait. Hesitantly, she picked up the receiver.

"I'm sorry," said a different, but equally polite, voice at the Plaza. "There's no answer in Mr. Stanton's suite now and I checked on the message you left last night. It's still here. It hasn't been picked up."

"I see," Julie said quietly, seeing only too well. Rigg hadn't even made it home last night. "Thank you. And please discard the message. It's no longer important." Julie hung up the receiver slowly. Rigg must have had quite an evening. She shook her head wearily. She certainly should be congratulated on her way with men. Somehow, she'd turned a passive archaeology professor into an appalling weirdo. And worse yet, having finally met a man who practically made her heart skip a beat every time he spoke to her, she'd driven him directly into the arms of some other woman! Yes indeed, she could probably give lessons on the care and feeding of men. But only to women who wanted every relationship they had to end up on the rocks.

The phone rang, interrupting Julie's self-recrimination. She stared at it warily. The way things were going it was probably an obscene caller. Reluctantly she picked up the receiver.

"Julie, it's Rigg."

Julie closed her eyes, trying to understand her own emotions. How could she be so happy to hear from him after he'd just spent the night heaven knows where? She bit back a hundred accusing questions and managed, "Good morning. I'm glad you phoned."

"I just wanted to say goodbye before I left."

"Well, before we get to goodbyes, Rigg, I have some news. I called your suite to tell you about it last night but I guess you didn't get my message." Julie tried to sound nonchalant. She was certain she'd failed miserably.

"I didn't make it home last night, Julie. In fact, I haven't been back to the Plaza yet. I'm still at my office. I just kept on working here after you left yesterday and it got to be so darn late I sacked out on one of the couches."

Julie took a deep breath. No blonde...no brunette...no other woman. She felt as if the weight of the world had just been lifted from her shoulders, as if fate was offering her a second chance with this man.

"What were you calling me about, Julie?"

Rigg's question jolted her back to reality. "Oh, Rigg, it's good news as far as your company's concerned. This whole mess never had anything to do with your audit. Bob Cramer was behind my break-in...and all of the other crazy things. I'm sure of it. I had dinner with him last night. Well, we didn't actually get to the dinner part. What we got to was a terrible fight." Julie could feel herself getting upset again, merely thinking about Bob. "It's a long story, Rigg. I'll tell you about it sometime but—"

"How about right now?" Rigg cut her off. "There are later planes out today. I can be at your place in ten minutes, as long as you don't mind a man who's unshowered, unshaved and who slept on a couch all night."

Julie laughed. "Just don't let any of the other tenants see you on your way up. I wouldn't want them to think I was running a soup kitchen." She hung up the receiver and hugged herself. Suddenly, everything was right with the world—at least, with her tiny bit of it.

Chapter Seven

Julie opened the door to Rigg's knock and surveyed him with a grin. "Were you really intending to get on a plane looking like this? Airport security would probably have searched you for concealed weapons."

Rigg smiled, relieved to find the Julie Lind of Friday and Saturday standing in her doorway. The anxious woman who'd been in his office yesterday had vanished. "Actually, I wasn't planning on going anywhere looking like this. I intended to go by the Plaza before I headed for La Guardia. I'd have gotten cleaned up then." He rubbed the stubble on his jaw, realizing just how grubby he must look. "Maybe I should have stopped off before I came here."

Julie laughed. "Rigg, this is the second time I've seen you in the morning, before you've transformed yourself into Mr. Executive. I didn't scare off on Saturday, so you don't need to worry about it today. New Yorkers are tough. We can handle a lot of pretty ghastly sights."

"That's a fine way to talk about a client, Julie," Rigg teased. "You'd better watch your insolence or I'm liable to report you to Ray."

Julie made a face at him. "If you're considering doing that, I don't think I'll tell you the story about Bob, after all."

"That's blackmail! And I ran four red lights getting over here to hear that story!"

"Only four? It's worth at least a dozen but I'll make you a deal. I tell you the story and you don't tell Ray how disrespectful I can be."

Rigg listened to Julie's account of her meeting with Bob quietly, not interrupting at all. She'd expected his face to mirror her own relief. Instead, he seemed to become progressively more worried as she spoke. Even when she'd finished the entire story, he merely nodded and rubbed his jaw thoughtfully.

"Well?" she prodded.

"So, Bob didn't admit to being involved."

Julie merely shook her head.

"No. No, of course he wouldn't have," Rigg said slowly. "He may have been angry but he's obviously not a fool. Even with him denying it, though, you must have been awfully upset by the time you got home last night, Julie. And then to get his crazy call about the letters on top of it all. Why didn't you phone the police?"

She felt suddenly guilty, recalling that her primary concern at that point had been getting in touch with Rigg. "It occurred to me that I should. But Wilcott had mentioned he'd be off duty until tomorrow, and I couldn't face starting in on the details all over again with someone else. I'll call first thing in the morning."

"Promise?"

"I promise." Julie paused. "What will they do about Bob?"

Rigg shook his head slowly. "I imagine Wilcott will have a long talk with him. But unless he confesses, which is pretty unlikely, I suspect there won't be much the police can do. He's already denied being involved, he can prove he was out of town, and, even though his 'get out of New

York' line strikes you and me as pretty damn significant, it certainly can't be considered hard evidence. Even the fact that he has the letters—if he actually does have them— doesn't mean much one way or the other. He could have had them all along or they could have appeared last night. Who's to know? I wish there were something else, something that would leave no shred of doubt.''

Julie bit her lip nervously. ''Well, I really can't believe it wasn't him. But even if he doesn't confess to Wilcott, I'm sure I'll never hear from him again, not after that scene.'' She eyed Rigg's thoughtful expression, his non-committal silence making her anxious. Did he think she was wrong? That it hadn't been Bob after all? Was there something about her conclusion that didn't hang together? She tried to think. There was a nagging inconsistency she'd been pushing out of her mind. ''Rigg, one things bothers me. Why would Bob have had his own letters taken in the first place? That just sent the police running straight to his door.''

Rigg shrugged. ''Double whammy, I guess.''

''Double what?''

''Don't you read detective novels?''

Julie shook her head.

''Well, double whammy probably isn't the technical term, but what I mean is that the guilty party intentionally leaves an obvious clue pointing to his guilt. But he makes it so obvious the police discount him as a suspect.''

''Then,'' Julie concluded slowly, ''you're saying that was the purpose of the letters?''

''Could be...if it was Bob.'' It all added up, Rigg assured himself. It even made sense in a perverse, senseless sort of way. Damn! He so badly wanted to believe it was Bob; that they definitely did know who it was...that Julie would be safe from here on in...that there were no problems with the Stanton Group's eastern division. He just didn't want to convince himself of something that wasn't true. Because if Julie was wrong, then there was someone else out there, still loose, still unidentified, still dangerous as hell!

"Julie, there's something more, aside from the letters, there's Bob himself. Up till last night you kept insisting Bob wouldn't have had anything to do with this, would never have planned it. What made you change your mind?"

"I don't know, Rigg. I guess it was the way he was acting and the things he was saying. He seemed so desperate—capable of anything."

"Did he threaten you, Julie?" Rigg asked quietly.

"No . . . not directly."

"And he didn't say anything that would tie him in to the crime?"

"Not in so many words."

"But you're still certain it was him behind all this?"

"Yes, who else could it be?"

Rigg was quiet for a moment before he spoke. "I guess that's the million dollar question.

"Look," he finally continued. "Why don't you tell me some more about Bob. I gather he can't be a full-time lunatic or you wouldn't have gone out with him in the first place. What's he like?"

"Well," Julie began hesitantly. "Normally he's quiet, thoughtful, rational. He was always a perfect gentleman when we were seeing each other—always considerate. . . ."

Rigg grinned, seeing his chance to lighten the mood. "He sounds like ideal husband material. Maybe he just got overly frustrated because you didn't see it that way. But," he teased, still hoping for a clue about Bob, "if he's so wonderful, why didn't you marry him when he asked you in the first place?''

"No magic."

"Magic?"

Julie smiled a little. "I don't generally admit this," she told him slowly, "but I've never quite given up on fairy tales; never quite stopped believing the myth of Prince Charming; never quite accepted that, in real life, a lot of people get married who don't feel a sense of magic every time they're together." She laughed quietly. "I'm pretty cynical about a lot of things but I've managed to hold on to my belief that there's some sort of magic between certain people. I never felt any magic around Bob."

"Ever feel it around any man?" Rigg stared at Julie intently as he asked the question, his interest in Bob suddenly forgotten.

She glanced at him a fraction of a second too long for there to be no meaning in her look, and Rigg felt an intense surge of arousal.

Julie lowered her gaze. "That's a pretty blunt question."

Rigg continued to watch her closely, hoping she would give him yet another message. "Texans aren't noted for their subtlety, Julie. You can miss out on a lot of things in life by being too subtle. I've always thought if you want to know something . . . or you want something, you should speak up."

Julie looked at him again, her eyes locking with his, intensifying his arousal. "I'm not married, am I? There's been no magic, up to and including Bob."

Rigg looked into those deep, gray eyes, feeling an aching desire for this woman. He wanted to reach across the space between them and fold her into his arms. And if he did that, he doubted he could ever let her go. Whatever the mysterious force that made two people react to each other as if a giant magnet had been placed between them, it was drawing him toward Julie now. If she wanted to call it magic, that was fine with him. She could call it magic or predestination or even witchcraft if she liked . . . so long as she felt the spell, too.

He knew she did. And yet she'd been skittish, and stubborn, and she was undoubtedly still upset about things. And he was damned if he was going to blow the situation by pushing her. This woman sitting here, all warm and beautiful and simply exuding sensuality, was the Julie Lind he wanted, not the one who'd been cold as ice to him yesterday. He wasn't going to take any chances on overstepping whatever damn boundaries she'd established in her mind. He'd wait for her to make the next move if the waiting killed him. "Do I smell coffee?" he asked, intentionally breaking the spell.

"Oh, of course. Not much of a hostess, am I?"

Rigg merely smiled. "Mind if I call American? I'll have to book a later flight."

Julie nodded and headed into the kitchen, confused by Rigg's sudden switch. He'd come racing over to her apartment, practically seduced her with his eyes once he'd arrived, and now he was more interested in a cup of coffee than in her. Or maybe he'd merely rushed over to hear her story, eager to learn that his company would undoubtedly be getting an unqualified audit report from G and K. That certainly wasn't the message she'd read. But maybe she'd been misreading. She seemed to have been doing a lot of that recently. Maybe he was overly interested in that audit report after all.

No! All her suspicions about Rigg had been absurd. She'd realized that last night and she wasn't about to get onto such a foolish train of thought again. There was some other reason for his abrupt change just now. There had to be. Most likely her behavior yesterday...her bitchy behavior, she reminded herself grimly, was giving Rigg second thoughts.

Asset meowed at the sight of the milk container. Julie poured her a little milk, put the creamer on the tray and took Rigg his coffee. She stood awkwardly by the end table while he completed his call, uncertain whether to sit beside him on the couch or take the chair.

He replaced the receiver and smiled up at her. "I have a few hours before my plane leaves, Julie. How about lunch?"

"All right. That sounds fine. I'll just need a few minutes to get ready."

Rigg nodded. "Why don't you do that while I drink my coffee. Then we can head back to the Plaza so I can get presentable. We can go from there."

Julie eyed Rigg uncertainly. His face and voice were expressionless. He could be inviting her on a date or for a business lunch; she didn't have the slightest idea which.

RIGG CLOSED THE DOOR and Julie glanced about the French Provincial decor of his suite. The Plaza's elegance didn't stop in its lobby.

"I won't be long," Rigg promised. "Turn on the TV— or the stereo if you'd like."

Julie nodded absently, wandering over to the living room window. It overlooked Central Park. She could see the pond, almost directly below, and the zoo, all but hidden by trees, in the distance. Only remnants of pink and white clouds of magnolias and cherry blossoms remained, replaced over the past few weeks by fresh, leafy green. Julie smiled down on the park, her backyard in the midst of urbanity.

She heard the shower running in the background and her thoughts turned back to Rigg. He was going to be flying out of her life in a few hours. He'd be back, she assured herself. He'd said he'd be back in a couple of weeks, that he'd want to see her then. And when had he said that? On Saturday. Not today. And certainly not yesterday. Maybe he'd changed his mind. She couldn't blame him if he had...she could only blame herself. She'd given him a whole lot of mixed messages as far as her interest in him was concerned. So, where did they stand?

What had he told her earlier? *If you want to know something...or you want something, you should speak up.* Julie sighed. She had no difficulty speaking up within the framework of business, but when it came to her personal life, being forward with men wasn't her style at all. And yet...*if you want something, you should speak up.* Should she? There definitely was something she wanted. She'd realized last night there was absolutely no doubt about that. She wanted Rigg Stanton. But that wasn't something she could say. Julie stood gazing, without seeing, out the window.

Rigg paused in the living room doorway and watched Julie for a moment. She was obviously lost in thought, hadn't heard him return. "Well?" He interrupted her reverie. "Do I pass inspection?" He slung his suit jacket casually over one shoulder and struck an exaggerated pose.

Julie laughed, then smiled warmly across the room at him, making him feel ten feet tall. "Sounds to me as if you're fishing for a compliment," she teased.

"So...do I get one?"

She laughed a second time. "I'll go as far as admitting you look better than you did half an hour ago."

"Is that the nicest thing you can say about a man who rearranged his entire itinerary just so he could buy you lunch?"

"Well, all right then. You look an awful lot better than you did half an hour ago."

Rigg shook his head. "That's your idea of a compliment, Julie? You're supposed to tell me I'm the most handsome man you've ever met and you'd have died of a broken heart if I'd left town without calling you this morning."

Julie gazed at him evenly; her smiled faded. "All right."

Rigg wasn't certain, for a moment, what she meant. His expression must have told her that because a slight smile returned to her lips and she shrugged.

"All right, Rigg. You're the most handsome man I've ever met and I'd have died of a broken heart if you'd left town without calling me this morning."

She took him completely by surprise. He stared at her questioningly, unsure whether or not she was still joking. There was no clue in her eyes. "I'm worried there might be an echo in here, Julie," he finally tried. "I'd be a lot more likely to believe you meant that if you used your own words."

Julie looked steadily into his eyes. "You can believe that I meant it," she told him quietly.

He took a step toward her and she flashed him a broad, mischievous smile, once again making him uncertain.

"Well, hold on for a minute and let me rephrase your statement a little, Rigg. I wouldn't want your ego to become completely overbearing. You just *may* be the most handsome man I ever met and I'm very happy that you didn't leave town without calling. How's that?"

"Julie—"

"Wait. I do want to say something of my own, Rigg," she interrupted softly. "I want to apologize for my behavior yesterday. I was extremely rude to you and I had no reason to be. I'm not generally like that. Things just got a little hard to handle there for a while."

"You don't need to apologize for anything, Julie. I understand." Rigg walked forward, ordering his feet to stop moving. He had no intention of pushing this scene but his feet wouldn't listen to his brain. He reached Julie and his hands refused to listen, either. He tossed his jacket onto the couch and took her firmly by the shoulders. "Julie, you're making it extremely difficult to be just friends."

"Well...maybe I should apologize about that, too. I get some pretty foolish ideas sometimes."

Rigg willed her to continue, to say more, but she stood quietly, not pulling away from his hold, but making no movement toward him. She merely stood before him, watching him, waiting. Waiting for what? For him to stop or to continue? He didn't know. He only knew that Julie Lind was irresistible.

Despite his resolve, Rigg bent to kiss her. Her lips were soft and lush against his, and at the probe of his tongue they parted, allowing his mouth to possess hers. He gripped her shoulders more tightly, pulling her close to him so that her breasts crushed warmly against his chest. He smoothed his hands slowly down her back, willing her to feel the same emotions he felt, wanting her to respond to his body touching hers.

Finally, she did. Her tongue probed, tentatively at first and then demanding his. He offered it willingly, explored the sweet recesses of her mouth in return, overwhelmed by the needs she was creating within him. And then her hands encircled his waist, drawing him even closer to her. Her fingers tugged his shirt free and he gasped in a sharp, involuntary breath as her hands began to roam up his back. Her palms slid slowly across his skin, tantalizing him with the feather-light friction of their motion, and Rigg ached with the arousal her touch engendered.

He kissed her even more deeply. She tasted so incredibly sweet, smelled so unbelievably good. Her hair had a scent like new-mown hay, her body was so warm and yielding against his that he wanted to kiss every inch of it, wanted to know every inch of it. Her nipples were hard with arousal, pressing against his chest, telling him she felt the same desire that he did, making him long to caress her breasts.

Rigg's back was firm and muscular beneath Julie's hands. The nearness of his body, the maleness of him, fresh from the shower, the feel of his naked skin against her palms, excited her beyond belief. Her own boldness astonished her. This wasn't her! She simply didn't behave this way, didn't take the initiative! She had to stop this, stop it before things went any further... before they went too far. But Rigg's lips were doing incredible things to hers, heightening her longing for him by the moment.

His hands moved across her back, then stopped, cupping the sides of her breasts. His lips began a trail of kisses down her neck, a warm, moist trail that sent hot shivers through her. He nuzzled the hollow of her throat, his hands moved hungrily across her breasts, his fingers began to stroke her already taut nipples through the silk of her dress.

Rigg continued to caress one of Julie's nipples, making it ache with delight; his other hand began to unbutton her dress. And then his fingers slid under the silk of her dress, under the silk of her slip, the lace of her bra, to claim the nakedness of her breast, to slowly circle her nipple with a light, rhythmic motion. An involuntary moan escaped her throat.

Rigg's kisses trailed lower, his lips lingered warmly on the swell of her breast and her body began to throb heavily with desire. Rigg's breath was hot against her flesh; when he spoke, his words were strained. "Julie... I want you. You can tell how much I want you."

His fingers continued their caress, making Julie long to have him go on touching her, kissing her, making her want him to make love to her. *Magic!* She'd always looked for magic. But this man was no mere magician. He was a wizard, a sorcerer. He had to be, had to have woven a spell over her. No ordinary man could make her feel like this! But everything had been happening so fast, with such intensity. She couldn't think...and she didn't want to make a mistake, a mistake she might regret. Nothing had been what it first seemed over the past few days. What if Rigg wasn't what he seemed, either? What if he was... She caught his hands in hers and pulled away a little.

"Rigg... I want you too... so much that it amazes me. But this has all been so sudden I can barely believe it. Rigg, I'm sorry. I can't tell you how sorry I am. I shouldn't have started something I'm not ready to finish, but I have to go more slowly, have to go one step at a time." Julie forced herself to move backward, away from Rigg. It was almost impossible.

Rigg shook his head as if she wasn't speaking a language he understood. "Julie, do you have any idea what you're doing to me? Physically? Emotionally?"

"Oh, Rigg, I'm so sorry! I must sound like a broken record but I don't know what else to say. You were kissing me and I wanted to kiss you back. But I didn't intend to get carried away. I only wanted to be sure you realized I'm interested in you. I've been acting like such a fool that I was afraid you'd decided I wasn't worth the effort. And when things got started, I didn't want to stop. But I had to, Rigg. It's all been too fast, too confusing...and I need to be certain."

Rigg exhaled loudly. "All right, Julie. I guess it isn't really your fault." He was clearly finding it difficult to keep his voice even. "I started things. But when you responded the way you did, when it became so obvious that you wanted me as much as..."

He shook his head ruefully. "That was definitely what I'd call a deflating experience. Promise you won't ever do it to me again."

"Rigg, I don't know what's the matter with me. I know better. I'm twenty-eight years old and acting like thirteen...an immature thirteen at that. I just seem to have a major problem thinking straight around you." She shrugged, feeling like an utter fool.

"You haven't promised me you won't ever do that again, Julie," Rigg reminded her quietly.

"I promise," she whispered, overwhelmed with relief that he still thought there might be an again.

"Okay. Let's go out and get some lunch." Rigg began tucking his shirt back into his suit pants.

Julie glanced down at her unbuttoned dress. The gray silk was incredibly crushed; bits of it were moist from Rigg's kisses. She couldn't go out of here looking like this!

"It's Memorial Day, Rigg. A lot of restaurants will be closed. How about room service instead?"

He shook his head firmly. "I don't think I could handle being alone with you in a hotel suite just at the moment, Julie. Trust me. Getting out of here is a good idea." He opened the door and waited.

An elevator arrived immediately. Rigg turned to her as its doors closed.

"Julie, tell me precisely what the hell it is you do want, will you?" he whispered. "You just may be the most confusing woman I've ever met. What exactly do you want me to do from here on?"

Rigg's whisper filled the elevator. Julie cringed, glancing pointedly at the rigid back of the elevator operator.

"He's paid not to listen!"

Rigg's whisper hadn't dropped a decibel and Julie sighed silently with relief as the elevator stopped on the next floor and an elderly woman, bedecked in fur, got on. They rode the rest of the way down in silence.

Rigg took her arm once they were in the lobby and propelled her to the street outside. "We'll walk some place for lunch, Julie. And while we're walking you can answer my question. What the hell is it you want?"

She knew what she didn't want; she didn't want this conversation. But there was no escaping it. "I'm not exactly sure, Rigg," she admitted slowly. "I've never found myself in quite this situation before—not understanding my own emotions. It's a little scary. But I think I just need time. I want to see you when you're in New York, want to get to know you better.... You confuse me, Rigg."

"No." She shook her head. "No, that's not right. My own reaction to you is what confuses me. I've always managed to run my life pretty well. I have a responsible job, don't have any major hang-ups. I thought I was doing just fine, that I was emotionally all grown-up, could handle anything that came along. Then you came along. And every time you're near me I feel as if I'm under a spell. I keep doing things that are totally out of character, things I don't mean to do... that just sort of happen."

Julie shrugged ruefully. "And, even now, I'm babbling on, making it sound as if I'm blaming you for my own behavior."

Rigg steered her into a restaurant. She was only vaguely aware of the maître d' leading them to a table, of Rigg ordering something to drink.

"Julie," he said softly, taking her hand across the table and gazing at her with a look that almost made her melt. "It isn't only that I'm making you feel as if you're under a spell. *I* feel the same way when I'm around you. Julie, I've heard it said that falling in love makes people crazy. Do you think that could be what's happening to us?"

Julie stared across the table at him. Suddenly, after all the horrors of the past few days, the most wonderful man in the world was sitting right here in front of her, holding her hand and telling her, with his soft smile, that every recollection of her foolish behavior could be swept quietly under the carpet, explained away by this wonderful possibility.

She nodded, not trusting her voice.

Rigg's smile grew. "Does that nod mean," he asked quietly, "that you've started to feel a little magic?"

"I guess it does," Julie admitted, fighting back the grin she felt spreading across her face. She'd obviously lost the battle because Rigg grinned broadly back at her.

Finally, she gave up and laughed. "Rigg, I wouldn't be the least bit surprised if you appeared wearing a top hat and started to pull rabbits out of it. Yes, there's magic. It must be that. I can't imagine anything else that could have been making me feel and act the way I have been since we met."

Rigg exhaled slowly and sank back in his chair. "Julie, you have no idea how that makes me feel—sort of relieved and ecstatic, all rolled up in one. I was so worried you weren't feeling what I was, that you might even have been resenting me for being a part of all this mess. It sure looked that way yesterday. I was worried sick about what might happen to you and you just strolled out of my office as if being there with me was giving you a royal pain."

"It wasn't you, Rigg. It definitely wasn't you. At least, not the real you. It was just my imagination running wild. I hadn't been able to figure out anything that was going on. I didn't even know who the good guys were and who the bad guys were."

Rigg grinned. "Think you've got it straight now?"

"No doubt about it. I guess my perceptual difficulties have corrected themselves."

"And none too soon. You had me so I didn't know whether I was coming or going."

Julie laughed again. She felt like wrapping her arms around Rigg and never letting him go, but that would have to wait. A New York restaurant was hardly the right surroundings for what she had in mind.

"As I recall," she teased, "you were going. All the way back to Houston."

Rigg shot her a wry glance. "You know that isn't what I meant, Julie. Right at the moment, anywhere away from you is the very last place I want to go. And I'll be back here just as soon as I can. I have a feeling I'll be spending a lot more time in New York in the future.

"But, Julie," he continued seriously, "I can't see how in hell I'm going to be able to make it back for a couple of weeks. And I hate the idea of leaving you here, alone." He squeezed her hand, looking at her worriedly.

"I'll be fine, Rigg." She could barely believe it but that statement had come out sounding almost sincere. Maybe she had some acting ability after all.

"I'll call Wilcott in the morning, Rigg, and, as I said before, there's no way Bob's going to try anything else. Actually," she added, as much to convince herself as Rigg, "the timing works out well. I'll be finished the audit in a couple of weeks. And, even though I've been pretty silly about it, I'll still feel a lot better if no one knows anything about us until after it's done."

Rigg shook his head. "So," he asked with apparent amusement, "you're just going to pretend I don't exist until the next time I show up?"

"Absolutely not! That's stretching things way beyond what's possible. I'm nowhere near imaginative enough to pretend you don't exist. But . . . I am imaginative enough to figure out how wonderful things will be once the audit's done and you're back." She smiled across at Rigg and he squeezed her hand once more.

"Julie, you can't possibly begin to imagine how wonderful things will be."

Lunch passed in a happy daze. Julie was vaguely aware of someone serving them food, but she might have been eating the tablecloth for all it mattered. Then, after what seemed like ten minutes, Rigg was looking at his watch and telling her he had to leave.

"It can't be that late already, Rigg!"

"'Fraid so. We've been here for two hours. Come on. Let's get a cab. I can drop you off on my way."

Rigg cuddled Julie closely to him in the back seat of the taxi. She hoped the ride would never end; they reached her apartment house in seconds.

Rigg walked her to the front door and kissed her. Julie sensed Robert, the doorman, looking at her with disapproval. She didn't care in the least.

"I'll miss your magic, Rigg," she whispered as he released her from his embrace.

He leaned forward again and kissed her quickly on the nose. "It's going to seem like forever until I see you again, Julie. I'll be traveling for the next few days and it might be difficult for me to get in touch with you. But Julie, if anything at all happens that bothers you, call the ranch. Leave a message with my father and I'll reach you. Otherwise, I'll call you when I get a chance.

"Or, if I can contain myself," he told her with a grin, "maybe I'll just surprise you and call you the instant I'm back. Yes, I like that idea better. I'd far rather talk to you face-to-face than over the phone." He touched her cheek gently. "It's such a lovely face."

Rigg turned to go, then paused and looked back for a moment. "Please be careful, Julie. And remember—if you need me, call. I'll get back here somehow."

Julie waved at the back of the taxi as it disappeared down East Sixty-ninth. Then she floated past Robert, into the building and up to her apartment.

Chapter Eight

The elevator door opened onto the Stanton Group offices and Tracy looked up from her desk, flashing a welcoming smile across at Julie. "Morning," she called, getting up. "You're here bright and early."

Julie glanced about. Neil Overbach was visible through his office doorway and two women were working in the back of the open area. "It certainly doesn't look that way. In fact, it seems more like I'm the last one in."

"Well, you work for G and K." Tracy shot a grin at Neil as he strode out of his office. "We're used to the slave driver here. Neil's an awfully hard taskmaster. Early as you are, if you worked for the Stanton Group, he'd probably give you a lecture on tardiness."

Neil returned Tracy's grin with a look of absolute adoration. Julie smiled at how improbable looking a couple they made—tiny, vivacious Tracy and overweight, balding Neil. The vice president pushed his heavy, horn-rimmed glasses up on his nose as he walked. "And, if Julie paid as much attention to one of my lectures as you ever do, I could save my breath, couldn't I?" He turned to Julie. "Nice to see you again. I hear you've got the audit practically completed already."

Julie laughed. "I think someone's been exaggerating a little, but we are in pretty good shape. The verification letters are set to go out and I called our courier before I left home. A driver should be by to pick them up shortly. After that, it'll be a matter of running a few system tests, checking all the data as the letters are returned, and then writing up the audit report."

"Well, if you need any help from me, just stick your head into my office. I imagine it's Tracy you'll want to spend most of your time with, though."

Julie nodded. "Most of it. But I'll have to physically inspect a couple of properties, just so we can assure your investors the assets actually exist. I guess you and I should go out and have a look at a building or two, or at whatever projects you have underway."

"All right. We've got a redevelopment in progress near the South Street Seaport, so that wouldn't be a major trip. Or we could check out some of our rental buildings."

"The redevelopment and one rental would be good; preferably the rental you've acquired most recently."

"Fine. I have nothing pressing for the next couple of days. Whenever you want a break from Tracy's wisecracks, just let me know."

Tracy shook her head. "You see how it is around here, Julie? My wonderful sense of humor is simply not appreciated. Come on. We'll leave Mr. Overbach to his serious endeavors and I'll introduce you to the staff."

Tracy led the way to the back of the office area and introduced Julie to the two women working there. Betty-Anne Taylor, a woman Julie guessed to be in her early thirties, was attractive in a quiet, understated way—brown hair, brown eyes, wearing a conservative brown suit. Betty-Anne nodded shyly to Julie and resumed her work.

Francine Ruhling looked ten years younger than Betty-Anne and her attractiveness was the extreme opposite of understated. She sported rather brassy blond hair, cut in a short, avant-garde style that merely emphasized its dark roots. She had a well-proportioned size-ten figure and was wearing a red linen dress that either had shrunk to, or had been bought as, a size eight. Julie tried to imagine how many hours it took to apply Francine's perfect, if excessive, makeup. Her own face, she thought fleetingly, must seem positively naked to Francine. The younger woman eyed Julie warily, finally smiling an unfriendly smile when they were introduced.

"So, how was your long weekend?" Tracy asked as they walked back to her desk.

Julie grinned at Tracy's nonchalant nosiness. "Not bad, thanks."

"See any more of Rigg after Saturday?"

"A little," she admitted, wondering how she'd ever imagined she could keep the fact that she'd been seeing Rigg confidential. She couldn't picture Tracy as a secret keeper.

Tracy laughed. "I suspect your definition of a little is very different from mine. I'll bet you even saw him off at the airport yesterday."

Julie couldn't help laughing in return. "Not quite. He dropped me at my apartment on his way there."

Tracy shot her a know-it-all look. "I figured it from the moment I saw the two of you together. So, now he's been gone less than twenty-four hours and I'll bet he's already called you from Texas . . . right?"

"Wrong! And I'm relieved to hear you can't figure out everything to the letter. As a matter of fact, he said he probably wouldn't call me at all, that I wouldn't hear from him until the next time he's in New York. But," she admitted with a happy smile, "I think he will call then."

Tracy shook her head firmly. "I predict he'll call you long before that."

Julie suddenly felt she was being watched. Her glance flickered away from Tracy and across the office. She caught Francine staring at them and her smile faded. The woman was obviously listening and obviously upset. Julie caught Tracy's eye and gestured, almost imperceptibly, in Francine's direction.

Tracy looked casually over, then turned away. "Sorry," she apologized quietly. "You'd think by my age I'd have learned to keep my mouth shut. I'm forever putting my foot into it. Francine has an enormous crush on Rigg; not at all reciprocated, I should add."

She grinned and continued, her voice still low. "When we hired Francine, she looked like a recent escapee from a convent. Then, about two weeks later, Rigg arrived in town, spent a couple of days in the office, and she's looked like this ever since. I'd be willing to bet money that she prays every night for him to appear here the next morning." Tracy shrugged. "Don't let her bother you. But if she offers you any coffee, I advise you not to drink it."

Julie nodded ruefully. "Wonderful! Now I have to come to work and worry about being poisoned. And they say accounting is a dull profession!"

Tracy laughed. "Let's get to work and take your mind off Francine. She's hardly worthy competition. Although," she added teasingly, "I imagine she types a lot faster than you do.

"Everything still look good after I left on Saturday?" Tracy continued casually as she brought an accounts payable file up onto the computer screen for Julie.

Julie nodded. "Didn't see any problems at all. You know, the most . . ."

"Miss Lind."

The deep, male voice behind her startled Julie. She whirled around in her chair. "Detective Wilcott. You surprised me. I didn't expect to see you here." She glanced at Tracy and saw she was eyeing Wilcott with apparent interest. "This is Tracy Alders—Detective Wilcott."

Wilcott nodded to Tracy. "I'll be wanting to speak with you shortly, Miss Alders." He looked back at Julie. "Is there some place we can talk in private for a moment?"

"Use Rigg's office, Julie," Tracy suggested quickly, looking suddenly more anxious than interested.

Julie led the detective into Rigg's office, uncomfortably aware that several pairs of eyes were watching them. She closed the door and turned to Wilcott.

"I mentioned Saturday evening that I'd want to talk to Miss Alders and Mr. Overbach today," he reminded her.

Julie nodded. "Yes, but I left a message at the precinct for you this morning. Didn't you get it?"

Wilcott shook his head. "I came here directly from home."

"Well," Julie told him, "it seems likely that Bob Cramer was behind things, after all." Briefly, she recounted their meeting and Bob's phone call.

The detective merely nodded when she'd finished, as if expecting her to tell him more. "That's not exactly conclusive evidence," he finally offered.

Julie stared at him, taken aback by his reaction. "You didn't hear the way he was talking! And how could those letters have simply arrived at his door? He must have had them all along."

"If he's got them at all."

"What do you mean if?"

Wilcott shrugged. "I mean that maybe his calling you with a story about those letters turning up was just childish retaliation, just a ploy he figured would upset you. He must have been awfully angry; you'd embarrassed him in front of a restaurant full of people."

Julie shook her head firmly. "Even so, the rest adds up. Bob must have been behind things!"

Wilcott rubbed his jaw. "Did you tell him you suspected him?"

"Yes, of course."

"And I assume he denied anything to do with it."

Julie nodded.

"Well, I suppose anything's possible. But to be frank, I suspect his temper simply overcame his common sense so far as his calling you goes. I have a lot of trouble buying the idea of a university professor, who you told me yourself is sensible and mild-mannered, hiring thugs and masterminding some completely illogical scheme to make you marry him after you'd given him the gate months ago."

"Are you saying it wasn't Bob?"

"I'm saying I have a lot of trouble buying the idea, Miss Lind.

"At any rate, I'll still talk with Miss Alders and Mr. Overbach while I'm here."

Julie watched the detective leave the room and stood quietly thinking for a moment. She had a feeling Rigg wasn't convinced Bob was guilty. And now Detective Wilcott had said just about the same thing. She bit her lip nervously. If they were right and she was wrong she could be in bigger trouble than she'd thought.

WILCOTT HAD SPOKEN with Neil first. After that, he'd taken Tracy into Rigg's office. Julie glanced nervously at the closed door. Why was he questioning them at such length? Almost an hour with Neil; already more than an hour with Tracy. Why…when it seemed so clear to her that it was Bob, that it had nothing to do with the Stanton Group? Or, might it have after all? Did it? Julie's thoughts whirled in confusion.

She looked over, through the doorway of Neil's office, wanting to ask him what the detective had said, what questions he'd asked. But Neil was poring over a stack of papers on his desk, either extremely engrossed in his work or studiously ignoring her. She suspected the latter. Whatever Wilcott had told him, it would have been obvious that she'd suggested the possibility of irregularities within the company. Both Neil and Tracy were bound to be thrilled with her! An auditor who called in the police certainly wasn't going to get the prize for winning friends and influencing people.

But what if it wasn't Bob? Then they were back to the missing file…back to a suspect within the Stanton Group. Julie swallowed hard, trying to force the lump from her throat, the tightness from her chest. The effort was futile. She stared at the computer screen in front of her. The figures blurred into one another, making no sense at all.

Julie jumped at the sound of Rigg's office door opening. She looked over and Wilcott motioned her to join him. Tracy glared across the room, then marched into Neil's office and closed the door tightly. Julie rose and walked quickly toward Wilcott.

He pushed the door shut behind her. "Both of them claim there's absolutely nothing out of the ordinary going on here. That's not exactly a surprise." He paused and then continued. "But you haven't noticed anything peculiar as far as the audit goes."

"No, not a thing."

"And you said you've had no further trouble. Nothing's happened since the van?"

"Nothing except the incident with Bob."

Wilcott shrugged. "Well then, I think we've probably been tilting at windmills. I'm not going to bother talking to the other two women. I can't imagine anyone putting much over on Miss Alders or her boss. I'll still call on your Mr. Cramer, but my feeling at this point is that you simply had a very offbeat burglary, that none of the things taken had any special significance at all. And I suspect, as far as the van is concerned, Mr. Stanton's imagination got a little carried away."

Julie frowned. Wilcott sounded so certain. "Then," she concluded tentatively, "you're saying I've really had nothing to worry about these past few days after all, that there's no problem in the Stanton Group and Bob wasn't involved at all."

Wilcott nodded. "That'd be my opinion."

Julie sighed wearily. The detective hadn't gotten where he was by being a fool. That meant he was probably right. The knowledge half filled her with relief that all her fears had been groundless, half filled her with dismay about the terrible things she'd said to Bob; about Wilcott questioning Tracy and Neil. "I certainly hope you're right," she told Wilcott. "But, if you are, I could easily spend the next month apologizing to people for everything stupid I've said and done—including wasting so much police time." She thought, momentarily, about having to call Bob and apologize. No, she told herself firmly. That was one instance where it was best to let things lie.

The detective shook his head. "You had a good reason to be concerned. And we had to check things out. But I think the odds are you've seen the last of your trouble. Call me if there does turn out to be anything further. And I'll hope I don't hear from you," he added with a wry smile.

Neil was hovering in his doorway when Julie and Wilcott came out of Rigg's office. The three of them walked to the elevator and chatted about nothing until it arrived. The door closed on Wilcott and Neil turned to Julie. "Is there anything I should know, Julie? Is there actually something wrong?" His concern was clearly audible in his voice.

She shook her head, feeling incredibly guilty. "I'm sure there isn't, Neil. I've seen nothing at all. It was just the coincidence of the initial audit being stolen that started all of this. I'm sorry it's ended by upsetting people here."

Neil regarded her seriously. "You would tell me if there was something... wouldn't you, Julie?"

She nodded. "Neil, I would and there isn't. The audit's going smoothly. I should be able to wrap up everything except a few details by the end of this week."

"I'm glad to hear that. I'd hate Rigg to think he has any problems in New York."

Julie forced a smile, trying to look reassuring. "No problems, Neil."

Neil merely nodded and turned toward his office. The worried expression had faded, but not completely disappeared, from his face.

Tracy hadn't been in sight when Wilcott had left, but she was back at her desk now. "I'll be going out for lunch shortly," she told Julie, her voice icy. "Is there anything else you need before I leave?"

"Tracy, I'm sorry about Wilcott coming here. I realize you—"

"I thought you said you hadn't seen any problems, Julie."

"I haven't," Julie protested. "It was just that with my break-in and Mark's file being taken—"

"You told me you hadn't even looked at Mark's file before it disappeared," Tracy reminded her sharply.

"I . . . I hadn't." Julie paused, trying vainly to think of something reassuring to say. "We just thought there might have been something in it," she added lamely.

"The man talked to us for more than two hours, Julie. There must be more to it than that!" There was a question in Tracy's statement.

Julie felt absolutely miserable. "There's nothing, Tracy. I guess he was just doing his job."

Tracy's face said she was certain Julie knew more than she was telling. She opened her mouth again, then closed it quickly without speaking, eyeing Julie suspiciously for a moment before turning abruptly away.

Julie watched the other woman walk stiffly to the elevator, realizing it was likely to be an awfully uncomfortable week for her at the Stanton Group. She worked through lunch, sure that, had it not been for Wilcott's visit, Tracy would have suggested lunching together. A little after one, Tracy reappeared and Julie breathed a sigh of relief when she smiled and headed across to her.

"Sorry I was so short with you, Julie. It was just Wilcott's visit, the implication that I'm not doing my job properly, that was so upsetting."

"Everyone knows you do a good job, Tracy."

Tracy smiled again. "Well, I guess I'll feel better after I've seen your unqualified audit report. Just let me know when you need help with anything."

BY FOUR O'CLOCK Julie had reached a good breaking point. She said brief farewells to the others and left. The day had seemed ninety hours long; she definitely deserved a treat. She walked a few blocks to a stretch of fashionable clothing stores and wandered in and out of a few of them, absently looking for something suitable to wear to the G and K clients' reception Friday evening, thinking a new dress might improve her feelings about the event. The annual reception was a command performance for all G and K staff, but she always dreaded the prospect, hated the inane chitchat that passed for conversation at cocktail parties.

In the fourth store, Julie tried on a lacy black suit and smiled at herself in the mirror, realizing that no matter what outfit she looked at she was trying to imagine it through Rigg's eyes. Rigg...for all the distress of the past little while, things had certainly worked out well for her in one respect. Worked out well? What an inadequate expression that was! How about things had worked out wonderfully, marvellously, incredibly? There simply weren't sufficient words to describe the fact that Rigg thought he was falling in love with her.

The stores were beginning to close before Julie finally chose a pale blue, raw silk dress. The dress box tucked under her arm, she hailed a cab. It crawled through the rush hour traffic toward East Sixty-ninth. She scarcely noticed its snail's pace, was barely aware of the driver haranguing his cohorts. Her mind was oblivious to anything that might interfere with her thoughts of Rigg Stanton.

JULIE CLOSED her apartment door and bent to stroke Asset. The cat rubbed affectionately against her ankles.

"Just let me get this dress hung up, Asset. Then I'll find you some dinner." Julie took the dress box into her bedroom, reached into the closet for a hanger and heard a quiet knock on her door. Quickly, she thrust the dress onto the hanger and hurried back along the hall. Charlie Thomas's beaming face greeted her through the keyhole.

She opened her door and saw the cause of the super's expression. He was holding a long, white florist's box.

"This was delivered about half an hour ago, Miss Lind. I guess you got home a little later than usual, huh?"

Julie nodded, smiling at the box. There was only one person who would be sending her flowers—the man she hadn't expected to hear from for the next two weeks. "Thank you, Charlie. I appreciate you taking them in for me."

"No problem," Charlie assured her, backing away. "I saw your taxi arrive and thought I'd bring them right up."

Julie laid the box on the kitchen counter and searched through a drawer for a sharp knife to cut the string. She opened the box, folded back the waxy green wrap inside and the faint scent of roses wafted upward. Yellow roses...the yellow roses of Texas. Julie smiled, lifting one of the long-stemmed beauties from the box and smelling its delicate perfume. She picked up the small envelope from the midst of the foliage and opened it to reveal the card inside. "Change of heart," the message read in a precise florist's script. "I'll call you tonight. Rigg."

Julie grinned happily to herself, stuck the card onto her fridge door with a ladybug magnet and began to arrange the dozen roses in a large, crystal vase—one of the delicate breakables that her mother hadn't transported to Phoenix.

Satisfied with the arrangement, Julie moved the vase to the end table in the living room and began making dinner, looking at the small card on her fridge each time she reached for something inside it.

After dinner, she curled up in the wing chair with a novel, glancing intermittently at the roses and the phone . . . and waiting.

A little after ten-thirty, Julie walked across the room and picked up the receiver. The dial tone buzzed loudly into her ear. Another good theory down the drain; her phone was working just fine. Slowly, Julie replaced the receiver and sat on the couch, near the phone, no longer even trying to concentrate on her book. What had Rigg told her? He'd be traveling for the next few days. It might be difficult to get in touch with her. That was the logical explanation. He'd planned on phoning but had gotten tied up. She reached over and touched the velvet petals of one rose. She was being silly. He'd sent her flowers and he'd call as soon as he could get to a phone. She'd wait a while longer and then go to bed. She'd hear the phone ring when Rigg called.

WEDNESDAY MORNING, Julie lingered over her coffee, watching the silent phone, resisting the urge to check the dial tone again. Her phone wasn't the problem. And she'd slept fitfully last night, waking at the slightest sound—a neighbor in the corridor, Asset rustling in her closet. She hadn't missed Rigg's call; he hadn't made one.

She shook her head ruefully at her own foolishness. He'd been busy and it had gotten too late to call. She'd hear from him today. She stuck her coffee cup into the dishwasher and headed out for the Stanton Group offices.

Once there, Julie's mood brightened. Tracy had completely reverted to her bubbly self and chatted merrily away. "Talk to Rigg last night?" she asked after they began working through a sample account at the terminal Julie was using.

Julie said she hadn't, then smiled at the look of concern that appeared on Tracy's face. "You're just worried about your prediction not coming true, Tracy," she teased.

"No. I'm just a little surprised."

"Well, maybe I should admit he sent flowers." The grin that appeared on Tracy's face made Julie glad she'd told her.

"He'll call you today," Tracy declared confidently. "And my predictions really don't fail very often. No man sends flowers without a follow-up call. They enjoy being told how thoughtful they are."

The two women worked through the morning and, after only a brief lunch break, pressed on. Near the end of the afternoon, the phone on Francine's desk rang and Julie glanced over in amusement at the saccharine voice Francine used to answer it. "Mr. Overbach's office... Oh yes, Mr. Stanton," she purred silkily. "I'm afraid he isn't in his office at the moment. Is there anything I can do for you, Mr. Stanton?"

Julie felt a surge of annoyance, imagining there wasn't a whole lot Francine wouldn't be happy to do for Mr. Stanton. She watched, not even attempting to conceal her interest in the call, curious to see the look on the young woman's face when Rigg asked to speak to her. The awareness that she would undoubtedly feel a malicious satisfaction at Francine's expression didn't make her feel even a tiny bit guilty.

"Certainly, Mr. Stanton. One moment and I'll transfer you." Francine glanced over at Julie and Tracy. "Mr. Stanton would like to talk to you, Tracy. Should I transfer him to that line or to your desk?"

Tracy shot Julie a puzzled look and shrugged slightly before turning back to Francine. "Transfer it over here, Francine." She picked up the receiver on the first ring.

"Hi, Rigg. What's up?" She listened for a moment. "I'm not certain about that. I'll check with Neil as soon as he gets back. He shouldn't be long. Is there a number he can reach you at?" Tracy wrote down a telephone number. "Area code 713?" she asked, jotting those numbers at his reply. "Fine." She glanced at Julie. "Did you want to talk to anyone else, Rigg?"

The pause, Julie thought, lasted forever.

"Fine . . . I'll have him call, then." Tracy hung up and looked anxiously at Julie. "I guess he was in a rush."

Julie answered carefully, hoping her disappointment wasn't obvious. "I guess he was."

Tracy tapped the area code. "He's in Houston—or around there some place."

Julie merely nodded. Traveling? That was Rigg's idea of traveling? A suburb of Houston? And there was certainly no dearth of telephones around Houston. . . . He'd obviously managed to find one to call Neil. Well, she assured herself, Tracy was right. He'd been in a rush. He'd phone her tonight. She glanced at Tracy and forced a smile. "You're more concerned than I am, Tracy."

Tracy hesitated, then grinned. "Yeah! Silly, isn't it. Guess I'm just the romantic type."

JULIE GLANCED from her watch to the roses to her silent phone. She could understand Rigg getting tied up last night, being too busy to talk with her at the office this afternoon, but tonight . . . not calling for the second evening in a row after he'd made a point of letting her know he would? *Change of heart. I'll call you tonight.* But that had been last night. This was beginning to make no sense at all.

Julie fingered Rigg's business card. She flipped it over and absently underlined his residence number in Houston with her nail. He'd told her to call the ranch if she had to get in touch with him. Well, she didn't have to. But she wanted to. He'd said she probably wouldn't hear from him until he was back in New York. Fine...she could have lived with that. But why the change of heart? Why the roses and the promise to call her if he hadn't intended to? It was almost as if he were playing a game with her.

The thought that something was wrong flashed through her mind. She doubted that was it. He'd called the office this afternoon. Nothing had been wrong. And why hadn't he talked to her then...even just for a moment...even if only to explain why he hadn't phoned last night?

Julie firmly replaced the card beside the phone. She had to get to bed. There must be an explanation but she couldn't spend the entire night waiting up for a call that might not come.

JULIE AWOKE ON THURSDAY morning more tired than she'd been when she'd gone to sleep. She'd dreamed about Rigg...several times. And each time she'd woken up in a cold sweat. In every dream Rigg had been laughing at her, mocking her. His warm eyes had been stone cold and his lazy smile had been a sardonic sneer.

Each time she'd wakened, Julie had been more certain that Rigg was playing some game, that he was punishing her for something she'd done. She'd lain awake since dawn, trying to determine what, precisely, he was up to.

And gradually, she'd realized the truth. Her suspicions from days ago had come trickling back. Rigg's only interest in her had been as his company's new auditor. His only concern had been whether or not Mark had found a problem, whether she would find a problem. And once that possibility had been ruled out, once she'd told him there was nothing wrong, that she was sure Bob had been be-

hind the file disappearing, she was of no further interest to
Mr. Rigg Stanton.

She'd conveniently confessed to suspecting Bob and
Rigg had flown off to Houston, secure in the knowledge
that there was no longer any need to be charming to her.
And all that had happened between her story about Bob
and Rigg's departure had been lunch . . . and that scene at
the Plaza. Her face burned, just thinking back to it. What
a fool he must have thought her! What an idiot she'd made
of herself! She buried her head in her hands, not wanting
to even think about how she'd encouraged him, how she'd
almost . . .

Well, thank heavens she hadn't! Things had gone too far
as it was. He'd likely been laughing at her the entire time.
Falling in love with her! Falling in love with her, indeed!
Magic . . . Oh! She groaned quietly at the recollection of
that discussion. She felt like kicking herself. He hadn't
phoned because he'd never had any intention of calling her
again . . . from Houston or from New York.

But the roses . . . why the roses? She couldn't figure out
that piece of the puzzle at all. Why would he have wanted
to upset her this way? She shuddered to think. Her judgment of people was going from bad to worse. There was
only one explanation for the roses and the card. Rigg
Stanton had a mean streak a mile wide.

Chapter Nine

The day dragged slowly and Julie found her attention faltering each time a phone rang. When the call wasn't for her, she'd force her mind back to work, ordering herself to stop thinking about Rigg Stanton. But almost every piece of paper she looked at was a *Stanton* Group invoice or *Stanton* Group letterhead. By two o'clock she didn't think she could stand seeing that name one more time. She wandered over to Neil's office, trying to look a whole lot cheerier than she felt. "Feel like a break, Neil? What about doing those inspections this afternoon?"

Neil nodded. "Sure. How thorough do you have to be? If a look-see is enough for the rental, we can just stop off at it on our way to the redevelopment. There are copies of the ownership records in the files here you can use as checks."

"I guess a drive by would be enough," Julie agreed, realizing she was being a little lax, that she'd be willing to agree to almost anything to escape from the office. She'd inspect the project carefully, she told herself. That would make up for the cursory look at the rental.

Tracy watched curiously while Julie packed all the leftover work into her briefcase. "Taking everything home?"

"Yes, I might feel like working on it tonight." She might, she realized, be glad of something to keep her mind occupied. She was relieved to see Neil approaching, relieved Tracy wouldn't have a chance to launch into another reassuring monologue about how busy Rigg must be.

Julie and Neil rode the elevator down in silence. Neil, she had realized, was not of Tracy's forgive-and-forget persuasion. He'd remained somewhat cool to Julie since Wilcott's visit.

Neil hailed a cab in front of the building. "Head toward the Trump Tower," he told the driver.

Julie grinned, determined not to let Neil see how down she was. "That isn't your latest rental acquisition, is it?"

Neil laughed. "No, we aren't quite in that league. But we do have property in some very pricey districts."

The building Neil finally directed the driver to, a rather nondescript office building, definitely offered no architectural competition to the glittering glass of the Trump Tower. The cab waited, meter clicking, as Julie and Neil poked briefly about the exterior and main floor lobby.

"Certainly looks like a viable asset to me," Julie offered. "I'll get the figures on it from the files."

Neil turned back to the cab. "We're going down to the Seaport district," he instructed, getting back inside.

The driver nodded. "It's your meter that's running."

Half an hour later, they pulled up at an old brick building a few blocks from the Fulton Fish Market. The building's main floor had been boarded off from the sidewalk and men in work clothes were visible on the floors above the hoardings. Neil paid the driver through the open window and turned to Julie. "Wait here while I find the contractor. He's not going to want you wandering around in there without a hard hat on."

After a few minutes Neil reappeared, a hard hat now perched crookedly on his head. He was accompanied by an extremely good-looking man in his late thirties.

"Julie Lind, Craig Howarth," Neil introduced them.

Craig removed his own hard hat, then glanced at his hand and rubbed it across one leg of his tight jeans, shooting Julie an open, engaging smile that deepened the crinkly laugh lines beside his blue eyes. "I won't shake hands with you, Julie. I'm afraid construction isn't the cleanest occupation in the world."

Julie smiled at Craig. His hair was blond, almost white, in fact—bleached, she imagined, by the same exposure to the sun that had produced his golden tan. He had the muscular physique of a man accustomed to physical labor, a build that some men paid a fortune to acquire in a gym.

"Want the royal tour?" Craig asked her.

"Well, at least a bit of it. I'd like to see exactly how you turn something that looks like this into a building people enjoy working in."

Craig glanced at Neil.

"I think I'll pass this time," Neil answered. "Here." He handed his hard hat to Julie and took her briefcase from her.

The hat slipped down far over her forehead, pushing her bangs so low she had to brush them from in front of her eyes so she could see again.

Craig laughed. "At least no one can accuse you of having a swelled head, Julie. Just be sure you can see well enough not to step on anything you shouldn't." He glanced down. "High heels aren't the recommended gear for inspecting a site like this."

Craig's eyes, Julie thought, lingered a little too long on her ankles, traveled a little too slowly up her legs.

The two of them wandered around the site, Craig pointing out what changes were being made, how they planned to retain the original character of the building while completely modernizing it.

"I must be lacking in the imagination department," Julie told him with a wry grin. "I can't believe this is going to end up as attractive as the Stanton offices."

Craig smiled. "We're hoping it'll be better—practice makes perfect and all that. I'll have to invite you back to see it when I'm finished...show you what I can do." He shot her an extremely suggestive look.

Julie merely nodded, revising her impression of Craig Howarth downward several notches. She studiously kept her eyes off the contractor until they'd completed the tour and rejoined Neil on the sidewalk outside the hoardings. The vice president had a taxi waiting.

Neil glanced at his watch as he clambered into the back seat after Julie. "It's quitting time. Want me to drop you off at your apartment on the way back?"

Julie nodded. "That would be great." She gave the driver her address and the cab lurched forward.

"What did you think of the project, Julie?"

"Looks good. Does Craig do all of your renovation work?"

"Pretty well. He's consistent and he does a first-class job."

Julie glanced across at Neil. There was an unspoken *but* at the end of his statement. There was something about Craig Howarth that bothered him. She wanted to ask what it was, certain it had nothing to do with Craig ever having looked lustfully at Neil's legs. She decided to mind her own business. For all Neil had been consistently polite to her, she sensed he wasn't about to tell her much he didn't have to. The taxi pulled up in front of her apartment house.

"Well," she said, opening the door, "see you in the morning, Neil."

"Yeah, see you, Julie."

JULIE'S CLOCK RADIO clicked on. "Wake up, New York!" The announcer's voice was a grating intrusion. "It's Friday, folks. The weekend's almost here!" he continued with annoying cheerfulness. If she could have reached the radio without rolling over, she'd have turned him off. Instead, she merely glanced over at the clock, realizing through her tired haze that she'd gotten to sleep last night, after all. It must have been four, four-thirty at least before she'd managed. If she had no other reason to be furious with Rigg, Julie reflected bitterly, he'd caused her to lose a lot of sleep this week.

She pulled the pillow down over her head, thinking she'd be hard-pressed to make it out of bed, let alone through the entire day. She groaned, remembering that the clients' reception was tonight, and pressed the pillow more tightly against her face. If she smothered to death, she wouldn't have to get up.

Telling herself not to be overdramatic, Julie dragged herself out of bed, pulled the drapes open and groaned. Rain was pouring down from a gray sky; her bedroom window was smeared with tiny rivulets of wet dirt.

In the bathroom, Julie splashed cold water on her face and peered into the mirror, instantly wishing she hadn't. "Ugh!" She groaned again. The face creating that reflection shouldn't be let loose on an unsuspecting world. She stared into the mirror, flirting with the idea of playing hooky. Why not? There wasn't an awful lot more she could do on the Stanton audit until all the verification letters were returned. Why not stay home, get some sleep and gear herself up to being civil at the reception tonight. Yes. She'd call Tracy and tell her she wasn't feeling well...which was certainly far from a lie.

Julie lingered over coffee until she was sure Tracy would have arrived at work and then dialed, feeling guilty. Maybe she should simply tell the truth—that she needed to take the day off, that she hadn't been sleeping well. And what would Tracy conclude? That Julie was so upset about Rigg's not calling she hadn't been able to sleep, couldn't face coming in to the Stanton Group? Likely she would. Tracy seemed to have a sixth sense about that sort of thing. And she'd tell Neil...and Neil might tell Rigg. Damn! She wasn't going to let any of them know how badly Rigg had hurt her.

Tracy answered the phone and Julie mumbled her story.

"That's too bad, Julie. Is it the flu or what?"

Rats! She should have known Tracy would press for details. "Uhh...migraine," she explained.

"Migraine..."

How, Julie wondered, could Tracy say one word and tell her she knew she was lying? Migraine! What a stupid thing to say. She didn't even suffer from hay fever, let alone migraines.

"You took a lot of files home with you yesterday," Tracy reminded her.

"Yes, sorry, I'd forgotten about that. Is there anything you'll need today, Tracy? I could stick them in a cab for you."

"No...no, I don't imagine I'll need them before next week," Tracy told her slowly. "But if I do, will you be at home?"

"Yes, yes, of course."

"Do you think you'll be feeling better by tonight, Julie?"

"Tonight?"

"Yes. Will we see you at the G and K reception?"

"Oh, yes. At least, I hope so. I hadn't realized you were going."

"Neil thinks someone from the Stanton Group should go. And, since Rigg isn't in New York, that leaves us."

"Yes. Well, I'm sure I'll be feeling better by then. I'll see you there." Julie hung up, wondering how some people managed to lie glibly. Tracy hadn't believed her migraine story for a second.

Julie sat with her coffee, staring absently at the roses. They were fully open now, absolutely gorgeous. And they were sitting there, on her end table, silently mocking her. She'd really begun to hate those roses—those yellow, Texas roses. She should throw them out. *Don't be childish,* she rebuked herself. *They're just flowers.* Julie eyed them for a few moments longer, then went into the kitchen and got a green garbage bag from under the sink.

JULIE TOOK A DEEP BREATH and fixed a smile firmly on her face as the elevator slowed at the tenth floor. The last time she'd been to the office in the evening was when she'd come to retrieve Mark's non-existent backup file on the Stanton Group. If that backup had existed she likely could have wrapped the audit up in a day or two and wouldn't have needed to spend time at Rigg's offices, time with Rigg. Things certainly would have been different.

The elevator doors opened onto the G and K reception area. Much of the brass and glass furniture had to be removed for the evening, making the space look far larger than it normally did. The coatrack, to her left, was already filled with raincoats and umbrellas, many of them still dripping. Julie added her umbrella to the collection and crossed the room toward the welcoming group of senior partners, her determined smile already beginning to make her face ache.

Ray Brent smiled warmly at her. "Nice to see you, Julie. I was starting to worry that we'd lost you permanently to the Stanton Group."

"Not a chance," Julie assured him. *Not a chance in the world,* she added ruefully to herself. "I should be back here by Tuesday."

"Got things just about wrapped up then?"

She nodded.

"Good. I appreciate the time you put in last weekend. You deserve to give yourself a few days off once it's all done."

Julie felt a twinge of guilt and hoped Ray didn't learn she'd already given herself one today.

"The bar's set up in there." Ray's gesture indicated one of the conference rooms off the reception area. "Why don't you get something to drink and circulate a little? The Stanton people came in a while ago."

The only place Julie wanted to circulate was back onto the elevator and home. Instead, she obediently headed in the direction of the conference room, glancing absently around the crowded reception area for Tracy and Neil. She spotted them, standing by the windows on the far side...standing with Rigg! Standing with Rigg and the gorgeous brunette whose shoulder his arm was possessively encircling!

A knife twisted inside Julie's stomach, sending pain up all the way into her heart. What was he doing here? What was he doing with that woman? Why was he doing this to her? She had to get away. She couldn't; her feet were rooted to the floor. And then Rigg saw her. His face broke into a broad grin. He spoke briefly to the brunette then strode toward Julie. She watched him, wanting to flee, unable to move.

He stopped in front of her, his grin a mile wide. "Well?" he demanded.

Julie stared at him, stone-faced, determined not to lose control of her emotions. *Well?* What the hell did he mean, *well?* There wasn't a single thing *well* as far as she was concerned. Quite the opposite! Things were about as far from well as she could imagine them getting, starting with no phone call and ending with a very amply endowed brunette.

"Well?" he repeated. "Did I surprise you? I knew you'd be here!"

Rigg beamed down at her and Julie had a most unladylike urge to ram her fist into those white, even teeth.

"Yes, I noticed you were looking for me," she snapped, delighted to hear her voice wasn't betraying the hurt she felt; it was only revealing her anger.

Rigg's grin turned into a puzzled frown. "Julie, I knew you'd be here so—"

"So," she cut him off, "you thought you'd bring a friend and we could make it a threesome, right?"

Rigg stared at Julie for a moment and then glanced back at the brunette. When he turned to Julie again he was clearly trying to keep from laughing. Her blood pressure leaped several points.

"Whoa!" Rigg raised his hands and backed up a step.

"Don't whoa me! I'm not one of your damn horses!" Julie snarled.

Rigg shook his head firmly. "Hold on a minute, Julie. I didn't bring Susanne. I just met her here . . . about ten minutes ago."

"Well, aren't you the fast worker then? But, I suppose I should know that, shouldn't I?" Julie vaguely realized people were staring at them, but she continued to glare at Rigg. How could she have ever thought this man was Mr. Wonderful? Mr. Jerk was more like it! Mr. Insincere Jerk to christen him with an appropriate first name!

Rigg glanced around. "Julie," he said firmly, "I need five minutes alone with you. Where's your office?"

Julie hesitated. Out of the corner of one eye she caught sight of Ray Brent watching them and pasted a smile back onto her face. "This way!" she hissed through her teeth, turning toward the corridor of offices.

Julie opened the door, annoyed that her hand was trembling. She switched on the light and walked around her desk to sit behind it, motioning Rigg to sit in the armchair on the other side of the desk.

Ignoring her gesture, he closed the door and leaned back against it. "I think I'll just stay here," he said evenly. "Just in case you get any ideas about leaving before we finish our discussion."

Julie glared at him.

"Look, Julie. I can understand how you might have jumped to conclusions about Susanne, but isn't your reaction a little extreme? I don't find jealousy particularly flattering."

"Don't even think about being flattered, Rigg! My reaction has nothing to do with your Susanne. She's just the capper to the rest of your games."

Rigg looked perplexed. "All right," he said slowly. "First I'm going to explain about Susanne and then you can explain what you meant by that remark. I arrived here precisely—" he paused, glancing at his watch "—thirteen minutes ago. And I arrived alone. Aside from Ray, the first person I saw that I recognized was Susanne. And she is not my Susanne. We went to school together years ago, in Boston. And that was all we ever did together. She was pinned to a friend of mine—eventually married him, for that matter. She's here tonight with her father, William Brooks, one of your senior partners. I'd just taken her over to introduce Neil and Tracy when I saw you.''

Julie felt her face flush, ordered herself to remember that Susanne wasn't the issue. She shrugged. "Fine. You're right. I jumped to the wrong conclusion about Susanne. But that's hardly the point, Rigg.''

"That's what I'm obviously missing, Julie. What is the point?''

"The point," Julie said as evenly as she could manage, "is that I think when someone says they'll do something they should do it.''

Rigg nodded. "So do I.''

"Then why," Julie asked, fighting to control the tears she felt forming, "did you tell me you were going to call me and then not do it? I have better things to do with my time than sitting around waiting for a phone to ring!''

Rigg ran his fingers through his hair. "Julie, there's been a giant misunderstanding here some place. I definitely did not tell you I'd phone you . . . not right away, at least. As I recall, I said you probably wouldn't hear from me for a couple of weeks, until I got back to New York. As it is, I worked my behind off in Houston rearranging my schedule so that I could spend this weekend with you. I knew you'd be here tonight. I wanted to surprise you!''

Julie was becoming more frustrated by the moment. There was no mistaking the message on that card. She couldn't have gotten it wrong. She'd read it four thousand times. "I guess it's my stupidity that's to blame, Rigg," she snapped sarcastically. "But when I read the words 'I'll call you tonight,' I assume they mean *that* night, as in the evening of *that* day. Is there some different meaning to a sentence like that in Texas?''

Rigg was looking at her strangely. "Julie, I don't have the foggiest idea what you're talking about."

"The card!"

"What card?"

Julie hesitated, suddenly uncertain. Rigg did seem totally confused. "The card that came with the roses."

Rigg slumped back against the door. "Julie, what roses?"

Julie stared across her desk at him, not quite sure she understood. "You didn't send me roses?"

Rigg shook his head. "If you got roses, they were from someone else. Do I have competition you haven't bothered mentioning?"

Rigg grinned unconvincingly after asking the question and Julie frowned, trying to make sense of this.

"You're telling me the truth, Rigg? This isn't some game?"

"Julie, why on earth would I be lying? If I wanted to lie I'd be taking credit for sending you the damn flowers!"

Why would he be lying? Why indeed? She gazed at him steadily for a moment. He looked so concerned, so intense. He couldn't be lying. Her thoughts whirled. It hadn't been Rigg, after all. That revelation was wonderful! But if it hadn't been Rigg, then who?"

"This isn't funny, Rigg," she murmured slowly. "The card was signed with your name. The roses were yellow; I automatically thought of Texas. And the message on the card was from someone who knew you'd told me you wouldn't be calling. It said *'Change of heart. I'll call you tonight.'*"

"And the flowers arrived . . ."

"Tuesday evening."

Rigg moved away from the door, sank into the armchair across from Julie. "And so you thought . . ."

Julie nodded.

"Then I'm starting to understand why you were upset."

Rigg reached across Julie's desk and took her hand in his. His gesture of understanding made her feel guilty about everything she'd been thinking.

"I just kept getting angrier all week, Rigg." She tried to explain her feelings. "Especially when you called the office and didn't even talk to me. You obviously weren't too busy to phone people."

Rigg squeezed her hand reassuringly. "You don't know how much I wanted to talk to you then. But you were the one who'd been going on about not letting anybody know about us. I figured asking Tracy to let me speak with you was the last thing you'd want me to do!"

He smiled ruefully at her. "Julie, I'm sorry. I wouldn't have knowingly upset you for the world. We're going to have to work on our communication skills. But first, we have to figure out what's been happening. Tell me again what the card said.

"Let's think this through," he suggested once she'd repeated the message. "It's pretty unlikely that the doorman at your apartment house is a spy. That means whoever knew you weren't expecting me to call had to be someone you told. Who?"

Julie thought back. "Tracy," she said hesitantly.

Rigg tossed that aside. "Tracy makes no sense. Who else?"

Julie thought again. "Nobody else. I'm not very open about my personal life. I only told Tracy because she was so persistent about knowing." As she spoke, Julie recalled Francine listening to her and Tracy, the expression of dismay on Francine's face. Had it been the conversation about Rigg not intending to call until he returned that Francine had overheard? She couldn't remember.

"I'm not certain, Rigg," she said slowly, "but I think Francine heard Tracy and me talking about it. And," she added thoughtfully, "if she did, then Betty-Anne likely did as well, maybe even Neil."

Rigg gazed at her anxiously for a moment. "Anyone else, Julie? Anyone not at my offices?"

Julie prodded her memory again. "Only a friend. She called me Monday evening to talk about our weekends. She did ask if I expected to hear from you again soon, but she certainly wouldn't have anything to do with all this."

"Does she know Bob? Any chance she'd have told him?"

Julie looked at Rigg blankly, then suddenly realized what he was getting at, realized he was missing a whole lot of information. "No, Rigg. Things have changed since last weekend. It turns out I was wrong...it probably wasn't Bob, after all. More likely, the burglar wasn't anyone, at least not anyone I know. Nothing meant anything—not the letters or the file or anything Bob said."

Rigg's face told her he didn't understand what she was talking about.

"Let me back up." She started again. "This is confusing even for me and I've been here all week. Wilcott came to your office on Tuesday," Julie began, trying to produce a coherent account of what the detective had said, of what he'd concluded.

Rigg listened intently. "Do you really buy that theory, Julie?" he asked with apparent skepticism when she finished. "You really think it was simply a weird burglary after all...that the van was a coincidence...that Bob just happened to resurface in your life last week?"

Julie sighed wearily. "Rigg, I wish you wouldn't start giving me doubts again. It must have all been one giant coincidence. I'm sure Wilcott knows what he's talking about. And now that I've had a chance to think things through without something bizarre happening every time I turn around, I realize that any other conclusion is just too incredible."

Rigg nodded slowly, clearly not convinced. "But that leaves us with the mystery of the roses," he pointed out. "That malicious little trick was pulled by someone who wanted to cause you grief."

"Francine?" Julie asked hesitantly. "She's the obvious one."

"Francine?" Rigg repeated. "Why Francine?"

"Because she has a crush on you and she overheard Tracy and me talking and looked pretty upset."

Rigg looked at her doubtfully, then glanced at his watch. "Do you know which florist the roses came from, Julie? Friday night; it's probably still open."

"Trilliums. The name was stamped on the envelope."

Julie sat silently while Rigg called Information, then the florist. He hadn't been playing games after all. He couldn't have been! How could she have believed he didn't care for her? How could she have been suspecting the worst about him when he was so eager to see her he'd just flown halfway across the country?

She had to stop being such a damn fool! She gazed at Rigg, her mind swirling with relief that he wasn't a jerk after all. But, if Rigg wasn't, then someone else was.

Rigg hung up and shook his head. "Whoever bought them paid cash. I spoke to the sales clerk who wrote up the bill, but she couldn't even remember if it was a man or a woman." He paused, looking anxiously at Julie. "You

really think Francine might have done it? I didn't even realize she had a crush on me."

Julie laughed quietly. "That doesn't say much for your
powers of observation. According to Tracy, you'd have to
be blind to have missed it. But, to answer your question,
yes, I think Francine might have done it. But I also think
we should just forget about it because there's no way we're
going to find out for certain and it can't be worth worrying about."

She watched his face, trying to anticipate his response.
He was absolutely gorgeous. And he was back in her life
again. That fact was so wonderful she scarcely cared
who'd sent the flowers. What did it matter now?

"I can't simply let it drop, Julie. I'll have to talk to
Francine. I'll have to phone her. I can't possibly stay over
till Monday but I'll call her before I leave."

"Why bother, Rigg? I won't be in your office more than
another day or two. I can't think why anyone else would
have sent them, but if Francine did, she'll deny it."

"I don't like it, Julie. I don't like someone doing that to
you and I don't like not knowing who it was. You're
probably right about Francine denying it, though. I
wouldn't be able to get the truth from her. But Wilcott
probably could. Why don't you call him about this, Julie? We have to consider the possibility that it wasn't
Francine—that the roses are somehow connected to
everything else that's been going on."

"Rigg, I think you're overreacting. Wilcott must know
what he's talking about and he figures the burglary and the
van weren't related. He's sure there's no one out there
trying to get me...no rhyme or reason to the break-in. And
the roses were just silly. There was really no harm done—
except that I lost a little beauty sleep."

Rigg gazed across the desk at Julie for a moment, then reached over and ran his fingers gently along her cheek, sending a tingling sensation through her body.

"No one would ever notice you'd lost any beauty sleep at all." He glanced at the fingers that had just caressed her skin and grinned. "Not even a trace of powder. As for Francine, I've never even given her the time of day. I don't get involved with women who wear a lot of makeup."

Julie grinned back at him, feeling a million times better than she had a few minutes earlier. "I don't get involved with women who wear a lot of makeup either. I don't even get involved with women who don't wear a lot of makeup. But what's your point?"

Rigg laughed. "You'll notice I'm still laughing at your jokes, Julie. And my point is that some women aren't my type at all, and some, present company for example, very definitely are. If you weren't hiding behind that desk, I'd be delighted to show you just how definitely."

"Would you?" Julie stared across at him, challenging him to make good on his offer. "Well, Rigg," she teased, "the excitement of hiding is in being found...and I'm hiding right here, in plain sight."

Rigg gazed across the desk at Julie and realized he didn't resent a single minute of the long hours he'd worked in Houston the past few days. He rose from the chair, strode around the desk and, placing his hands firmly on Julie's shoulders, pulled her up. "Found you," he whispered. "And isn't there some rule about finder's keepers?"

Those deep, gray eyes regarded him steadily. "I think that all depends on how seriously you take your game, Rigg."

"If the stakes are high enough, I take the game extremely seriously, Julie. And the stakes here are just about as high as I could ever imagine them."

He bent to kiss her, running his hands down her body, resting them on her hips, pulling her tightly against him. Her mouth was soft and yielding against his, the nearness of her body exquisitely arousing. He pulled back a little. "Let's get out of here, Julie. I want to be alone with you...all alone, without a hundred people lurking practically outside the door. Can you leave the reception this soon?"

She grinned at him. She had the most delightful grin in the world. "Well, it is a reception for the clients, and you are a client. I'm supposed to be nice to you."

"And you are. You're being very nice. Let's go some place where you can be even nicer."

Ray Brent saw them coming back from Julie's office and looked over curiously. Julie swore silently to herself as he headed casually toward them. There wasn't going to be any sneaking out without an explanation.

"Leaving already, Julie?"

She nodded. "Migraine." Surely, if she tried that excuse often enough, someone would believe it.

Ray looked at her skeptically. "I didn't know you suffered."

"It's the weather, Ray." Rigg gestured at the rain-covered windows. "It's all the heat you've been having along with the humidity. Causes roller-coaster air pressure levels...that's the devil for bringing on migraines. Julie shouldn't even have come tonight," he added sternly. "And it's far too hot in here. She has to get out and cool off. I've offered to drive her home."

Ray regarded Rigg carefully. Julie wasn't certain if he believed Rigg, but he obviously wasn't about to contradict a client. She searched for her umbrella on the rack while Rigg continued to chat with Ray about the rain.

The elevator doors closed behind them and Julie collapsed, in laughter, against the back wall. "Rigg, you're an outrageous liar! And I think Ray almost believed you! Air pressure levels cause migraines? I hadn't realized you have a medical degree."

Rigg laughed. "Not quite, but I do have a kid sister who's in med school. Every time she's home for a visit she spends half her days telling us all sorts of medical facts that we have no interest in. It's nice to be able to use the odd bit of information now and then." He caught Julie's hand in his and pulled her tightly against him. "And you should be grateful for my secondhand knowledge. I don't think Ray believed you for a moment."

Julie leaned into Rigg's chest, delighting in the firmness of his muscles, the warmth of his body. "And you know what else I don't think he believed for a moment?"

"What?"

"That you have any intention of letting me cool off."

"Well, Ray didn't get to be a senior partner by being any dummy, did he?"

Julie reluctantly pulled away from Rigg as the elevator slowed. It opened onto the lobby and she exchanged a few pleasantries with a couple of G and K staff who were on their way up.

"Wait inside while I get the car, Julie. There's no point in both of us getting wet. And," he added with a grin, "we know what all that humidity out there does to migraine sufferers."

"Here. At least take my umbrella."

Rigg shot her a look of horror. "Real Texans don't use umbrellas, ma'am!"

Julie laughed quietly as he disappeared into the night. She couldn't remember ever being this happy before. What had started out as an evening of disaster was likely to end up as the most beautiful night of her life.

Chapter Ten

The curb lane in front of Julie's building was a solid row of parked cars. Rigg pulled the Mercedes to a halt. "I'll let you out here and go find a place to park. I'm assuming," he added with a grin, "that you intend to invite me in."

The wipers swished rhythmically back and forth in the darkness, counting the seconds until Julie replied. "Well," she finally teased, "I suppose...since you did come all the way from Houston to see me..."

Rigg leaned across and opened her door. "I'll be back in a couple of minutes." He watched as Julie navigated her way between two parked cars. She was holding her umbrella so low over her head that he didn't imagine she could see much, and he waited until she'd reached the brightly lit area near the entrance. Then he shifted into first and started slowly down the street. A few yards along, he took one final look into the rearview mirror and his heart stopped. In the mirror, a shape leaped from the shadows behind Julie, knocked her umbrella to the sidewalk and wrapped an arm around her throat.

Rigg ground the gearshift into reverse, floored the accelerator and screamed backward through the darkness. He slammed on the brakes and the powerful car skidded on the wet pavement. It was still moving when he hurtled from it toward the struggling figures.

He dived at Julie's assailant, locking his hands around the man's throat, yanking him away from Julie and shooting one knee viciously into his kidney region. The mugger grunted loudly, slumping to the sidewalk. He rolled to one side, struggled to his feet and staggered into the shadows. Rigg started after him, hesitated and glanced back at Julie.

She was leaning heavily against the building, looking as if she might collapse at any moment. Her umbrella lay, torn, on the wet sidewalk. Rigg focused on her face; her skin was ghostly pale in the streetlight's harsh glare.

He looked back into the street. The mugger had made it to the far side and was limping rapidly away.

"Damn you to hell!" Rigg swore at the retreating figure, then stepped quickly to Julie's side and hugged her tightly. "Julie, are you all right?"

"Yes," she mumbled against his chest. "Yes . . . I am."

Her voice quavered but she wasn't crying. Rigg glanced back at the street in time to see the mugger disappear into an alley. He put his arm protectively around Julie's shoulder and walked her to her doorway in silence.

The doorman appeared, flinging the door open as they reached the entrance. "Miss Lind! What happened? Are you hurt?"

"No. I'm all right, Robert."

"I'm sorry, Miss Lind. I was only gone for a second. I was just helping one of the tenants onto the elevator with some parcels . . . only for a second!"

"It's okay, Robert. I'll be fine."

Rigg glared at the doorman as they passed him and then paused, in the light of the lobby, to brush a lock of damp hair from Julie's cheek. Her face was still incredibly pale.

"Julie, are you certain you're not hurt?"

"Yes. I know I'm still shaking, but I'm fine. Really."

Both her face and voice told Rigg she was lying. "Come on. Let's get you upstairs." Rigg put his arm around Julie's shoulders once more and started to the elevators. He felt her hesitate.

"Rigg, your car's sitting in the middle of the street."

"To hell with my car! I'll worry about it later."

Julie shook her head and smiled. It wasn't much of a smile but it made him feel a whole lot better.

"Oh, damn! I guess you're right. It's still running, and the way things are going, that bastard is liable to come back and steal the thing!"

He frowned over at Robert, who was watching them with a nervous expression. "Think Miss Lind'll be safe here with you for a couple of minutes?"

"Of course, sir!"

Rigg nodded curtly to the man, then turned back to Julie. "Two minutes. That's all. Even if I have to leave it in a tow-away zone."

Julie waited in the lobby, telling herself to calm down. She was safe and unharmed. But the mugger had frightened the devil out of her. She closed her eyes, not wanting to think about what might have happened if she'd been alone. Rigg's two minutes stretched into five. By the time he appeared back at the door he was drenched.

They waited in silence for the elevator, Rigg's arm tightly around Julie's shoulder. The dampness of his suit jacket felt cold against the thin raw silk of her dress, but she wouldn't have had him remove his arm for the world. Neither of them spoke until Rigg closed the door of her apartment behind them.

He pulled her against him. "I just want to hold you for a minute, Julie . . . just need to feel you're really here with me, really safe."

Rigg hugged her so tightly she could scarcely breathe. The smell of wet wool filled her nostrils. The cold dampness of his suit made her shiver but his closeness made her feel secure; surely nothing could harm her as long as Rigg was nearby. Too soon, he released her. Then he looked down and grinned ruefully.

"I'm afraid I've done quite a number on your dress."

Julie glanced at it. The pale blue silk was soaked. The thin, wet fabric clung to her breasts, emphasizing their fullness, exposing the firmness of her nipples. "I guess I'd better change," she murmured, "and turn the air-conditioning off until we warm up a little."

Rigg removed his jacket. "Can I put this someplace?"

"I'll take it . . . and get you a towel. Your hair looks as if you'd just stepped out of the shower." Julie turned down the hall, quickly hung up the jacket in her den and grabbed a towel from the linen closet.

Rigg eyed her as she returned. "You're pretty well soaked yourself. Why don't you get into something dry right away, before we call the police?"

"Police?" She tossed him the towel.

He nodded, rubbing his hair.

"What about? That guy out there?"

"Julie," Rigg said slowly, lowering the towel. "That guy out there could have hurt you."

"I'm not making light of what happened, Rigg. I realize I was awfully lucky. But this is New York. Muggings are a dime a dozen. At least half of them don't get reported. And certainly not when nobody gets hurt and nothing gets taken." She smiled at him. "But I haven't even thanked you. If you hadn't tackled that guy I'd have been in serious trouble."

"It was a lot like throwing a bull."

Julie laughed. "That's one advantage to growing up on a ranch that never would have occurred to me."

Rigg didn't smile at her remark. "Julie," he said slowly, a deep frown spreading across his face, "what if that creep grabbing you wasn't some random mugging? I suspect it wasn't. I think it had something to do with your break-in, with the van, maybe even with those goddamn roses... I think this just shot Wilcott's coincidence theory all to hell!"

Julie walked wearily to the couch and sank onto it. She'd been trying to force that possibility from her mind but now it was out in the open. Rigg sat down beside her and she shook her head slowly, not wanting the incidents to be related.

Rigg took her hands in his. "Julie," he said quietly, "there've been too damn many coincidences. If you aren't going to call Wilcott, I am."

JULIE REPLACED the receiver and turned to Rigg. "He's not on duty again until Monday, Rigg. And I'm just not going to ask them to send someone else over to talk about a minor mugging when they don't know anything about the case. There's absolutely nothing they could do for us. I didn't even see the guy, you didn't get a clear look at him and he's probably home in the Bronx by now, nursing his bruises. We'd just be wasting everyone's time including our own.

"Besides," she added, forcing a grin, "I've gotten pretty tired of having the police on my doorstep every day. Wilcott is starting to seem like a long-lost uncle who's unexpectedly appeared and has no intention of leaving again."

Rigg exhaled slowly. Julie thought he was about to argue but he merely studied her for a moment.

"I guess you're right. There wouldn't be much they could do. And anyway, I didn't come all this way to spend time with the NYPD. I came to spend it with you."

He smiled at her so warmly that Julie practically melted.

"But I didn't come to spend time with you in a hospital ward. As sexy as you look in that wet dress, go and change into something dry before you catch pneumonia. I'll make us some coffee."

Julie laughed. "Are you going to tell me that's something else you learned from your sister, the doctor? That wet dresses cause pneumonia and coffee prevents it?"

"She's only a med student," Rigg corrected. "But Julie, I get the feeling that you have very little respect for all my medical knowledge!"

"That's not it at all, Rigg," Julie told him, backing down the hall. "It's just that we decided you're into magic. That means it's not medicine you practice at all, it's magic! And I think I should be awfully leery of that!"

Julie closed the bedroom door and pulled her dress over her head. Even her slip and bra were soaked, and her shoes, she noted with dismay, were ruined. The feet of her panty hose were sticking wetly to her skin. She peeled them off and discarded them, along with her bra and slip, in a heap on the floor. Then she hastily pulled on an oversize white, cotton-knit sweater that concealed her braless state, and a casual, Indian-cotton skirt that was so long it almost hid her bare feet. She took a quick glance into the mirror and paused to run a comb through her hair.

On her way back to the living room, she stopped in the den and pulled her stepfather's thick, terry-cloth robe from the closet.

"Here." Julie proffered the robe to Rigg. "You must be soaked right through. Would you like this? It's not exactly high fashion but it's dry."

Rigg eyed it, then Julie. "You keep a man's robe in your apartment?"

Julie tried to keep a straight face at Rigg's dismayed expression. "Of course. Why wouldn't I?"

"No reason, I guess," Rigg said slowly. "It just surprises me a little...more than a little. I don't keep any women's clothes at the Plaza." He paused, his look growing more wary. "I think I'll pass. Navy isn't my color... and I wouldn't feel comfortable wearing another man's robe in your apartment."

"Suit yourself." Julie grinned. "But I know Henry wouldn't mind you wearing it. He left it here last fall because it's so bulky to pack. My mother had done a lot of shopping and they ran out of suitcase space."

Rigg glanced at her wryly. "That was rotten, Julie! You know what I thought!"

Julie laughed. "Yeah...you thought you wouldn't look handsome enough in navy. Actually, my mother's housecoat is here, too. It's pink and fuzzy and about a size nine. Would you prefer it?"

Rigg reached for the blue robe. "I look even worse in pink. And, as long as this is Henry's, maybe I will get out of these wet things. After all, Henry and I are old friends. We've even talked on the phone once."

"Just throw whatever's wet over the side of the bathtub, Rigg. Smells like your coffee's ready. I'll get it while you change."

Several minutes later, Rigg poked his head into the living room. "I'm not sure you're ready for this, Julie. I almost put my wet clothes back on." He stepped into the doorway and grinned sheepishly. "I guess Henry isn't very tall."

Julie looked at Rigg's legs, their muscular nakedness exposed from the knees down. The sparse dark hair on them did nothing to hide the marks left by the elastic of his socks. The sight of him in Henry's bathrobe made her suddenly anxious.

She knew how this evening was going to end. And that was what she wanted...wasn't it? Then why the jitters? She was starting to feel thirteen years old again. She was being ridiculous! Damn! Why couldn't she be as casual about this sort of thing as any other liberated woman?

She forced a smile. "It's just as well I'm not a leg woman, Rigg. That's definitely not a pretty sight. Of course, Henry always has pajamas on under the robe, so I guess I'm not being quite fair to you."

"I don't suppose Henry left his pajamas here as well, did he?"

"Nope, they weren't bulky to pack."

Rigg slumped onto the couch beside Julie. "Well, at least I'm dry. Do I get some of that coffee to warm me up?"

Rigg leaned back against the couch, sipping coffee, glancing occasionally at Julie, apparently content to sit companionably with her. She gazed down at his bare legs. She'd lied. They were undoubtedly the best pair of male legs she'd ever seen.

And the bathrobe was open halfway to his waist, exposing a mass of dark chest hair that she felt an almost overwhelming desire to run her fingers through. But she wasn't certain how he'd take to that. At the moment, she wasn't certain about anything. Here she was, alone with a practically naked man, who was the sexiest thing this side of Hollywood, and she couldn't fully enjoy it because her stomach was doing nervous flip-flops.

There was no doubt she was in deep. And the idea of making love to Rigg Stanton was very, very appealing. She was crazy about the man and he simply had to be crazy about her. She smiled a little at that. No man who wasn't crazy would come all this way to surprise her. So why was he just sitting there, drinking his coffee?

She might be liberated but she certainly wasn't about to attack him. She glanced at her empty coffee cup. "Would you like a brandy?"

"That would be nice."

Julie took the coffee cups into the kitchen and poured brandy into two snifters. Her hands were trembling again. This time it wasn't with anger, or with fear. This time, she knew, it was with the excitement of anticipation.

She handed one of the glasses to Rigg and sat down beside him on the couch. "What shall we toast?"

"How about toasting you?" He raised his glass. "To the most beautiful accountant in New York."

Julie laughed. "All right. And, since you're willing to risk giving me a swelled head, how be we also toast the most beautiful Texan in New York."

Rigg grinned and looked down. "With these legs?"

"Well, they're not really so bad."

Rigg raised his glass. "To the accountant and the Texan, then. That's us, Julie.... To us."

Julie took a sip of brandy, gazing over the top of her glass at him. "I'll drink to that, Rigg. To us."

Rigg watched her quietly.

"I'm glad you came back to New York," Julie finally broke the silence.

"So am I."

Julie sipped more brandy, aching to have Rigg hold her. He had to realize what she wanted. Her desire must be plastered all over her face.

He drained the brandy snifter and put it on the coffee table.

"Would you like a little more, Rigg?"

Rigg reached over and brushed her cheek gently with his fingers. "What I'd really like, Julie, is you."

The warmth from his touch spread through her like the warmth of the brandy. "I'd like that, too, Rigg," she told him softly.

"Are you certain this time, Julie?"

She nodded slowly. "I've never been more certain of anything."

"And the audit . . . all your concerns about getting involved with me before it's completed?"

"The audit's almost done. And, from everything I've seen, there's nothing left to have a conflict of interest over. All that's left," she added quietly, "is the interest."

Slowly, Rigg took Julie's glass from her and drew her to him. His lips softly caressed her mouth, his tongue lazily sought hers, his hands slid slowly down the back of her bulky sweater, found its waistband, began to inch their way back upward, beneath it, his palms warm and enticing against her skin. His touch was gentle, yet so exciting. A deep, throbbing sensation began within Julie and she ran her fingers across the back of Rigg's neck, curling locks of his still-damp hair around them, pulling him more firmly against her, responding even more fully to his kiss.

Rigg's hands reached the center of her back, slid over to cup her breasts, making her shiver with desire. He pulled back a little and smiled teasingly down at her. "You cheated, Julie. You have half of your clothes off already."

"They were wet.... And a man sitting in a bathrobe isn't exactly in any position to talk."

"A man sitting in a bathrobe, talking, when you're beside him with half your clothes off and there's a bedroom down the hall, is a lunatic. And I certainly don't intend to fall into that category!"

Rigg stood up, gathered Julie in his arms and began carrying her to the bedroom. He grinned down at her. "I've never done this before...always laughed when I saw it in the movies. Maybe I am a lunatic after all! At the very least, I'm absolutely crazy about you!"

Julie wrapped her arms around Rigg's neck, feeling like the star of a romantic film, being swept off her feet by the handsome hero.

Rigg reached the bed, gently lowered Julie onto it and sat beside her. Slowly, he brushed her hair back from her neck and leaned forward to trail kisses across the hollow of her throat. The heat of his kisses inflamed her desire and she ran her fingers through Rigg's hair, lifted his head from her throat, met his lips with her own. He forced her head back onto the pillow with the firmness of his kisses and began to devour her mouth. His hands moved hungrily, beneath her sweater, devouring her breasts.

Rigg pulled his lips away for a moment. "Oh Julie," he whispered hotly against her neck, "you taste so wonderful, feel so heavenly. I could go on touching you, kissing you, forever."

He slid the sweater up. Julie twisted her shoulders, allowing him to pull it over her head and he moved lower, still fondling her breasts, now kissing them as well, firmly stroking her nipples with his tongue. Each of those probing caresses made her ache for more. Julie's hands slipped under Rigg's bathrobe, across his chest, kneaded his shoulders, delighting in the hard muscularity of his body.

He was pressing her down now, his length against hers. Her body was throbbing so heavily that she was certain Rigg could feel it.

And then his hands moved under the hem of her skirt, slid up her bare legs, began to stroke her thighs and, incredibly the throbbing increased in intensity. Rigg's terry-cloth robe and the voluminous cotton of Julie's skirt, crumpled around her legs, became obstacles, keeping Rigg's body from being close enough to hers. Julie ran her hands down his chest, pushing the bathrobe aside, reaching for the fabric belt. Frantically, as if Rigg might suddenly vanish, as if she might wake up and find this was all a dream, Julie untied the belt, realizing as the bathrobe fell open that Rigg was completely naked under it, completely naked and completely aroused.

He shrugged out of the robe and Julie's hands moved searchingly over his hips, across his stomach. She heard the sharp intake of his breath as she caressed him, felt his fingers fumbling with the button of her skirt. The zipper slid open and Julie arched her back as Rigg pulled the skirt down. Then slowly, gently, he slid off her silk panties and he was beside her, ever so close and yet not nearly close enough. His body was warm and strong and hard; he was intertwining his legs with hers, kissing her face, her breasts, her stomach, caressing her inner thighs, her most private places, using what had to be every ounce of his magic to drive her mad with desire.

Julie raked his back with her nails, wanting him nearer than was physically possible, wanting him to be part of her. Rigg moved his hips against hers and entered her with a hard thrust that took her breath away.

And then he began to move…slowly, deliberately. With each rhythmic thrust a new wave of excitement swept through Julie, barely subsiding before the next one rushed after it. Gradually, Rigg began moving faster, his rhythm became less controlled. His breath, hot against Julie's neck, grew ragged. Her body moved instinctively, in primitive response, beneath Rigg's. The waves of excitement came crashing faster, stronger, threatening to overwhelm her totally, until finally they did so with an incredible surge that left her quivering. Rigg's hands dug into her shoulders and his body collapsed onto hers.

After a few moments, he rolled onto his side, pulling Julie tightly against his chest. "Still glad I came back?" he whispered.

Julie stroked the arm that circled her waist. "That just might be the understatement of the century."

Rigg brushed her hair aside and nuzzled her neck. "The best part of all this is that the weekend's barely begun."

Julie shifted position so she could see Rigg's face in the dim light that strayed into the bedroom from the hallway. Softly, she outlined his even features with her fingers.

Rigg smiled a lazy smile at her. "Happy?"

"I'm starting to think you have a way with understatements. I'd have gone with ecstatic."

"I'm glad. I feel pretty ecstatic myself." Rigg kissed Julie's ear, sending a tingle through her body.

Slowly, he stroked her arm. "Ecstatic," he repeated, "but also contented. I can't imagine any place I'd rather be than here with you, Julie. You're the only thing I've been able to think about since the minute we met. All this week, I've been totally preoccupied with thoughts of you. I'd start working on something and then realize I didn't have a clue about what I was doing, that I'd been daydreaming about you again."

Rigg captured Julie's hands in his, exploring her eyes in the dimness. "Julie, I love you. I don't ever want to be apart from you.'' He leaned forward and kissed her tenderly.

Julie's mind whirled. Rigg loved her! He didn't merely think he might be falling in love with her. He wasn't just crazy about her. He loved her! This man, in her bed, kissing her this very moment, in a wonderful way that no man had ever kissed her before, loved her. And she loved him. And she didn't want to be apart from him any more than he wanted to be apart from her.

But his home was on a ranch, in the wide-open spaces of Texas, and hers was on the tiny island of Manhattan, in the middle of the largest mass of humanity in the country. And what the hell were they going to do about that major discrepancy?

''Julie, I want you to do something for me.''

''What?''

''I want you to come back to Houston with me on Sunday.''

Julie glanced at him, surprised. As much as she wanted to be with him, that suggestion was hardly a practical solution to the major discrepancy. She was about to speak but Rigg placed his fingers on her lips, telling her not to.

''Just for a few days, Julie. You said you couldn't finish up the audit until the rest of your letters were returned. And you worked all through last weekend. Couldn't you take a few days off? I absolutely have to be in Houston for a meeting on Monday and I just don't want you thousands of miles away. Especially not right now,'' he added slowly. ''I am definitely not convinced Wilcott's coincidences theory hangs together, not after tonight.''

Julie fought back her anxiety, wishing Rigg would stop telling her Wilcott could be wrong. She didn't want to think that might be true.

"Julie—" Rigg's voice broke into her thoughts "—what you said earlier was only too right. If I hadn't been here tonight, you'd have been in serious trouble."

"But you were...and I wasn't...and I did thank you."

"That isn't what I'm getting at; I'm not fishing for gratitude. What I'm getting at is that I almost wasn't here, almost wasn't with you. I worked every night this week so that I could get away, and even then I practically missed the flight because I got tied up in a meeting. And Julie, the entire week I kept worrying about you being back here by yourself. And I was right to worry."

Rigg caressed the side of her neck softly as he spoke. She ordered her mind to stay in control. That gentle touch might convince her of almost anything.

"Julie, the thought of you being alone in this city drives me bananas. I don't know if this guy tonight had anything to do with all the rest of your mystery or not. But whether he did or didn't, he's just gotten me even more concerned about you. Julie," Rigg continued slowly, "have you ever thought about living anywhere other than Manhattan?"

Julie shook her head, trying to decide whether this was déjà vu or a rerun. She'd always lived in Manhattan but suddenly people were telling her how foolish she was to be here. First Bob...now Rigg. What was going on? *Don't get too defensive about New York,* she warned herself. The last thing she wanted was an argument with Rigg.

She propped herself up on one elbow, wanting to watch his face while she explained. "Rigg, the New York you saw tonight—and last week—that isn't my New York. I've never had a break-in before, never been mugged before. It's as if all the odds ganged up on me at once. I realize New York isn't the safest city in the country but it isn't the most dangerous, either. I think," she continued, trying a smile, "that we're way down to number ten these days."

Rigg didn't return her smile but she pressed on.

"New York just gets bad press, Rigg; it's really a wonderful city. My New York is...I don't know... It's the whole atmosphere—ideas, conversation, galleries, museums. Rigg, the city's so stimulating that I can feel the air is charged with energy. You can do everything here. If I want, I can spend a Monday evening listening to Woody Allen play clarinet in a pub, or I can spend it at the opera." She tried smiling again.

This time Rigg smiled a half smile in return. "I understand what you're saying, Julie. But New York isn't the only great place in the world. Texas is pretty terrific, too. Haven't you ever listened to the lyrics Tanya Tucker sings?"

"Tanya Tucker? I don't know her music. Has she ever played Carnegie Hall?"

Rigg broke into a laugh and Julie sighed with relief. He shook his head ruefully at her. "You're a snob, Julie!"

"Maybe just a bit. Look, Rigg," she pushed on while he was still smiling, "I understand how you feel about New York, but the bottom line is I can't possibly go to Houston with you. Not on Sunday, not while I'm still your company's auditor. I know what I said before about that not really mattering now, but I still have a boss to consider. Ray would have a hundred fits if he even knew where you are right now, let alone if I blatantly traipsed off to Texas with you. I simply can't do it. I've already stepped a mile over the fine line of discretion. If Ray found out about you being in my bed, I'd be finished. Even as it is, after our little escape from the reception tonight, I'll likely find myself in line for a lecture on professional ethics."

Rigg ran his fingers through his hair, obviously trying to control his annoyance. "Julie, how can you be so damn rational? So damn logical? To hell with Ray Brent! I don't care what he thinks, what anyone thinks except the two of us. I have a hundred reasons for wanting you to come to Texas!"

"Rigg," Julie said softly, "it's not that I don't want to. It's that I have a very important reason for not going. I'd like to keep my job."

"Julie, I can understand that. But there are things more important than a damn job. I know this is going to sound chauvinistic, but I'm worried about you and I want to be certain you're safe. And that's just part of it. I want you to see Houston, stay on the ranch, meet my father and my sister.

"But Julie, there's one major reason that's the sum total of all the little ones. It's that I love you, Julie. Damn it! I love you . . . and you love me." He paused and looked at her anxiously in the dimness. "You do love me, don't you?"

Julie smiled at his question. How could he possibly doubt it? "Of course I do. You're here with me, aren't you? I certainly don't make a practice of this sort of thing. Although," she teased, "I think I might start doing just that!"

Rigg grinned broadly. "As long as it's me you're doing it with that's just fine. I love you, you love me. What a wonderful state of affairs! So come with me on Sunday, Julie."

Before she could reply, Rigg leaned closer and kissed her longingly.

Gradually his kiss ended, leaving Julie breathless and certain she was thinking less logically than she'd ever thought in her entire life. "Rigg, I want to see your ranch . . . and meet your family. Just as soon as the audit's done. Give me another week; maybe I could even come next weekend. But not on Sunday, Rigg. I simply can't. I have to be rational and logical. Otherwise, I'm going to find myself unemployed.''

Rigg exhaled slowly. ''Julie, I know it must seem as if I keep trying to tell you how to run your life. I don't mean to. I don't know how long it's going to take me to accept the fact that telling you what to do simply doesn't make you do it. I'm trying to keep quiet, but I'm finding it damn difficult. It's awfully hard not to suggest things when I just want to look after you, to protect you.''

Julie smiled, relieved he was making an effort not to push. ''Don't get all macho on me, Rigg,'' she teased. ''I really haven't done a bad job of looking after myself all these years.''

''No. That's obvious. But, Julie, you will come out for a few days . . . as soon as you can?''

''Scout's honor!'' She grinned, holding up two fingers in a signal.

Rigg laughed. ''You don't look much like any Boy Scout I ever met.''

''That's 'cause I'm a New York scout. We're much cuter than Texas scouts!''

''Well, I don't know about all New York scouts, but you're certainly cuter than any Texas scout I've ever seen. I'll grant you that. Especially,'' he added with a leer, ''when you don't have a uniform on.

''Does Cleo's deliver?'' he asked, switching subjects so abruptly he took Julie aback.

''Pardon?''

''Your corner deli, does it deliver?''

''Rigg, haven't you eaten dinner tonight?''

He grinned at her. "Yes, but I wasn't thinking about tonight. I was thinking about breakfast in bed tomorrow...and lunch...and dinner tomorrow night...and breakfast on Sunday...and..."

Julie laughed. "Oh, no you don't! Now that I've got you for the entire weekend, I intend to show you all the sights, show you all the wonderful places in New York."

"Julie, I've already found the most wonderful place there can possibly be in New York. It's right here with you." Rigg ran his hand along Julie's side, causing an ache of desire to start, once more, deep within her. He moved closer, pressing his body against hers, showing her how ready he was to make love again.

She wasn't at all certain she wasn't facing a weekend of Cleo's deliveries. And she wasn't at all certain she would mind a bit.

Chapter Eleven

SUNDAY AFTERNOON

Julie stretched luxuriously under the sheet. "This is the first time I've spent an entire weekend in bed since I was eight years old. Only then, I had the measles... and I got an awful lot more sleep."

Rigg grinned at her, tossing the *Times'* Sunday crossword puzzle to the bottom of the rumpled bed. "And this time you had me. Can I assume you enjoyed being in bed with me more than with the measles, despite the lack of sleep?"

"That goes without saying."

"Say it anyway. I'd like to hear it." Rigg leaned over and kissed her cheek.

"Mmm, I must have said it a thousand times, a thousand different ways. Isn't your male ego ever satisfied?"

Rigg didn't laugh. "I just need reassurance. Being here, with you, doesn't seem quite real."

Julie reached for his hand. "I know exactly what you mean."

Rigg glanced at the clock radio. "I've got to get going, Julie. I guess there's no point in asking you again, is there?"

"I'll come for a visit as soon as I possibly can, Rigg. I promise."

Rigg got out of bed, obviously not happy about her insistence on staying in New York. He dressed quickly then picked up Julie's robe from the floor and tossed it to her. "Here. It's hardly worth your while getting dressed just to see me to the door. Besides," he added with a grin, "I like you in that white robe. You never have anything on underneath it."

Julie slipped into the robe, watching Rigg straighten his tie in the mirror. "We should have gotten that suit to the cleaner's, Rigg. Or, at least, I could have pressed it for you."

Rigg smiled at her. "Julie, you did everything for me that I could possibly have wanted...and then some. I have to stop off at the Plaza anyway, to leave the car. I'll change and someone there can look after the suit."

He took her hand and led her slowly down the hall, lingering at the door, his arms around her waist, his expression worried. "I wish to hell I didn't have to go back, Julie. I hate leaving you alone here."

"Rigg, I'll be fine. I'm a big girl."

He smiled anxiously. "I'll call you tomorrow night. And, if you get any flowers with a different message, don't believe it!"

He bent to kiss Julie, his lips making her wish she could get on the plane with him today. She hugged him tightly when he began to draw away.

"Julie, I don't want to leave but I'm going to miss my flight."

Reluctantly, she gave him one last, quick kiss and released him.

"Don't forget to lock the door when I leave."

Julie rolled her eyes. "I'm a grown-up, Rigg. I can cope with these complicated routines."

She slid the lock behind Rigg and wandered back to the bedroom. Her apartment seemed empty. Rigg's presence had made it feel so full of life. But she was used to living alone. How could his departure make the rooms feel so lonely?

Asset had claimed the center of the bed. Julie picked her up and stroked her for a moment. "Sorry to depose you, Asset, but this bed's a disaster." She deposited the cat on the carpet and reached for a pillow. The pillowcase smelled of Rigg. She put it back on the bed. Perhaps she wouldn't change the linen after all. Perhaps she'd merely straighten the sheets and sleep on them again tonight.

JULIE WAS DREAMING of Rigg when the phone woke her. She tried to hold on to the threads of the dream, reached for the bedroom extension, blearily glancing at the clock radio. Seven-thirty. Who would be calling her this early? She picked up the receiver. "Hello?"

"Hello, Julie, it's Ray."

Her heart sank; she was instantly wide awake. There was only one reason her boss would be calling at this hour. She was in big trouble. "Morning, Ray," she managed. "What's up?"

"I didn't waken you, did I, Julie?"

"No, of course not. I was just having coffee." She crossed her fingers at the lies.

"Good. I wanted to catch you before you left for the Stanton Group. I'd like you to come by G and K first. There's something I have to discuss with you. Let's say we get together right at nine?"

"Fine. See you then." Julie hung up slowly, swearing silently at herself, knowing only too well what the something they would be discussing was. Why hadn't she been a little more circumspect on Friday? Why hadn't she and

Rigg left the party separately? Because, she swore at herself once more, she'd been so damned excited about seeing
him again she hadn't been thinking straight. And now she
was going to pay. There was no point in lying to Ray; he
was as sharp as they came. She'd just have to hope she
could get through their discussion without his guessing
how far things had actually gone between her and Rigg.

Julie got ready, grabbed her briefcase, still full of her
working papers and the Stanton files that she'd taken home
last Thursday, and caught a taxi to G and K. She rode the
crowded elevator up impatiently. Every button had been
pressed; every person who wanted off was standing against
the back wall. Her watch read three minutes past nine by
the time she reached the tenth floor. Julie squared her
shoulders and marched off the elevator toward Ray's office, feeling a close kinship to those long-ago Christians
who'd been thrown to the lions.

Ray's door was open. Julie paused in the doorway and
he looked up with a perfunctory smile. "Come in, Julie.
Please close the door." He gestured her into a chair and
clasped his hands on the top of his desk. "How are you
feeling today?"

"Fine, thank you," she told him nervously.

"Migraine completely better?"

Julie nodded, forcing a smile that she was certain looked
as phony as it felt.

Ray sat quietly for a moment, then began. "Julie,
there's no delicate way around this. I'm upset about you
leaving the reception with Rigg Stanton on Friday." He
paused, looking at Julie hopefully, as if expecting some
logical explanation. When she didn't speak he continued.
"I'm certain it was all perfectly innocent, but you know
how people talk. You've always been so careful about ap-

pearances as far as male clients are concerned that I was a little nonplussed.''

"I'm sorry, Ray. I realize it was a foolish thing to do."

Ray sat silently, obviously waiting for Julie to continue, to explain herself.

She couldn't. Whatever she said was only going to get her in deeper. She remained quiet, praying he'd let it go.

"Julie," he persisted, "it was perfectly innocent, wasn't it?"

Julie sighed. "Not perfectly, Ray."

"I see." Ray took his steel-rimmed glasses off, examined them for a moment, tapped them absently on the pile of papers before him. "Julie," he said finally, brushing his thinning, gray hair back with a nervous gesture, "I'm not going to ask you for any details. They're none of my concern. But what is my concern is the fact that you're socializing with the president of a company you're in the process of auditing. Julie, you realize that's against all the rules!"

Julie nodded, trying to recall if she'd ever felt more uncomfortable in her life. "Ray, the audit is almost completed. I'm just waiting for the final verification letters to be returned. And I've seen absolutely no problems."

"That's hardly relevant," Ray said sternly. "Getting involved with Rigg Stanton is totally unprofessional; your behavior has been extremely questionable. I don't have to tell you that conflict of interest is a very serious issue."

"I know that. I admit again that I was foolish. I have no excuse, no explanation. I apologize, Ray. I was wrong and I'm sorry and it will never happen again. My behavior with Rigg Stanton was a once-in-a-lifetime aberration." Julie stared at the floor, not wanting to face Ray's anger.

Her boss exhaled loudly. Julie glanced across the desk at him. He was shaking his head but there was a trace of a smile on his lips. "Julie, you know I've raised three daughters. We always had a houseful of their friends. I've seen that aberration many times before.'' He paused. ''With the girls, I just came to accept it. But I've always managed to think of you as an accountant first and a woman second. I'm not saying I don't disapprove of what you did, that I'm not distressed by it. I'm merely saying I understand.''

Julie breathed a slow sigh of relief. If she knew Ray's daughters and their friends she'd have made a point of thanking each and every one of them for existing.

Ray slipped his glasses back on. His smile had vanished; he was all business once again. ''I'll have to do a close review of your working papers on the Stanton audit, Julie. Get them to me as soon as possible.''

''I have them right here, Ray,'' Julie told him quickly, tapping her briefcase.

''Good. And once you've got all of the verification letters back, get the results in order and I'll go over them as well. We'll write up the report together. As far as G and K's concerned, I'll record the audit as a required collaboration with a senior partner. That'll wash; initial audits are sometimes sticky.''

''Thank you, Ray,'' Julie said quietly, barely believing he was going to let her off this easily.

''I don't have to tell you never to do anything like this again, do I?''

''No... of course not.'' Julie hesitated, knowing if Ray ever got the idea she was trying to put something over on him she'd be dead. ''But, Ray, there is something I should tell you.''

He regarded her warily.

''Rigg wanted me to go back to Texas with him for a few days. I promised I'd go there soon. Not until after the audit's completed,'' she rushed on, seeing the annoyed expression appear on Ray's face. "But after it's wrapped up I will be going. I just thought I'd better tell you," she added lamely.

Ray eyed Julie intently. "You've had a pretty rough couple of weeks, haven't you ... what with your burglary, that phone call to your mother and all?"

Julie nodded. Ray didn't know the half of it. "It's almost laughable, but I even got mugged on Friday night. No doubt it was some sort of divine retribution for sneaking out of here."

"Oh, Julie, I am sorry. Are you all right?"

"Yes. The gentleman I shouldn't have been with took care of the mugger."

"I see ... And then the gentleman you shouldn't have been with wanted you to get away from New York for a few days."

"I'm glad you have daughters. You don't need all the gaps filled in."

"Look, Julie, you've dug yourself into such a deep hole I don't imagine the reality can be any worse than appearances. I'm already going to have to do a complete review of your work. That isn't likely to help your professional reputation around here, but it'll squelch any potential criticisms about the audit itself."

Ray took a deep breath as if to clear his mind. "There can't be much more work you can do till all your data is in. If you want to take a few days off, go ahead. You have my permission. I can't see that what you and Stanton do at this point makes a lot of difference. Particularly," he added with a smile, "if you don't tell anyone else where you're going."

Julie grinned with a mixture of relief and joy. "Thank you, Ray. You don't know how much I appreciate the offer."

He chuckled. "The look on your face gives me a pretty good idea."

"Well, I'll think about it right now...let you know what I decide in a few minutes." Julie backed out of Ray's office, still smiling her thanks, and raced down the corridor to her own office. Should she go to Texas right away, after all? Rigg had wanted her to. But he was awfully busy. Maybe he wouldn't be able to free up much time to spend with her. And maybe she should wait until the Stanton audit was completed—make certain there would be nothing for Ray to find fault with. Then, once she had everything in order, she could stay in Texas far longer than if she had to hurry back to get the audit wrapped up. She couldn't decide which would be best. For starters, she'd call Rigg and see what things were like at his end.

Julie opened her office door, took a couple of steps inside and stopped abruptly. On her desk, looking as if it had been there forever, sat her antique clock...the clock that had been taken from her apartment. She swallowed hard, glancing quickly about the rest of the room. Then she swallowed a second time. A space had been cleared on her wall unit to make room for the photograph of her and her mother. Its silver frame glistened in the sunlight.

She could feel her heart racing. Keep control, she ordered herself. There's no danger here, at G and K, in the middle of the morning.

No danger? asked a disbelieving little voice inside her head.

Julie tried to think rationally. Sometime last week, while she was working at the Stanton Group, whoever had broken into her apartment had come into her office and left those things. Why? To mock her? To frighten her? To show her they knew where she was and where she wasn't all the time?

But who? Anyone! Anyone here at G and K could have wandered freely in. Did that mean it had been someone from the firm? That was crazy! Her mind pictured Ray, sitting across his desk from her, talking to her in a kindly, fatherly way. Good God! For all she knew, it could even be Ray Brent!

No... wait. More thoughts clicked over. She'd been in her office during the reception on Friday night. She and Rigg had been here and she'd sat at her desk. And there'd been no clock on it. So, someone had come in on the weekend, past security. It must have been someone with a legitimate reason for being in the building, someone who'd signed in. There'd be a record that Wilcott could check. Unless... unless someone had brought them in this morning. Someone who worked here could have simply come in early and left them for her to find.

Julie glanced nervously at her door. She had to get out of here. She didn't want to be at G and K. Damn it! She didn't want to be in New York. The only place she wanted to be was with Rigg! She shook her head ruefully. A week ago she'd been suspecting Rigg Stanton of being involved in all manner of crimes. At the moment, he was the only person on earth she'd feel safe with.

Fingers fumbling, she checked the clients list for the Stanton Group's number in Texas. She dialed and breathlessly asked the receptionist for Rigg.

"May I tell him who's calling, please?" the voice drawled.

Julie gave her name, relieved to find him in his office.

"Julie! What's wrong?" Rigg's voice leaped at her through the phone.

"Nothing, Rigg, nothing at all." She hoped her voice sounded normal. There was no point in upsetting him. There'd be time enough in Texas to tell him what had happened. "Nothing's wrong," she repeated firmly. "In fact, everything's right. That is, if you still want me to come for a visit. I've just been talking with Ray and he said I could take a few days off if I liked. I could be there tomorrow."

"Julie... could you be here today?"

A warmly reassuring feeling washed over her at his words. "I... I guess... If there's a flight."

"Julie, go home and start packing. I'll have someone arrange for your ticket and call your apartment in an hour with the flight number."

Relieved, Julie dialed Neil's office. She grimaced at Francine's saccharine voice; a moment later Neil came on the line.

"Good morning, Neil. I'm just calling to let you know I won't be in for a few days. It'll be the end of the week, maybe even next Monday, before you see me again. I have some of Tracy's files here. Would you mind telling her I'll be returning them by courier today?"

"No...of course I'll tell her. But what's up, Julie? Why the change of plans? I thought you were just about finished here."

"I am, Neil. The audit will be wrapped up on time. It's simply that something's come up." *Don't tell anyone else where you're going,* Ray had said. His advice made sense. Especially after this latest little discovery. "I'm afraid I can't really talk about it. But I wanted you to know you haven't been deserted. In fact," she added, "you're getting special attention. Ray Brent will be reviewing what I've done thus far."

"I see," Neil said quietly.

"Well, bye, Neil. See you in a few days...or next week." Julie hung up and rapidly began sorting through her working papers for Ray and setting aside the files that had to be sent back to Tracy.

In his office, Neil Overbach sat silently gazing out his window for a few moments. Then he buzzed Francine. "Get me Mr. Stanton in Houston, Francine."

Two minutes later, Rigg was on the line.

"Rigg, I'm not going to beat around the bush. I think Julie's found something wrong here." Neil's voice sounded more anxious than Rigg recalled ever hearing it.

"What gives you that idea, Neil?"

"She didn't show up this morning, just called me with some cock-and-bull story about not being in for a few days. And she mentioned that Ray Brent is reviewing the audit. I'm sure that's not standard practice, Rigg. I think she's found something and they want to have a thorough look at things before she comes back here."

Rigg smiled to himself. "Neil, I think you're jumping to conclusions. I'm sure there's some other, perfectly logical reason for her not being there today."

"No, Rigg," Neil insisted. "It's not only that. She had some detective here last week. None of it makes any sense unless there's a problem. In fact, now that I recall, she wasn't in on Friday. Thursday she walks out of here with a whole stack of our files—probably had them photocopied. Friday she calls in sick and today they've decided they need even more time. There's something wrong, Rigg and I have no idea what it is."

Rigg frowned. Julie had said she wasn't to tell anyone where she was going, but he couldn't let Neil worry himself sick about what G and K was up to. "Look, Neil, this is strictly between you and me, but I know all about this and there's no problem at all. Julie isn't coming in today because she's coming to Houston. And her visit has absolutely nothing to do with the company. It's personal... between her and me.''

"I see," Neil said slowly at the other end. "Well, thanks for letting me know, Rigg. I'd have been plenty worried by the time she finally showed up if you hadn't told me.''

JULIE TAPPED on Mrs. Benson's door before she even went to her own apartment. She was relieved to hear the response of slow footsteps inside.

"Julie, how nice to see you.'' The elderly neighbor smiled warmly at her. "The building's usually so quiet during the week when everyone's at work. You're all right? Not sick?''

"No, I'm fine. I just have some time off. Mrs. Benson, would it be a terrible imposition on you to take Asset for a few days?''

"Of course not, dear. Asset and I always have a fine time when you're away.''

"Oh, thanks, Mrs. Benson. I don't know what we'd do without you. And I'm sorry it's such short notice.''

"That's all right. Going to visit your mother?''

"No... No, I'm going to visit a friend in Texas—rather unexpectedly. But I won't be gone long. I'll be back by Sunday at the latest.''

Mrs. Benson smiled. "You stay as long as you want. I enjoy Asset's company. One of these times I'm not going to give her back!''

Julie laughed. "I'll bring her over in a few minutes if that's okay. And I'll leave you a number in Texas in case you have any problems.''

"I'll just go right now and organize that little space in the closet she's so fond of. You bring her over whenever you like.''

Julie walked along the hall to her own door, contemplating what she should pack. She'd never been on a ranch in her life. Jeans; her jeans were a must. Beyond that, it could get tricky. Her wardrobe was geared for a Manhattan life-style. It didn't take much imagination to conclude it might not fit in among a herd of Texas longhorns.

She tossed some probably inappropriate clothes into her suitcase, then called Wilcott. He listened quietly as she told him about the mugging and the mysterious appearance of her clock and photograph.

"Did you touch anything in your office, Miss Lind?"

"I used the phone and sorted through some files."

"But you didn't touch the pictures or the clock?"

"No."

"Good. We'll dust them for fingerprints. And we'll see what the security log shows as far as weekend visitors go. We just might turn up something useful. We're not likely to have much luck tracing your mugger, though." Wilcott paused.

"I think," he finally continued, "that getting out of town for a few days is a good idea. Do you have a number I can reach you at in Texas?"

"Yes." Julie gave him Rigg's number.

"Well, have a good trip. We'll try to sort this out while you're gone. If you don't hear from me in the meantime, call me as soon as you get back."

"Yes. I will. Thanks." Julie hung up the receiver, sank back into the couch and closed her eyes. Instead of feeling reassured about what Wilcott would be doing, she felt worse than ever. He obviously thought she was in danger.

THE 727 COMPLETED its initial climb and began swinging west over the Manhattan skyscrapers. Almost immediately, the plane broke into cloud cover and Julie leaned back from the window into the plushness of her first-class seat. Trust Rigg, she mused, to provide nothing but the best.

The space beside her was unoccupied. Across from it, in the aisle seat, sat a middle-aged man whose appearance made Julie smile to herself. If there were prizes for Texan stereotypes, he'd undoubtedly won his share. He wore a denim suit that sported a flashy, embroidered design across the shoulders, a leather string tie, cowboy boots and a Stetson.

A stewardess paused in the aisle between them. "Would either of you like a drink? We'll be serving a late lunch shortly." Her glance flickered from one to the other.

"Double bourbon for me, on the rocks," the man stated. "And what'll you have, little lady?" He peered across at Julie with a broad, friendly grin.

"Oh, nothing, thank you." Julie spoke to the stewardess but it was the man who replied.

"Nonsense!" he snorted. "The air in here's dry as yesterday's oatmeal. Little lady like you'll dry up an' blow 'way without somethin'."

Julie laughed. "Well, perhaps a little white wine."

"Some white wine for the little lady," the man repeated her request. The stewardess, to his mind, apparently required a man's instructions. "Joe-Bob Jackson," he declared, extending a fleshy hand across the aisle between them as the stewardess retreated.

Julie reached across the empty seat beside her. "Julie Lind."

Joe-Bob pumped her hand vigorously. "You all plannin' on visitin' Houston, ma'am?"

Julie nodded, certain that if she opened her mouth she'd laugh. Joe-Bob sounded like Rigg did when he was joking.

"Houston's grown so fast don't hardly know it anymore. I'm from Dallas, myself."

"Dallas, that's interesting... I've never been to Houston before. Is it nice?" This, Julie realized ruefully, was far more painful than cocktail party chitchat.

"T'ain't Dallas!" Joe-Bob scoffed. "'Bout all Houston's got worthwhile's the Oilers, but we got the Cowboys, so that tells all, don't it?"

Julie tried to remember if the names were those of baseball or basketball teams.

"Other thing they got's Gilley's. Gotta see Gilley's while you're there, hear now?"

"Gilley's," Julie repeated blankly.

"Great honky-tonk," Joe-Bob explained. "Got a rodeo arena right next door!"

Julie smiled politely, relieved to see the stewardess approaching with their drinks. As she'd suspected, given Joe-Bob's red jowls and expanse of stomach, he seemed inordinately fond of bourbon. His first double was quickly followed by a second and he was soon asleep, leaving Julie to her thoughts.

Before meeting Joe-Bob, she'd known Houston was famous for oil wells and the Johnson Space Center. Now she could add a sports team of some variety and a honky-tonk. Houston, she thought ruefully, was a long way from the bustle of Broadway or the Metropolitan Museum. And the distance was more than miles. But Houston, she reminded herself with a slow smile, had Rigg.

JULIE FOLLOWED the other passengers to the baggage area, keeping a lookout for Rigg. Suddenly, she was lifted off her feet and whirled around in midair. Rigg held her aloft for a moment, then swept her back down to the ground, folding her into his body with a hug, and the Houston airport became the most wonderful place on earth.

He beamed down at her. "It seems like forever since yesterday, Julie. I'm sure glad you're here."

Julie's gaze swept over the cowpoke who was holding her. His faded, checked shirt looked as if it should have been relegated to a ragbag. Pressing uncomfortably into her midriff was a large belt buckle. She stepped back and glanced down at his wide, hand-tooled leather belt. Below that, a pair of faded jeans stretched tightly, sexily, across his hips. He was about three inches taller than usual. She didn't have to look any further to know he was wearing cowboy boots. She'd been right. Underneath the veneer he wore in New York, Rigg Stanton was the Marlboro Man incarnate.

"I thought you were coming straight from the office." She eyed his outfit questioningly.

Rigg grinned. "I did. The meeting I had to get back here for was with a group of ranchers. When in Rome..."

"Wear a toga," she concluded with a laugh. "This may take me a little time to adjust to. I don't think I've ever seen the president of a New York company in anything but a three-piece suit."

"It's a different culture, Julie."

"That's what I'm leery of, Rigg," she told him, only half in jest, "culture shock."

Rigg put an arm around her shoulder. "Come on. We'll find your luggage. Once I get you to the ranch and into some jeans you'll feel like a native."

Rigg grabbed Julie's suitcase off the baggage carousel and, one arm firmly around her waist, headed toward the exit. He opened the door of the air-conditioned terminal and the humidity hit them; Julie guessed the temperature was well into the nineties. She silently thanked the powers that be for both her straight hairstyle and air-conditioned cars.

"I'm not parked far, just along this aisle here." Rigg stopped at a battered pickup, glanced at Julie's white linen dress and grimaced. "Sorry about the transportation. When I took the truck this morning I didn't know you'd be coming."

He helped Julie into the passenger side; the vinyl seat scorched through her clothes.

Rigg got into the truck, pulled her against him and kissed her longingly.

"Rigg," she whispered as he released her, "At the risk of sounding like a Southern belle, I'm positively going to faint if we don't get some air in this truck!"

He laughed and started the ignition. "And you told me New Yorkers were tough! This is only spring! We're barely half an hour from the ranch. Think you'll make it without expiring?"

Julie made a face at him, then turned to stare out the open window, grateful for the wind that rushed noisily in. Instead of the barren sagebrush she'd expected, lush, green pastures sped by. The scenery was positively pastoral; she could feel the tension that had gripped her for the past days begin to ease.

Twenty minutes later, Rigg wheeled off the highway onto a side road and grinned over at her. "Almost home." A little farther along he turned onto a tree-lined drive. The sunlight that had been beating down on the truck now filtered softly through the leaves of enormous trees; the temperature dropped a good ten degrees.

Rigg pulled the truck to a stop. "This is it...the old homestead."

Julie gazed through the dusty windshield at the stately white house. A balcony wrapped around the entire second floor, and four enormous pillars stretched two stories high to support the overhanging roof.

"Rigg, it looks like something out of *Gone with the Wind*!"

Rigg smiled, clearly pleased at having impressed her. "It's an old plantation house. Most of the ones still standing are farther north, near Jefferson, but there's the odd one around here."

A man strode through the front door and down the wide staircase. He headed toward the truck, his face wearing a wide, familiar-looking grin. Opening the truck door, he offered Julie his hand.

"I'm John Stanton, Julie. Welcome to Texas."

Julie smiled at this older version of Rigg. "Thank you. I hope I'm not putting you out. This visit is on such short notice."

"Not at all. I'm very pleased you've come. You're all I heard about last week...and last night. And now I can see why."

He glanced knowingly at Rigg. "Why don't you show Julie to her room? Then you can both join me on the terrace. Maria's just made some lemonade."

Rigg hoisted Julie's suitcase from the back of the truck and they followed his father to the house. Julie paused inside the doorway, gazing at the interior. The foyer was open to the ceiling of the second floor and an enormous brass chandelier hung from a ten or twelve-foot-long brass chain. A wide, oak staircase led up from the center of the foyer. To either side lay the living and dining rooms—both formal, both exquisitely decorated.

Julie smiled ruefully at Rigg. "If you knew what I'd pictured in my mind when you talked about your ranch house, you'd laugh at me."

"The whole house isn't like this, There's a family room and a terrace across the back of the house. We spend most of our time there. We're not really as formal as this suggests."

"Come on." He wrapped his arm around Julie's waist. "Let's get you settled in."

Rigg stopped at the second door along the upstairs hall, preceded Julie into the room and put her suitcase on the bed. "This do?"

"Do? You're back to understatements, Rigg. It's beautiful."

The room was decorated with pale pink silk, accented with snowy white and carpeted in a deep rose plush. Julie looked over at Rigg. He was watching her closely, obviously trying to read her reaction. "I love it, Rigg."

He stepped closer, taking her hands in his. "That's good, Julie. It's important to me that you like it here."

He bent to kiss her, his lips firm and demanding against hers. His hands slid up her back, drawing her against him, the heat of his body far hotter than the surrounding air. Gradually, he released her from his kiss, as if it was the last thing he wanted to do, and gazed down at her. "I'm glad you're here, Julie. And," he teased, "if I don't let go of you right now, I'm going to end up showing you precisely how glad and we'll miss dinner let alone Maria's lemonade.

"This heat does have its drawbacks, but," he promised with a grin, "things get better at night." He gestured at the side window. "There's an air conditioner you can turn on if you like. Want me to help you unpack?"

"I didn't bring much. Why don't you go on down before your father starts wondering what we're up to? I'll only be a few minutes."

"Just put on jeans and a T-shirt. As I said, we're not formal. The terrace is off the kitchen—through the back of the foyer."

Rigg closed the door and Julie glanced around the room again. It was beautiful. French doors opened onto the balcony and she walked over to look out. Her room was on the back of the house, overlooking a meadow that merged into a heavily wooded area. The view was gorgeous. But as she stood gazing out, a little voice inside her head asked if she could look at it every day without missing New York City.

Julie turned away from the view, not wanting to answer the little voice; not just yet. Quickly, she unpacked and changed from her dress into jeans and an emerald T-shirt she'd bought from a street vender near Washington Square. She grinned into the mirror at the shirt. It was decorated with the hand-painted head of a furry white cat.

Julie turned to go, sticking her hand into her jeans pocket to smooth the denim, and felt a key. She pulled it out and turned it over in her hand. A number 411 key...the mysterious key she'd found taped in the Stanton Group folder at G and K. She eyed it thoughtfully. She hadn't had her jeans on since that night, had completely forgotten about the key. It had to belong to something at the Stanton Group offices, something she hadn't noticed last week. Rigg would recognize it. She shoved it back into her pocket and headed downstairs. First things, first. And the first thing on her mind was a cowboy named Rigg Stanton.

Chapter Twelve

John Stanton poured Julie another glass of icy lemonade then pushed back his chair.

"Need a hand with anything?" Rigg asked.

"No, you two stay on the terrace and enjoy the breeze. I just have a little organizing to do before we can eat. Maria's decided it's too hot to cook indoors tonight so we're going to barbecue."

He rose and grinned sheepishly down at Julie. "Somewhere along the way our housekeeper took over a lot of the decision making. I'd put my foot down if she weren't so darn good at it." John glanced over at his son. "I'll go get some roastin' ears to thrown on the barbecue."

Julie swallowed hard, choking on her latent vegetarianism. Roasted ears had to fall into the same unpalatable category as oxtails, tongue and sweetbreads.

"Something wrong, Julie?" Rigg asked.

"No. . . . I mean I don't want to be difficult. . . . It's just that I have trouble eating anything that looks like it could still be attached to an animal. I can't even look at pigs' knuckles in a deli."

Both Rigg and his father regarded her strangely. "I don't follow," Rigg told her.

"Roasted ears... I won't be able to cope." She shuddered, unable to repress a grimace.

Rigg and John looked at each other and simultaneously broke into hearty laughter. Rigg shook his head. "Julie, Dad didn't say roasted ears, he said roastin' ears...roasting ears." He enunciated the words precisely.

Julie looked at him blankly. Roasted, roastin', roasting. They were all ears.

Rigg's eyes sparkled and his grin threatened to turn into laughter again any second. "Corn, Julie...ears of corn. We roast them on the barbecue...roastin' ears."

Julie felt her face flush.

Rigg quickly took her hand across the table. "Sorry. We shouldn't laugh."

Julie shook her head ruefully, trying to hide her embarrassment. "Do you have a Texas phrase book around here some place? I obviously need to work on my vocabulary or I'm liable to get myself into real trouble."

Rigg squeezed her hand. "No trouble allowed. That's what you're here to get away from."

"No need to be embarrassed, Julie," John added. "Last time I was in New York I sure didn't catch all the pitches. There are a lot of regional differences."

Julie forced a smile, thinking just how large some of the differences were.

"Well," John told them, standing up. "I'm off to get the roastin' ears."

Julie watched him head along a path behind the house. Now that she was alone with Rigg, she should tell him about what had happened this morning. She didn't relish the prospect. The story would just upset him. Maybe she'd start by asking him about the key and work her way up to the rest. She pulled it from her pocket.

Rigg glanced at it disinterestedly. "Suitcase key?"

"No. You don't recognize it?"

Rigg eyed it more carefully. "Doesn't look familiar. Should it?"

"I thought it might. I found it in the Stanton folder at G and K . . . that first night, when I went down to pick up the nonexistent backup file. This key was the only thing in the folder. I took it, figuring it must belong to the filing cabinets at the Stanton Group. But I'd totally forgotten about it until I put my jeans on upstairs and found it in my pocket."

Rigg took the key, examining it with interest. "I don't think it fits anything at my offices," he told her less certainly. "Maybe Neil ordered a cabinet that I haven't noticed." He turned the key over. "But why would Mark have left this in the empty file?"

"I wondered the same thing." Julie took the key from Rigg. "I'll ask Tracy about it when I get back. I remember you once admitted," she teased, "that you didn't know much about the nitty-gritty in the New York office."

Rigg laughed. "I'll admit to not knowing much about the nitty-gritty in Houston, either. That's why I have vice presidents. If I spent my days on the office details I'd never have time for the important things." He reached over and took Julie's hand once more. "Important things like freeing up time to spend with you this week."

"I was wondering how you were going to manage that. I thought you were incredibly busy."

Rigg grinned. "I've brought a whole new dimension of meaning to the word delegate!

"I want to spend the week showing you Houston, Julie. Maybe in the morning I'll take you shopping at the Galleria. You'll like it; it has branches of a lot of the New York stores—Tiffany's, Neiman-Marcus. . . ."

Julie laughed. "Rigg, I can see New York stores in New York. I want to see the real Texas. I want to see an oil well and the space center, maybe the Astrodome . . . and definitely Gilley's!"

"Gilley's? Where did you ever hear about Gilley's?"

"I have confidential sources."

"Well . . . Gilley's isn't exactly the Metropolitan Opera House; it isn't even the Grand Ole Opry House. But you're absolutely right. You should see the real Texas. Instead of going shopping in the morning we'll go riding, explore the ranch, introduce you to a longhorn or two."

Riding . . . as in riding horses, Julie realized. The Galleria's appeal suddenly skyrocketed; she tried to recall how many years ago she'd last ridden a horse. She'd barely been into her teens. And she'd never been any Dale Evans the few times she'd tried it.

"You do ride?"

Rigg's voice told her it was inconceivable that she didn't, so she nodded slowly. "I'm just a little rusty." Why should Rigg have a monopoly on understatements? "And I didn't think to bring any boots," she added as an inspired afterthought.

Rigg glanced down at her feet. "A lot of my sister's clothes are here. Lynn's boots will likely fit you well enough for riding. If not, Maria's might. We'll find you a pair," he assured her.

Julie smiled weakly. "Good," she managed.

Rigg reached over and took her hand. "I'm awfully glad you decided to come today, Julie."

"Rigg, about that decision. I haven't had a chance to tell you all the details yet."

Rigg looked at her expectantly and she launched into a summary of her visit to G and K that morning.

"Oh, Julie," he murmured when she finished. "This just keeps getting worse and worse for you. But at least Wilcott should be able to put the pieces together by this point. Lord knows there are enough of them."

"He was hopeful there might be fingerprints in my office. Luckily, I didn't touch anything. I just wanted to get out of there. And, unless someone brought the things in this morning, there'll be a signature on Security's log. It's not easy to get into the offices on the weekends without someone stopping you."

Rigg exhaled slowly. "Julie, it hasn't been easy to do a lot of things your mystery man has done. He seems to know so much about you—where you live, where you work, your mother's number. Julie, did Wilcott get around to talking to Cramer a second time—after he phoned you claiming those letters had been delivered to his door?"

"I'm not sure. Until this morning, I hadn't spoken to Wilcott since last Tuesday—since he came to your office and saw Tracy and Neil. He told me then he'd talk to Bob again but I didn't think to ask him about that this morning. I told him about the mugger on Friday and about the clock and picture appearing in my office over the weekend. But I didn't ask about Bob. Why? Do you think..."

Rigg released Julie's hand and began to tap the table quietly. "I don't know, Julie. This has all been so crazy. I keep coming back to Bob. He seems to me to be the only logical one—the only person who would know enough about you. And he would have a motive, even if it was a pretty warped one. *The scorned lover.* Maybe he took your breaking up with him a lot more seriously than you realized. After all, he still wanted to marry you."

Julie sighed unhappily. "I don't know, Rigg. I keep going back and forth about Bob, too."

"Julie," Rigg asked slowly, "you weren't playing games with Bob, were you? You didn't lead him on or anything?"

Julie glanced at him sharply. The question he'd left unspoken was only too obvious. "No. I wasn't playing games and I didn't lead him on. I'm not that type, Rigg. I'm surprised you feel you had to ask."

Rigg slid his hand across the table in a conciliatory gesture. "I'm sorry. Really. It was a rotten thing to say. Just jealousy, I guess. Just a little insecurity on my part. I'm sorry."

Julie covered his hand with her own. "It's all right. This whole situation has got both our emotions riding pretty high. But there's no reason to feel either jealousy or insecure. Whatever feelings Bob had for me weren't reciprocated to any great extent. And whatever feelings you have for me certainly are—in spades."

"All set to go," John's voice interrupted them from the doorway. "I just need a volunteer or two to shuck this corn."

"COME ON, JULIE." Rigg removed his arm from around her shoulder and stretched. "If we don't get to bed soon you won't feel like going riding in the morning."

Julie resisted suggesting they continue talking all night. Rigg turned out the single remaining light in the family room, took her hand and led her upstairs.

Julie opened the door to her room and cooler air rushed out at them.

"I turned the air conditioner on earlier," Rigg told her. "Let's get inside before all the cold escapes into the hall." Quickly, he ushered her in, turned on a light and closed the door behind them.

Julie looked anxiously at the gleam in his eye. "Rigg...you aren't thinking about staying here, are you?"

He laughed quietly. "I'm certainly not thinking about staying anywhere else. Unless you don't like this room. There are others we could use."

"You know that's not what I mean. I mean you can't stay with me. Not with your father and Maria in the house!"

"Feeling as if you're thirteen again, Julie?" Rigg teased her gently.

"No...I just don't want them to think..."

"Don't want them to think what? That I love you? That I want to be with you? What do you figure they think already? That I invited you to Texas because I thought you needed a little fresh air?" He smiled slowly at her, taking her hand.

"Julie, no one's going to come skulking along the hall to see where I'm sleeping...or not sleeping. My father and I may both live here, but we live our own lives. And he certainly isn't going to think you're a scarlet woman because you're in love with me."

Rigg brushed her cheek with his fingertips, then circled her waist with his arms, drawing her toward him so that her body nestled against his, so that her pulse began to race at his nearness. He leaned down and kissed her softly on the mouth, then pulled back and gazed at her for a moment. "Julie, I love you more than anything in the world. Do you think my father can't see that? Good grief, Julie. Anyone who isn't blind could see it."

"I love you, too, Rigg," Julie told him softly.

He smiled a lazy smile down at her. "Then what's bothering you about my sleeping here? It was fine in your apartment."

She felt silly even trying to explain. "I guess it seems as if we're getting closer and closer to each other and we're so wonderful together. But I keeping thinking how improbable we are at the same time. The closer we get, the more I worry about how improbable...impossible...it is."

Rigg watched her intently. "Nothing's impossible, Julie, so let's just concentrate on the wonderful aspect for the moment."

Rigg's mouth covered hers, his hand slid beneath her T-shirt, unsnapped her bra, pushed it aside and began to fondle her breasts, gently caressing her aroused nipples. A rush of warmth pulsated through Julie's body at his intimate touch and she reached for the buttons of his shirt, quickly undid it to the waist and slid her hands over the muscles of his naked chest, up the warmth of his broad back.

Rigg pulled Julie's T-shirt over her head, slipped her bra off and shrugged free of his own shirt. He bent to nuzzle her breasts, knelt to trail his tongue down the tender expanse of skin beneath them, causing her to quiver with the excruciating delight of his mouth on her body. He unzipped her jeans and pulled them slowly off, kissing her bare legs with tiny, biting kisses. He slid the silkiness of her panties down and his hands and lips caressed her thighs. Julie's fingers entangled themselves in Rigg's hair, pulling him against her, wanting him closer, ever closer.

Rigg paused, momentarily, to remove the rest of his clothes. He gazed at Julie, drinking in the beauty of her nakedness, then switched off the light and drew her urgently onto the bed, into his arms, tightly against the length of his body. Her skin felt soft and smooth on his, she smelled of an intoxicating combination of perfume and herself. He could barely believe she was here with him, safe in his arms, exciting him so incredibly.

Rigg stroked Julie's back, her hips, the firmness of her behind, each stroke drawing her softness nearer, more tightly against his own hardness, each movement molding the curves of her body into his, heightening his longing beyond anything he'd ever known before. She ran her hands down his back making him shiver at her delicious touch. He ached with desire for this woman, wanting her, yet wanting to move slowly, patiently, and then she reached for him, telling him she wanted him now and he entered her with a thrust of ecstasy.

Julie's arms wrapped about his shoulders, her legs about his waist, pulling him deeper, her responsiveness heightening his own excitement, making control impossible.

"Don't hold back, Rigg," she whispered hotly against his ear.

He felt Julie's body responding, felt the pressure of her thrusting up against him, carrying him beyond feeling anything except the sudden explosion that overwhelmed him.

Slowly, he became aware of the sound of his own ragged breathing filling the silence that followed.

"Mmm...that was wonderful," Julie murmured. "I guess," she said, running a finger down Rigg's arm, "it's true that practice makes perfect."

Rigg smiled at her, reaching to brush damp bangs from her forehead. Whether or not that saying was true, he knew he wanted nothing more than to keep practicing with Julie for the rest of his life.

THEY REACHED THE STABLES before nine but two horses were already saddled and waiting for them.

"That's Ranger and this is Belle." Rigg indicated the smaller of the two. "She's pretty gentle. I hope you don't find her too tame for a good ride."

Julie gazed at the enormous animal, certain Belle's being too tame was the last thing she had to worry about. She watched carefully as Rigg placed a foot into the stirrup of Ranger's saddle and effortlessly swung his other leg across the horse's back. She adjusted the Stetson Rigg had insisted she wear and placed her foot in the stirrup, contemplating how much effort it would take to get herself up.

"Julie, have you done much riding?"

"There are stables in Central Park." Riding was obviously important to Rigg. She had no intention of being found out if she could possibly fake her way through this.

"That wasn't what I asked, Julie."

Julie glanced over at him and saw that he was grinning broadly down at her. She hesitated. "Why are you asking me?"

"Because you have the wrong foot in the stirrup. If you continue the way you're going, you'll end up with a fine view of Belle's tail."

Julie looked at her foot, then at the saddle. Spatial relations had never been her strong suit but it was obvious Rigg was right. She laughed. "I guess I'm more than a little rusty. In fact, come to think of it, I haven't been on a horse for about fifteen years."

Rigg swung off Ranger, shaking his head. "We don't have to go riding, Julie."

"No...I want to, really. How can I visit a ranch and not go riding? I just need a little refresher course."

"You're sure about this?"

"I'll be fine, if I can just get up."

Rigg laughed, lifted her other foot into the stirrup and hoisted her into the saddle. "I'll ride right beside you, tell you what to do with the reins as we go. If all else fails, just grab the saddle horn and hang on."

Julie looked at him skeptically, unimpressed with the idea of things failing.

"We'll just walk them for a while," Rigg told her once they'd reached an open field. "If you feel like getting more adventurous later, we'll have a bit of a gallop."

"Oh, this speed is fine!"

Rigg grinned at her. "You're doing great." He pointed off into the distance. "If we ride out toward that ridge a bit, just past that stand of cactus, we'll likely come across one of the herds of longhorns and you can—"

Ranger snorted and reared, pawing the air wildly. Belle danced about in excitement at the activity. Julie grabbed the saddle horn and hung on for dear life.

Rigg had his horse under control in a moment, rode over to Julie, retrieved her reins and handed them to her. "Sorry about that; it was just a snake." He pointed to a long shape slithering off into the grass. "They're all over the place but most of them won't hurt you."

Julie watched it disappear, her skin crawling. Just a snake...all over the place... Snakes were definitely not on her list of favorite things.

Rigg was eyeing her anxiously. "Want to go back, Julie?"

She shrugged, glancing at her bare arm. "I hate to sound like a city slicker but I burn easily. I packed so quickly I didn't even thing about bringing a sunscreen."

Rigg reached for Belle's bridle and reined Ranger around. They rode the short distance back to the stable in silence.

"Need help getting down?" Rigg asked, dismounting.

"I don't think so. It would be pretty difficult to get off backward." Julie clutched the saddle horn firmly and swung her right leg over Belle. Her foot hit the ground and the moment she put a little weight on it, she knew she was in trouble; it felt like rubber. She glanced over at Rigg, her left foot still in its stirrup. "Is your offer still available? I don't seem to have any strength in my leg."

Rigg strode over, wrapped his arms around her waist and helped her the rest of the way down. He nuzzled the back of her neck and she breathed a silent sigh of relief that he wasn't annoyed with her. As far as fitting in at the ranch went, she was racking up a pretty dismal score.

"Your legs will feel all right in a minute or two. We didn't ride long enough to give you a serious problem."

JOHN STANTON STARED across the dinner table at Rigg. "Gilley's?" he asked with apparent amusement. "You aren't really going to take her to Gilley's!"

"It's her idea."

John glanced at Julie. "You don't strike me as the type who'd be up on the turkey trot, Julie. You look more like a ballroom dancer."

"Actually, I'm not much of a dancer of any kind. But the turkey trot can't be that hard, can it?"

Rigg rested his arm across the back of Julie's chair. "Julie just wants to soak up a little Western culture while she's here. Being a New Yorker she feels a bit deprived when it comes to culture."

She made a face at him but he just laughed.

"Come on." He squeezed her shoulder. "If you're going to insist on dragging me off to Gilley's, let's get going."

Rigg helped her into his yellow Corvette. "You haven't seen anything of Houston yet, Julie. Why don't I take the long way 'round while it's still daylight."

Julie agreed with as much enthusiasm as she could muster. Rigg started the car, switched the air-conditioning on and they headed off.

"Is the traffic always this bad?" Julie asked once they'd turned onto the main highway.

"Traffic and air pollution...just like New York," Rigg joked. "But we're better organized in Houston. If you've got far to go you can always travel around the city by helicopter."

"Well, at least in New York distances are short. Here," she teased, glancing at the sprawling suburbs they'd reached, "it looks as if the city grew like Topsy. Didn't you ever let any town planners near Houston?"

"One sneaked in once," Rigg drawled, "but we shot 'im."

Julie laughed and stared back out the window into the hazy twilight. It looked as if Rigg was right. What New York and Houston had in common were traffic and air pollution.

Rigg drove forever, finally pulling into a gigantic parking lot. "This is it. As you requested, Julie, the infamous Gilley's Club." He took her hand and led her through the sea of parked cars to the building.

Rigg opened the door into the carnival that was Gilley's. Inside were wall-to-wall people and such a strong smell of beer that Julie almost sneezed. The biggest bar she'd ever seen was surrounded by mechanical bulls, punching bags, pool tables, pinball machines and rows of video games. "This place is enormous!" She realized she was shouting above the noise.

"About five acres," Rigg shouted back.

"It's absolutely incredible! Do you come here often?"

"No...well, not recently. Let's grab a table." Rigg pulled out a chair for Julie and sat down himself. "It's a little hard on the eardrums but they're just having a good time. Once the entertainment starts, though, we won't be able to hear ourselves."

"Pardon me?" Julie grinned at him. "I can't hear you."

Rigg laughed.

A waitress, carrying a huge tray laden with pitchers and overflowing mugs of beer stopped at their table. "Howdy, Rigg. How 'ya doin' sugar? Haven't seen you here in a dog's age!"

Julie glanced at Rigg; he looked appropriately sheepish. She turned her gaze to the waitress—skin-tight jeans, luminous green eyeshadow all the way to her eyebrows and a cowboy shirt open far enough to expose a generous amount of cleavage.

"The regular, Rigg?" the waitress asked cheerily.

"Beer okay, Julie?"

Julie nodded. That was obviously the regular.

A frothy pitcher of beer and two chilled glasses arrived. There was little point in attempting to talk over the noise and Julie sipped her beer quietly, trying to reconcile the fact that New York and Houston were cities in the same country.

"Let's get going." Rigg's voice interrupted her thoughts. She glanced at the table. Their beer was barely half-finished, but Rigg was already on his feet, holding out his hand to her.

"Gilley's isn't exactly what I'd have shown you if you hadn't insisted, Julie," he finally said once they were in the car.

"It was interesting." Julie grinned, unable to resist. "Especially the well-endowed waitress who knew your regular drink."

Rigg glanced over quickly, obviously assuring himself she was teasing, and laughed. "I grew up around here, Julie. I know a lot of people. But, I've told you before, women who wear a lot of makeup aren't my type."

The highway traffic had diminished and the Corvette raced along through the night. In no time at all, Rigg was turning into the drive. He stopped the car a few hundred feet from the house. "Roll down your window, Julie. The darkness smells as good as it looks in the country."

The cool night air was sweet and fresh; the chirping of crickets surrounded the car. Rigg placed one arm around Julie's shoulder and gently stroked the back of her neck.

The fine hairs on her neck were instantly electrified. How could such a casual caress set her afire for this man? He barely had to touch her and she wanted his arms around her, his mouth on hers. She turned toward Rigg in the darkness, her lips reached for his, her hands moving lightly down his chest. His kiss burned with a fever of excitement and she unbuttoned the top few buttons of his shirt.

Rigg caught her hands in his. "Julie, I can't make love to you the way I want to with a gearshift in the way." He restarted the car. "Let's go inside where we can continue in a lot more comfort."

Rigg pulled the Corvette up beside the house. The sound of the motor hadn't completely died before the front door opened and John stood in the doorway, his dark figure outlined from behind by the bright lights inside.

Rigg and Julie walked rapidly up the steps. "What's wrong?" Rigg called as they neared his father.

"Sorry. I didn't mean to startle you; just didn't want to miss you when you arrived. A courier came with something for Julie shortly after you'd left. I assumed it was important."

Julie glanced anxiously at Rigg. There was no one she could imagine sending her anything in Texas.

He squeezed her hand. "Let's see what it is, Julie. It's probably nothing." His voice belied his words.

"It's over there." John gestured to the heavy oak hall table. He hesitated and then headed in the direction of the stairs. "I'll be going on up now."

"Good night, John . . ." Julie could barely tear her eyes away from the manila pouch. "Thanks for waiting up," she added, walking toward the table, eyeing the padded envelope. She could see there was a flat, rectangular object inside. She ripped one end open, reached inside and withdrew a videotape. She looked at Rigg.

He took it from her and glanced at it quickly. "It'll work on my machine. It's on the TV in the family room."

Grimly, Julie followed Rigg to the back of the house, certain she wouldn't want to see whatever was on this tape. Rigg slid the tape into the VCR and pushed a couple of buttons. With a quiet whir the tape began to play. Julie stared at the screen, waiting, not knowing what to expect. All she knew was it wouldn't be good.

Chapter Thirteen

Julie slumped on the couch, her eyes glued to the TV, waiting for the gray glare to be replaced by an image. An involuntary gasp escaped from the back of her throat when the image appeared. She stared at the screen as it filled with a picture of the hallway in her apartment. Her familiar Monet prints hung in place along the wall.

"What is it, Julie?" Rigg reached for her hand. His voice sounded anxious but he clearly hadn't realized that it was her apartment on the screen.

"Rigg . . ." Her lips mouthed his name; no sound came out. She tried again but her words died as the picture swept slowly down the hall toward her bedroom.

"Oh my God!" Rigg exclaimed. "It's your apartment!" He wrapped his arm around Julie's shoulder and held her as if he thought she might try to escape.

She knew there was no escape. She couldn't have moved if she'd wanted to; could merely sit, transfixed by this latest macabre gambit.

Her bedroom was on the screen now.

Rigg grabbed the remote, snapped off the VCR and hugged Julie close, uncertain what else he could do, feeling an overwhelming sense of helplessness, not knowing what was going on, who was behind this. The only thing that was clear was that Julie wasn't safe, not even here in his own house. Whoever her enemy was knew exactly where she was, exactly how to get to her.

Julie's hands pushed gently against his chest and he loosened his hold.

"Rigg...I have to see the rest." Her voice sounded terribly anxious but controlled.

"There's no point, Julie. What good would watching the rest do? It could only make things worse."

"I have to see it, Rigg," she insisted.

He picked up the remote and snapped the VCR back on. The picture was focused on her dresser. Then the camera moved upward, revealing the mirror above. Smeared on the glass, in vibrant purple, was a huge question mark.

"It's a different message, Rigg," Julie whispered. "He's been back! What the hell is going on! I have a new lock and it doesn't matter! He wanted to get in again and he did! But why? Why, Rigg?"

He shook his head; he had no answer. The image was changing once more. He watched, morbidly fixated, as the picture panned across the bed. It paused, capturing Asset in the center of the bedspread, green eyes staring indolently at them from the screen. Julie's body shuddered against his own.

"Asset!" she whispered. "What if he's done something to Asset?"

Rigg snapped the tape off again but the screen had already gone gray. The message was finished...whatever it was.

Julie pushed against Rigg's chest, struggling to get up. "I have to call Mrs. Benson and make sure Asset's..." Her words trailed off and her hands relaxed, dropping from his chest. She leaned back against the couch, gazing at Rigg with a confused expression. "Asset isn't there, Rigg. She's perfectly safe. My neighbor has her. And that means the tape was made before I left New York." Julie paused. "What's going on, Rigg?"

He swore silently, wishing to hell he had an answer for her. "You're certain your neighbor wouldn't have put Asset in your apartment for some reason? Why don't you phone her and check."

Julie glanced at her watch. "She'd be in bed. It's past her bedtime in Texas, let alone New York. But I know she wouldn't have. I don't think she lets Asset out of her sight when she'd looking after her. And besides, she doesn't have a key. No. That tape couldn't have been made yesterday or today."

"And your lock was changed the day after the break-in," Rigg said thoughtfully, trying to connect the facts that were part of this enigma.

Julie nodded.

"Then the tape was probably made when he was in there to take the things. He was likely never back again."

"Do you really think so? That he was only there once, I mean?"

"Well, it's possible someone got hold of a key for your old lock at some point. But how could he have gotten one for the replacement? Besides, can you really imagine someone breaking into your apartment to steal a weird collection of things and then going back again to make a stupid tape? Even making one while he was there seems crazy!"

"But the message, Rigg, the question mark."

"I just don't know, Julie. Film one message on the mirror and then replace it with another one for you to find? I can't begin to imagine the point. I can't imagine the point of any of this."

"Play the tape again."

"Look, Julie, you got upset enough the first time, I don't think—"

"No. It won't bother me. It was just the initial shock and then seeing Asset there that frightened me. Play it again. We might have missed something that would give us a clue."

Rigg rewound the tape and started it once more. Julie sat motionless, eyes glued to the screen. The tape ended with a lengthy shot of Asset, and they sat watching the gray screen in silence. Finally, Rigg switched off the VCR.

"I don't understand any of this, Rigg. You're right about the tape being stupid. It's just a stupid tape with a stupid message that doesn't mean anything. Nothing makes any sense. Why take those things? Why make a tape? Why send it here? No sense," she repeated tiredly.

"Let's try a different angle," Rigg suggested. "Who could have sent it? Who knows you're here?"

"Ray Brent and the neighbor who's looking after Asset, Mrs. Benson."

Rigg's thoughts clicked over. "Mrs. Benson is looking after Asset; Asset was on the tape." He looked at Julie questioningly but she shook her head.

"Mrs. Benson is a sweet old lady. I've know her all my life. And she always asks me for a phone number when she's looking after Asset. I always tell her where I'm going."

"And you told no one else?"

Julie frowned. "I told Wilcott . . . and my super."

"The guy we got your new key from? That muscle-bound jerk with the beady eyes?"

"Beady eyes? I hadn't noticed. But I left New York so fast it seemed like a good idea to leave him your number . . . in case my mother got worried that I wasn't answering the phone. She made a point of getting Charlie's number from me last week."

"How long have you known this Charlie?"

"No time at all. The old super retired a few weeks ago. Charlie just started then."

"Before or after your break-in?"

"A few days before."

"And he has a master key..."

"That doesn't mean anything, Rigg. Do you have any idea how carefully supers are screened before they get a job like that? He probably had years of experience and a hundred excellent references."

Rigg checked himself. He was letting his imagination go running off half-cocked. He was no detective. Two minutes ago he'd been ready to leap on an old lady as a possibility. Now Charlie seemed suspicious—on the basis of being new kid on the block and having beady eyes—hardly conclusive evidence.

Another thought struck him. "I told Neil you were coming here," he admitted. Julie glanced at him sharply and he shrugged. "Sorry. It's another instance of seeming like a good idea at the time."

"So," Julie concluded caustically, "we can narrow the suspects down to your vice president, my senior partner, a NYPD detective, a kindly old lady who likes cats, a beady-eyed building superintendent...and anyone else in the world any one of those five might have told I was here."

Rigg exhaled slowly. "Julie, sarcasm doesn't become you. But you're right. We're not going to be able to narrow it down. All we know for certain," he added anxiously, "is that someone either wants to scare the hell out of you or—"

"Damn it, Rigg! I don't want to hear any ors! I'm already scared. I'm scared spitless! But I have to get this over and done with. I can't sit around your ranch, pretending I'm just here for a vacation when I'm really here because we're both terrified of what might happen to me.

"I'm going to have to go back to New York right away, Rigg. I'll go tomorrow. I have to take the tape back to Wilcott so that we can get this damn mystery solved. There's no way I'm going to put up with being... being terrorized. That's the only word for it! I can't handle a whole lot more of this...this...this shadow following me around, dumping nasty little surprises on me when I least expect them!"

Julie stopped, horrified by her own outburst. "I'm sorry, Rigg," she said quickly. "You're the last person I should be exploding at. You're the only one I'm sure is on my side; the only one I'm certain isn't part of all this. Rigg, I just don't know what to do anymore." She clung tightly to him, pressing her face against his chest, against his warmth. If she could simply stay right here, forever, simply never move from Rigg's side, maybe everything would be all right. But that was an impossible dream.

Rigg stroked her shoulder softly. "Julie, let's go to bed. You need some sleep... and I do mean sleep. We'll talk about all this in the morning. Maybe by then we'll be able to figure out what the hell's going on here."

Rigg turned off the lights and, one arm tightly around Julie's waist, walked her upstairs. He paused at her door. "Get into bed, Julie. I'll be back in a minute."

Julie pulled off her clothes and crawled between the cool sheets. Rigg quietly opened the door and came in. His right hand held a gun. Julie shuddered at the sight of it. "Rigg?" she murmured nervously.

"Just in case, Julie... just in case."

He undressed and crawled into the other side of the bed. Julie turned toward him and he reached for her, his arms enveloping her with his strength. He pulled her tightly against him and gently kissed her lips. "Let's get some sleep, Julie," he whispered. "That's what you need most right now."

Julie fell asleep in the safe circle of Rigg's arms, to the soft caress of his hand on her back. He was the only one in this whole crazy thing who didn't seem like a player in her nightmare.

JOHN STANTON PASSED the breakfast muffins to Julie for at least the nineteenth time. For at least the eighteenth time she forced a smile and shook her head. Her stomach felt none too settled.

Rigg glanced anxiously across the table at her. "How about a walk?"

"Sure."

Rigg took her hand as they crossed the terrace and led her silently along a trail toward the wooded area her bedroom overlooked. They neared the woods and he turned down an almost invisible path, stopping when it reached a clearing. "Let's sit here for a bit, Julie."

Early-morning sunlight drifted lazily through the overhanging trees, casting lacy patterns on the ground. A small stream meandered through the clearing; a bright orange butterfly drifted slowly past. Rigg sat beside the water, under a large tree, pulling Julie down beside him, both her hands in his.

"Julie," he said softly, "you were pretty upset last night when you talked about going back to New York today. Let's reconsider that idea. The thought of you going back there right now scares the hell out of me. Send the video-tape back to Wilcott. Let him solve the mystery. But don't go back, Julie. Don't ever go back. Stay here with me. Marry me?"

Julie closed her eyes. It would be so easy to say yes. Because, if she lost this man it would be the worst thing that could ever happen to her. And she would be so happy...for a while...when Rigg wasn't a thousand miles away some place. But this life on the ranch was his life, not hers. No matter how much she loved Rigg she couldn't live someone else's life; not in the long run. "Rigg," she said softly, "I love you...but I can't live here."

He gazed at her evenly, his dark eyes telling her he didn't want to hear what she was saying.

"Rigg, I don't fit in Texas. That's what I meant when I said our being in love was impossible. I fit with you. There's no doubt I fit with you. But I, me, Julie Lind the person, I fit perfectly in New York."

"How much do you love me, Julie?"

"It isn't quantifiable...more than anything in the world at the very least." She could hear her voice thickening with tears.

Rigg pulled her against his chest. "Julie," he whispered, "as long as you love me that much, everything else can be worked out."

Julie fought back the tears. "That sounds so simple, Rigg, but it isn't. I've spent my whole life in New York. It's my home, just as much as the ranch is yours. And I love it the same way you love it here. In New York, I'm a competent person, have a responsible job. Here, I'm the most incompetent person I know. I can't even get on a horse properly...mount a horse properly," she corrected herself. "You see? I don't even know the language—*mount* and *roastin' ears* and who knows what else?"

Rigg kissed her cheek. "Julie, you're making a mountain out of a molehill. Nobody cares if you mount a horse or get on it. And you don't need a job. I have enough money for both of us."

"Rigg, I do need a job. Money isn't the issue. Four years at NYU wasn't exactly a cotillion. I didn't spend all that time studying so I could sit around in a hooped skirt watching the magnolias bloom!"

Rigg pulled back and grinned at her. "Fine, have a job, Julie. Get a job in Houston. Do whatever you want. Just do it here, with me."

"Rigg, I couldn't have a job in Houston. I wouldn't be able to get to it. I can't drive! I can't do anything that's essential here. I couldn't have a job in Houston unless they ran a taxi service to the ranch. I can't drive and I can't ride!" She glanced down at her reddened arm. "I get a sunburn after ten minutes on a horse, I'm practically phobic about snakes, which you tell me are all over the place in Texas, and I wouldn't recognize the damn turkey trot if I saw someone dancing it in the street!"

Rigg stopped her words with a deep, demanding, probing kiss that took her breath away. "Marry me, Julie," he said again, releasing her. "If you don't want to learn to drive I'll get you a chauffeur. I'll get you anything you want, Julie. I'd do anything to make you happy."

Julie sighed heavily. "I know you would, Rigg. I'm never happier than when I'm with you. But be honest with me. How much time do you spend away from the ranch in a month?"

Rigg shrugged. "Maybe a week in New York and another week someplace else…maybe a few other days here and there. But I'm almost always home on weekends."

"So, I'd see you on weekends. And for a week or so each month you'd be here in the evenings."

"Julie, a lot of men travel."

"I know that, Rigg. I understand your work involves travel and that isn't the problem. I'd rather have you part of the time than have anyone else all of the time. But it can't be here, Rigg. I just couldn't adjust. Maybe, just maybe, it would work if you were always here. But you're not.

"Rigg...I want to marry you. But I want to stay in New York. You spend a week there as it is. Maybe you could spend a little more time. We could alternate weekends between here and there. It would work, Rigg. We'd have each other, you'd still have the ranch and I'd still have New York and my life there."

Julie gazed at him, painfully reading his answer in his eyes before he spoke.

"I won't marry you under those circumstances, Julie. This is my home. It has to be my wife's home as well. I want her, you, right here all the time. I just couldn't settle for a commuter marriage, Julie. That's not something I could live with. It has to be all or nothing."

"What you mean," Julie managed precisely, fighting back tears, "is that it has to be all your way or no way at all."

Rigg glanced at her. "You're twisting what I'm saying, Julie. I'm not playing Mr. Macho but it drove me crazy leaving you alone in New York last Sunday...and the time before that. I won't live my life constantly worrying about my wife's safety, about whether she's being burgled or mugged, about whether some lunatic is playing a game, with her as the prize. I simply couldn't handle what you're suggesting."

"And I simply couldn't handle what you're suggesting, Rigg. You wouldn't be here half the time and, whenever you weren't, I know I couldn't look at your corn patch and your horses and your cows without wishing I was in New York. And, eventually, I'd come to resent you for that." She stopped, praying Rigg would say something magic.

After an eternity of silence, she spoke again. "I guess we have nothing more to talk about." She pushed herself up off the ground and walked slowly back toward the house, knowing Rigg would come after her, listening for him to call her back. She reached the house alone and in tears.

JULIE WAS PUTTING the last of her clothes into her suitcase when Rigg tapped on the open bedroom door. She watched silently while his eyes swept down her white linen dress to her high heels, and back up.

"I take it you haven't reconsidered leaving."

She placed the videotape into the top of her hand luggage. "I told you last night, Rigg. I have to see an end to all this. I can't stand it going on any longer. I have to go back to New York."

"Julie . . . you never really left."

She swallowed hard, not trusting her emotions enough to challenge his remark. But it just wasn't fair! She'd given his ranch a chance, damn it! She simply wasn't naive enough to belive there was a happily-ever-after ending here. Maybe for a little while but not forever after; not with her stranded in the middle of nowhere, while Prince Charming gallivanted all over the country.

She took a deep breath, ordering her voice to be calm. "My flight leaves in just over an hour. I'm afraid I need a ride to the airport."

Rigg exhaled slowly. "I'll go back with you, Julie."

She glanced at him, not breathing, unsure of his meaning, hoping against hope he meant what she was almost certain he didn't.

"I'll go back to New York with you for a few days. I've freed up the time here, anyway. And surely, between this tape and those things appearing in your office, Wilcott can figure out what the hell has been going on. But you shouldn't be all alone until this is over."

Julie paused, repeating Rigg's *until* in her head. "And once it is over," she finally said, "you'll come back here."

It wasn't really a question. She knew the answer. Was she becoming masochistic? How many times did she need the reality of this situation pounded into her head?

"This is my home, Julie."

She nodded. "A ride to the airport will be enough, thanks."

"Julie . . ."

"Rigg, don't do this! Every day I spend with you is making it harder for me to think about going back to a life without you. My heart and my brain are already having one hell of a fight. And I have to listen to my brain, Rigg, because I don't want to make a decision that we'll both regret down the line.

"I'm going to arrive home in the middle of the afternoon in broad daylight. And I'm going to call Wilcott the minute I get there. I'll be all right.

"Rigg, you said you couldn't handle worrying about me. Well, you might as well stop right now. There's no point in spending a few more days together. It would only make things worse for both of us. You stop worrying and I'll start getting used the you not being in my life. It'll give me something to concentrate on, keep me from thinking about anything else." She looked down and snapped her suitcase shut.

Wordlessly, Rigg walked over, picked up the case from the bed and strode out of the room with it.

Julie closed her hand luggage and walked over to the French doors. She stared down at the peaceful scenery below, her vision blurred by tears. She needed a few minutes alone before she walked out of Rigg's life forever.

JOHN WAS STANDING at the bottom of the stairs. He glanced at Julie's suitcase. "You going with her, son?"

"She doesn't want me to."

"She say that?"

Rigg nodded, wishing his father would mind his own business.

"People don't always mean what they say, Rigg."

"She won't live here, Dad. She means that. She definitely means that!"

"Maybe she does. But just at the moment, we aren't talking about where she's going to live for the rest of her life. We're talking about what's going to happen to her over the next few days.

"Rigg, all I've heard from you for the past little while is how wonderful Julie Lind is and how worried you are about her. And if that tape arriving last night is any example of the sort of things that have been happening to her, I can certainly see why you've been worried. But now you're going to let her go back to that lunatic asylum she calls a city all by herself?"

"What do you expect me to do? Hog-tie her? She may be wonderful but she's also stubborn as hell! And every time I try to make her do anything for her own good she yells 'chauvinist' at me."

John's face reddened. "What I expect, Rigg, is you to make damn sure she comes out of this mess alive and safe. What happens after that is between the two of you. But damn it, Rigg, she came here because she was frightened. She came to you! She didn't go to her mother in Phoenix or to anyone else in the world. She came to you! If you can't read between the lines of that one you're a damn sight stupider than I've given you credit for all these years."

Rigg gritted his teeth, shifted Julie's suitcase into his other hand and stomped out to the car. His father stared after him, clearly angry, then turned as Julie came down the stairs.

She managed a smile for John when she reached the foyer.

"Sorry you've had to cut your visit short, Julie. I've enjoyed having you here. Rigg's waiting for you out front. I'll take your hand luggage out for you."

"I can manage, John. And thank you for your hospitality. I've enjoyed being here." Her voice cracked; she had to get away.

John put his arms around her and hugged her. Tears escaped down her cheeks and she bit her lip in a futile attempt to stop them.

"Do be careful, Julie."

She nodded, unable to speak, then turned and, wiping her face with one hand, walked toward the front door.

The Corvette's trunk was open. Rigg put her hand luggage into it and opened the car door for her.

They drove in silence. Julie concentrated on the scenery rushing by, uncertain if the car's speed or her own tears were causing it to blur. By the time they reached the airport, she'd regained some semblance of control.

Rigg waited with her at the counter, walked with her to the security check area. She stopped at the entrance, unable to think of anything to say, uncertain if she could even manage to speak.

Rigg placed his hands on her shoulders. "Julie... please change your mind."

She couldn't bear to meet his eyes, couldn't stand his gentle touch. It simply hurt too much. She turned and fled through the doorway, not looking back, not wanting Rigg to see the tears streaming down her face, not wanting to change her mind.

JULIE CARRIED her suitcase and hand luggage into her bedroom and looked about. Everything was as she'd left it. She glanced into the mirror, grimaced at the red eyes and blotchy tearstained face. This was certainly not the time to ask the mirror who was the fairest of them all. It definitely wasn't her.

In the bathroom, she splashed cold water on her face until the redness faded a little and then went along the hall to Mrs. Bensons's.

"You're back early, dear. Nothing wrong, is there?"

"No. Just a change of plans. Did Asset behave herself?"

"Oh my, yes. She was good as gold. I must tell you some of the cute things she did. Would you like some tea before you take her back?"

"Thank you, but no. There's something I have to do. But I'll call you tomorrow. Let me make the tea and you can tell me all about what the two of you got up to."

Julie carried the cat back to her own apartment, hugging her closely. "It's just you and me again, Asset," she whispered, closing the door. She put the cat down and it stalked into the living room to claim the white wing chair.

Julie checked Wilcott's number and dialed.

"I'm sorry," a voice told her, "Detective Wilcott is out of the precinct at the moment. He's expected back in two to three hours."

Julie swore silently. "Please leave him a message to call Julie Lind as soon as possible." She gave the man her number and hung up. Two to three hours. What was she going to do for all that time? Sit here and think about

Rigg? No! She had to keep busy. She dialed the Stanton Group.

"Hi, Tracy, it's Julie."

"Oh…hi. I wasn't expecting to hear from you. Neil said you were away for the week."

"Yes . . . well, change of plans. I thought if the verification letters have all come back, I'd drop by and pick them up in the morning."

"They're here waiting for you. The last one came in this morning."

"Fine. Thanks, Tracy. I'll see you in the morning, then. Oh, one more thing. I'd forgotten all about it but in Mark Thompson's file I found a key stamped with number 411. Is there a filing cabinet in the office there that has a lock with that number?"

"411," Tracy repeated slowly. "No. That's not a number I recognize."

"Well, just thought I'd check. See you tomorrow."

Julie hung up and looked at her watch. Great. She'd killed a whole five minutes. Absently, she took the small key from her purse and sat looking at it for a moment. It didn't belong to anything at G and K or at the Stanton Group. The only other logical explanation was that it had belonged to Mark.

She pulled out her G and K staff list, sat tapping her finger on Mark's home number. Why had the key been in the Stanton file? Did Mark have something that related to the audit? Julie shook her head. What did she care? The audit was virtually finished. And she wanted nothing more to do with Rigg's company than was absolutely necessary.

Firmly, Julie placed the key by the phone, picked up the novel she'd started last week and sat down on the couch. Fifteen pages later she didn't have any idea what was happening in the story. It was impossible to concentrate on the plot. Her eyes kept wandering back to the key... to the phone. She shouldn't even be considering phoning Mrs. Thompson, should she? But if she didn't, Wilcott certainly would. Impulsively, she snapped her book shut and reached for the phone.

Julie spoke briefly with Mark's widow and waited anxiously while the other woman went to check his filing cabinet.

"Yes," Mrs. Thompson came back on the line. "Yes, the lock is number 411. I haven't been able to find a key in the apartment to unlock it. I'm going out in about an hour, but if you could come over right now I'd be glad to let you see if the papers you're looking for are in it."

"Thank you. I really appreciate this. I'm not far from your place. I can be there within half an hour."

Quickly, Julie changed and glanced in the mirror to comb her hair. Her face looked more or less back to normal. She phoned for a cab. The number was ringing when the knock sounded on her door. She stared fearfully over at it wondering, not for the first time, if she'd made the biggest mistake of her life by coming back.

Chapter Fourteen

Putting the receiver down, Julie moved quietly, anxiously to the door. She glanced through the peephole, then closed her eyes, certain they were playing tricks on her. She reopened them... Rigg hadn't disappeared, he was still there. She fumbled with the lock, flung open the door and threw her arms tightly around his neck.

"Well," he murmured into her hair, "your reception certainly makes this trip to New York worthwhile." He half carried her back inside and closed the door.

"Rigg, what are you doing here?"

"Hugging you ... and kissing you." He bent to give her a long, loving kiss. "I couldn't let you leave like that, Julie. I sat in the parking lot for a while, telling myself it was for the best. Then I got five miles away from the airport and turned around. Your plane was already taking off so I caught the next flight. We have to work this situation out, Julie. We just have to! I tried to think things through on the plane but all I could think about was how awful my life would be without you."

Julie tried, unsuccessfully, to stop grinning. There was going to be a happy ending in this someplace after all! "I couldn't believe my eyes when I saw you standing in the hall. How did you get into the building?"

"I wanted to see the look of surprise on your face, so I convinced Robert to let me past. I think he figured he should try to get out of my bad books."

"Well, I'm glad you got here when you did. I was just calling a cab." Briefly, Julie recounted her conversation with Mark's widow.

"I told her I'd be right there, Rigg," she concluded. "Much as I'd rather stay here with you, we'd better get going."

"Julie, don't you think we should wait for Wilcott before we do anything?"

"We'll be there and back before he returns my call, Rigg. It isn't far and there can't be anything dangerous about going to her apartment in the middle of the day."

"I guess you're right," Rigg agreed slowly, "but we don't need a cab. I stopped off at the Plaza to get into some New York clothes and pick up the Mercedes. It's out front."

RIGG SAT IN THE MERCEDES, outside the Thompson apartment house, anxiously waiting for Julie to reappear. When she did, she was carrying a flat, legal-sized envelope. She slid in beside him and handed it to him.

"Photocopies, Rigg, photocopies of payments the Stanton Group made to Brocca Building Supplies."

Rigg pulled the papers out of the envelope and looked through them briefly. "I recognize the name. It's one of Craig Howarth's suppliers, isn't it?"

Julie nodded. "As a matter of fact, it's one of the companies I sent a verification letter to. They returned it immediately and, according to them, the Stanton Group records correlated perfectly with theirs."

"Which means?"

Julie shook her head. "I don't know. It should mean exactly what it said, that everything's A-okay. But why would Mark have made photocopies of these payments if there weren't something fishy about them? I ran a quick total in my head. There's more than two hundred thousand dollars' worth of payments in there."

Rigg glanced at the address on one of the copies and handed the stack back to Julie. "Let's go see what the people at Brocca Building Supplies have to say."

He drove silently through the traffic, his worst suspicions all but confirmed. Something was going on in his company, something he didn't know about, something Mark Thompson had uncovered. But what? Who? He glanced at Julie, realizing he should have given this idea a little more thought. Maybe he should turn back, let Wilcott talk to Brocca's owners. They were probably involved in whatever was going on. He couldn't simply march in and start asking questions; couldn't risk Julie's safety. He glanced at the street number they were passing. The address he wanted wasn't more than a block away. He'd drive by, have a look. Then he'd get Julie to the police.

Rigg slowed the car as they neared the address. There was no sign of Brocca Building Supplies. He pulled up at the curb. "Double-check one of those photocopies, Julie. This address can't be right."

She glanced at a page, then at the building Rigg had stopped in front of. "It's the right address." She looked at him questioningly. "Gino's Pizza Parlor?"

Rigg opened his door. "Stay here."

Julie opened hers. "No way!"

Rigg started to object, reminded himself Julie didn't take kindly to being told what to do and took her hand.

The fellow behind the counter shook his head silently at Rigg's questions, suspiciously eyeing first one, then the other of them. He glanced pointedly through the window at the Mercedes. "You ain't cops, is you?"

Rigg took out his wallet, reached inside and pulled out a hundred-dollar bill. He laid it on the counter. "If you've never heard of Brocca Building Supplies, just give me a small pizza and the change."

The man reached for the bill and stuffed it into his pocket. "All I know's a guy rents a room on the second floor. He comes around now and then, picks up mail addressed to the company. That's all I know, man."

"You know what he looks like?"

The man shrugged.

"A hundred bucks buys a lot of pizza, fellow. Should buy a description."

"I don't take much notice. He's your average guy. Thirty-five, forty...tall...blond. Just your average guy. That's all I know, man."

Not Neil. Rigg breathed a sigh of relief. Not Neil...but possibly Craig Howarth? It wasn't much of a description. "Let's get going, Julie."

"Wilcott can take it from here," he told her as they headed back out to the car. "The best thing for us to do is go back to your place, pick up the videotape and take both it and those photocopies straight over to Wilcott's office. I don't want to just sit around, waiting for him to call, when we have no idea what the hell's going on."

Rigg slid into the driver's seat and glanced worriedly across at Julie. "What's your best guess about all this?"

She answered slowly. "I'd say Brocca's a phony company that someone's using to skim money from the Stanton Group. Mark discovered the fraud; that's why he made the photocopies."

Rigg exhaled slowly. He'd known the answer to his question. Had he really thought Julie might have come up with a different one? "And what's your best guess as to who?" he forced himself to ask.

"I don't know enough about Craig Howarth's operation to guess at that one. But Brocca's supposedly one of Howarth's suppliers, so it has to be either Craig himself or someone in his company—someone who works on his accounts. I imagine the police will be able to determine who it is in no time."

"But," Rigg said slowly, "Neil authorized those payments."

Julie quickly flipped through the stack of photocopies. "Unless someone's forged his signature, he's signed every check."

Rigg peered closely at the top copy. "Definitely looks like Neil's signature to me." Glumly, he started the car, his mind turning over the possibility of Neil being in cahoots with Howarth...of the Stanton Group's vice president, his right-hand man, being a thief.

RIGG CLOSED the apartment door behind them.

"The tape's in my bedroom," Julie told him, heading down the hall. She glanced into the den on her way past; the message light was flashing on her machine. "Wilcott may have phoned back already, Rigg," she called. "There's a message here. I'll check it." Quickly, she pressed *Rewind*, then *Play*.

"Hi, Julie," the voice began, "it's Tracy. I got to thinking that I'll practically be going past your place after work. I can drop those letters off...save you a trip in the morning. If you're not home, I'll just buzz your super and leave them with him."

Julie glanced at Rigg, standing in the doorway of the den, and then at her watch. "I don't imagine she's been by yet. Want to wait for her or want to get going and let her leave them with Charlie?"

Rigg frowned. "I'd just as soon keep beady-eyes out of our business. Maybe we'd better sit tight until she gets here."

"All right. I'll put on some coffee and feed Asset."

JULIE AND RIGG had barely sat down with their coffee when Tracy arrived. Julie buzzed her into the building and waited by the door, hoping Tracy wouldn't expect to be invited in. Other than Rigg, Wilcott was the only person in the world she wanted to talk with at the moment.

There was a light tap on the door. Julie peered out at Tracy, turned the lock and opened the door.

"Hi, Tracy. I really appreciate you . . ." Her words died and she felt her smile freeze as Craig Howarth stepped into view with a gun pointed at her chest.

"Get inside, Julie," Tracy hissed.

Craig gestured with the gun and Tracy stepped forward, shoving Julie back so that Craig would close the door behind them.

"Tracy?" Julie forced out a whisper. "Tracy . . . what's going on?" Even as she asked, the pieces of the puzzle were falling into place in her mind. It had to be Tracy and Craig who'd set up the phony Brocca account.

Tracy glanced past her and Julie turned her head. Rigg walked out of the living room, stopping in midstride.

"Tracy . . . what's going on?" His deep voice echoed Julie's whispered question. He looked at Julie and Craig, focused on the gun and lost three shades of his tan.

"We're not playing Twenty Questions, Stanton," Craig snapped. He grabbed Julie's arm, poking the gun against her ribs. She could hear her heart pounding, feel herself trembling. Craig's body pressed menacingly against her own; the gun jabbed into her side as he spoke again.

"I think I'd prefer you sitting down, Stanton. Back it up!"

Slowly, obediently, Rigg backed into the living room.

"On the couch," Craig ordered. "And you sit in that white chair, Tracy. I don't want you in the line of fire if your boss gets any foolish ideas." Craig pushed Julie ahead of him, his gun painfully thrust into her ribs. "We'll just stay over here by the wall, Julie. I wouldn't want the cowboy to try anything. I've heard how tough he is; he even takes on muggers."

"Shut up, Craig!" Tracy snapped.

Craig grunted. "What's the difference? They're on to us. Whatever they got at Thompson's led them straight to Brocca's."

Julie forced her mind to think. "You followed us," she managed to get out. She had to stall for time. Wilcott would be calling soon. And Tracy was a talker. If they could just get her talking they'd be buying time. She glanced at Rigg, praying he was thinking along the same line. His face was a tense mask.

"Of course we followed you! After you told me you had that key... the key you found in Mark's file, we knew for sure you were onto us. We were outside your building within fifteen minutes, Julie, waiting to see if the police showed up or not. But the only person we saw arrive was Rigg. Of course we followed you. We had to know where you were going, what you were up to.

"Telling me you found that key in Mark's file was really stupid, Julie. You blew it! Until then, you almost had me believing you'd never looked inside that file before I took it out of here. Almost had me believe that Craig and I had gotten everything Mark left about the Stanton Group. But you took that key out before I got to the file, didn't you? You took the key out and it eventually lead you to the evidence.''

Julie's mind raced. Tracy had been the one in her apartment, the one who'd taken the file. She tried to remember what she'd told Tracy on the phone earlier. She'd said she'd found the key in Mark's file. She'd meant the virtually empty, backup file, of course, but how was Tracy to know that? Julie had said the wrong thing and now she and Rigg were in this mess! She focused on Tracy, wondering if there was any way out.

The other woman was staring at the envelope on the end table, the envelope full of copies of the phony Brocca receipts.

Tracy stood up, walked over to the envelope and riffled quickly through its contents. ''Bingo!'' She beamed at Craig. ''This is it! I thought it looked like the envelope she got at Thompson's. This is the evidence. We're home free!''

''Not quite, Tracy,'' Craig snapped. ''They've seen the evidence. We've got no choice now, Tracy. It's them or us. And it's not going to be us. It's just a question of how. How do we do it so we're sure to get away with it?''

It! Julie's throat grew tighter. She didn't need to read murder mysteries to know precisely what Craig meant.

''Look, Tracy,'' Rigg's voice broke in, sounding strained. ''Whatever's been going on at the Stanton Group isn't murder. Whatever it is, it can't be worth killing Julie or me over. That would mean life in prison, Tracy. Fraud's a few years, maybe not even that. Murder is life.''

Tracy glanced over at Craig.

''I've told you a million times, Tracy,'' he snarled, his breath repulsively hot against Julie's ear. ''If the police ever learn about the fraud, they'll reopen the file on

Thompson's death. I lucked out when they decided it was suicide, but if the fraud comes out, that'll change things. I'd be done, Tracy! No jury'd buy a self-defense plea. Not when the victim's an accountant in a three-piece suit and I killed him in his own office!''

Julie swallowed hard, unable to catch the horrified gasp that escaped. "You killed Mark," she whispered.

"It was an accident! Thompson pulled the gun! It was his own gun...his own damn fault! Mr. Holier-than-thou Accountant who uncovers a scam and, instead of reporting it, invites me down to his expensive office and tries to blackmail me!''

Rigg glanced back at Tracy, realizing she was their only hope. "Mark's murder is Craig's problem, Tracy. But what about you? You weren't involved in that. You'd be crazy to risk doing anything to us.''

Tracy shot him a mean smile and his heart sank.

"Crazy, Rigg? I'm hardly that. Maybe a little resentful toward you—you and Neil. Not to name a lot of other executives I've worked for. I've been running your damn eastern division since day one, you know. No...you don't know. Neither you nor Neil has ever given me much credit...or much pay. Why should I settle for less than I'm worth?

"You men are all alike. You think you're so very clever. But I can fool Neil with nothing more than a loving smile, and Blondie over there has you coming and going at the bat of an eyelash.

"No, I'm not crazy, Rigg. I'm just someone who looks out for number one. You and Neil aren't nearly as smart as you think you are. Neither of you had a clue anything was going on. And my scheme was so simple. All I needed was Craig's help and it was a case of take the money and run. Only, we hadn't taken enough to run quite as far as we wanted before Miss Super-Snoop got in on the act. But we'd gotten almost enough, Rigg. And I'm not about to give it up by backing out now."

"Good girl, Tracy!" Craig said. "And don't worry about the money. We've got enough."

"Yeah. You're right Craig. At worst, we'll have to cut the odd corner."

Tracy shot one of her loving smiles at Craig. Julie eyed her closely. That smile might fool a man, but Julie read the distinct message that Craig was one of the odd corners Tracy wouldn't have the slightest hesitation cutting. The irony, she realized, would be amusing if she and Rigg weren't in the midst of this horror show.

Tracy gazed at Craig thoughtfully for a moment. "How about a murder-suicide, Craig? How about Julie dumping Rigg and him rushing from Texas after her and killing her?"

"You *are* crazy!" Rigg exploded. "No one would ever believe nonsense like that!"

Tracy shrugged. "I don't see why not. Julie called me earlier today, you know. And I clearly remember the fear in her voice when she told me about you threatening to kill her before she fled from Texas."

Rigg began to rise, anger surging through him.

"Down, Stanton!" Craig ordered. He jammed the gun barrel into Julie's side and Rigg slumped furiously back onto the couch.

Craig grinned across at Tracy. "That's what I love best about you. You've got a good imagination. Murder-suicide it is!"

"You can't!" Julie's whisper echoed fiercely across the room. "You'd never get away with it! You only got away with Mark's murder because you had a lot of luck! When his secretary found his body she went into hysterics. She wasn't certain he was dead, tried to help him, disturbed his body, disturbed all kinds of things in his office.

"The detectives were awfully upset about that. But Helen messing up the scene was a lucky break for you. That and the fact that Mark had just bought the gun. Now I realize he bought it to protect himself from you, Craig, but they concluded he'd intended to kill himself."

Rigg wrenched his gaze from Julie, wanting to see Tracy's reaction. She eyed Julie suspiciously.

"So what?" she asked belligerently. "Who cares if luck was involved? Maybe that's a good sign! Luck comes in threes. That takes care of Mark . . . Rigg . . . and you," she concluded with a cruel chuckle. "And, as long as no one finds out about the fraud, nobody's going to relate Mark's death to yours. And there's nothing to tie Craig or me into being here!"

"Oh, yes, there is!" Julie snapped. "Neil knows you're here! If you kill us, the police will talk to Neil and he'll tell them you were coming here."

"Neil doesn't know anything about it; I didn't tell him."

Julie shook her head firmly. "But I did. After I got your message I called your office to tell you not to bother bringing the letters over, that there were some other things I had to check in the morning, anyway. You'd already left but I talked to Neil."

Rigg held his breath, knowing Julie was lying, praying that Tracy wouldn't. Tracy looked decidedly worried.

"I don't believe you," she said nervously.

"It doesn't matter what you believe, Tracy." Julie's voice was amazingly controlled. "It's only what the police believe if you kill us that matters."

Tracy bit her lip. "All right!" she finally snarled. "We can't take the chance that Neil knows I was coming here.

We can't kill them here. We'll have to take them somewhere else.''

Rigg wanted to catch Julie's eye, ordered himself not to even look at her. There was no way Craig was going to get the two of them out of this building...no way Rigg was going to allow it. They weren't going to kill Julie! Not even if it meant he got himself killed avoiding it!

Craig grinned menacingly. "You liked the redevelopment I'm working on, didn't you, Julie? How'd you and your boyfriend like to become a permanent part of its foundation?''

Hold on, Julie, Rigg prayed. Her entire body was rigid, her arm still firmly in Craig's grip. She didn't say a word.

Craig looked over at Tracy. "Let's get them down to the van, Tracy. I've got a place in the building we can dump the bodies where they'll never be found. The two of them will just disappear from the face of the earth. You go check the hall; make sure there's no one around." Craig gestured to Rigg. "You follow Tracy, Mister. And no tricks. Anything even looks like a trick and Blondie here gets it first. Then you. Then Tracy and I take our chances with what the police think."

Tracy crossed to the hall, the envelope clutched tightly under her arm and opened the door. "All clear," she whispered.

"Go down and get the elevator," Craig told her. He nodded to Rigg. "Get going."

Rigg pushed himself up off the couch, watching Craig, watching for any chance, any mistake. There was going to be an opportunity. There had to be! Probably once they were out of the apartment. Maybe in the hallway, in the elevator, the lobby. There had be a chance and he'd grab it.

And then the miracle happened. A crash came from the kitchen! Craig whirled at the sound, releasing his hold on Julie. His gun flashed toward the noise and Rigg hurtled himself through the air.

One fist drove Craig's head into the wall. His other hand chopped viciously at the gun. Simultaneously, Rigg heard a snap, a scream of pain, the smash of Craig's skull against plaster and the soft thud of his gun hitting the carpet.

"The gun, Julie!" Rigg screamed.

Julie leaped toward the gun, picked it up, glanced back at Rigg and Craig. Craig was slumped, motionless on the floor, his eyes closed, the wall propping him up. Rigg stood over him, breathing raggedly.

She glanced at the open door, then ran out into the hall. Tracy stood at the elevators, looking back, her eyes wide, clearly aware something had gone wrong with Craig's plan. Julie stared down at the gun in her hand, realizing she'd never held a real gun before. She heard the elevator door open, looked back along the wall, saw Tracy bolt into the elevator, watched the door slide shut.

Julie stepped back inside her apartment, closed the door and walked shakily to the living room. Craig was still on the floor. His eyes were open, his face was contorted with apparent pain. He was holding his right wrist gingerly in his left hand. Julie handed the gun to Rigg. "Tracy made it onto the elevator."

"That's all right. She's not going anywhere. Call 911, Julie."

She nodded, staring down at Craig. Clearly, he wasn't going anywhere, either. "I'll call in just a second," she told Rigg, turning toward the kitchen. She paused in the doorway. Asset looked up; the long fur beneath her mouth was wet. The creamer Julie had left on the counter lay shattered on the floor. The ceramic floor tiles were liberally splashed with milk. Julie picked up the cat, doubting she'd ever again be angry when Asset knocked something off the kitchen counter. "You've had enough, Asset. There could be glass splinters in that milk."

She carried the cat over to the phone and dialed.

"SIT HERE, beside me, Julie."

Still holding Asset, Julie sank onto the couch beside Rigg, her body totally drained of energy, her mind totally drained of emotion. Rigg put one arm firmly around her shoulder and gestured, with the gun, across the coffee table at Craig, slumped in the wing chair. "Mr. Howarth is going to fill us in on the details of their little plot, Julie."

"Go to hell! You broke my damn wrist. I'm not filling you in on anything."

Rigg leaned forward. "I'd say the police won't be here for at least ten minutes," he said coldly. "Do you have any idea how many more bones could get broken in ten minutes? Do you think the police are going to care if you're in worse shape when they arrive than you are now? That's your choice, Howarth.

"On the other hand, Julie and I would be real interested in hearing some details. Why don't we start with the fraud? How much were you skimming?"

Craig swore, eyed the gun and exhaled wearily. "Two percent," he admitted haltingly. "We were skimming two percent on each of my jobs. All we needed was a couple of years and we'd have had a small fortune, enough to retire in luxury. Two percent is pretty easy to hide, and on million-dollar projects, its adds up quick." He paused, shaking his head. "Everything was going smooth as silk," he added ruefully. "Tracy was doing her phony lovey-dovey routine on Overbach and he never suspected a thing was wrong; just kept signing everything she put on his desk."

"Poor Neil," Julie murmured quietly. "He's going to be devastated."

"But then Thompson caught on," Rigg prodded.

Craig merely nodded.

"How?" Julie demanded. How had she missed whatever Mark had caught?

"Just a fluke," Craig muttered, his voice bitter. "He knew the neighborhood where Brocca's was supposed to be located and he couldn't recall any building supply company. So he drove by to take a look. It was just a damn fluke!"

"And then," Rigg concluded, "Thompson tried to blackmail you and you killed him."

"That was an accident!"

Rigg ignored the protest. "Then," he continued, "you broke into Julie's apartment to steal the audit file because you thought there might be evidence in it."

Craig nodded, staring at the floor.

"How did you get in?" Julie asked.

Craig didn't answer.

"The lady asked how you got in." Rigg waved the gun in Craig's direction. "Let's not have any more pauses in the conversation."

Craig sank a little further into the chair. "Your doorman seems to take a lot of breaks. And your super's none too bright. I got him into the lobby, flashed my contractor's ID at him, and told him one of the tenants had called me about an emergency repair, that I had to get in real fast or there'd be water damage.

"Then Tracy started pounding on the front door as if she was being attacked and I got your super to give me his master key for a minute while he saw to Tracy. I unlocked your apartment so Tracy could get in later, gave him his key right back, and he was none the wiser."

"And everything except the file was taken so I wouldn't be certain what you were after?"

"Partly. But partly we figured we could use them to scare you off if you started causing trouble. Didn't want to find ourselves unprepared when it was murder we were involved with. If you uncovered the fraud, Thompson's death would have been reexamined under a whole different light. We had to make sure you didn't pick up on anything."

Julie stared at Craig. Incredibly, his voice had taken on a note of pride. His words were beginning to tumble out; he was clearly becoming eager to tell them the details.

"Tracy knew you'd be under time pressure to get the audit completed," Craig volunteered. "We decided our best bet was to scare you enough to keep you off balance. Then, if you did have any suspicions, you'd be less likely to follow them up. We figured if we kept it up long enough, you'd come to the conclusion that the audit was jinxed, and the sooner you got rid of it the better. After all, you didn't want to end up like your predecessor, did you?"

Julie's thoughts whirled. All these warped, bizarre things that had terrified her had been part of their crazy plan...their senseless, crazy plan. The whole idea that she would think the audit was jinxed and she could wind up dead, wasn't even logical. No, she told herself, that wasn't entirely true. After all, she'd been thinking along that line several times.

"You were about to tell us why Tracy took the specific things she did," Rigg reminded Craig.

He shrugged. "There was a message on the answering machine from Bob Cramer. Tracy listened to that and then, when she came across his letters, she took them, figuring that would throw suspicion onto him."

"The letters," Julie murmured. "But then . . . you had them returned to him?"

Craig nodded. "We were watching you, Julie. One of us was always watching you. That's how we knew where you and Rigg were walking when I came at you with the van. You know, my van, Julie. I told your mother about it. And after that scene in the restaurant, Tracy decided sending Cramer his letters would be a master stroke."

"Wilcott was right," Julie said guiltily to Rigg. "Those remarks of Bob's really were just a coincidence."

Rigg squeezed her shoulder reassuringly. "You couldn't have known that. And the clock, the photograph?" he asked, turning his attention back to Craig.

"Things that Julie would instantly recognize as hers. We wanted her to know she wasn't safe . . . that someone was still around, still knew where she was, what she was doing."

"How did you get into my office with them?"

Craig grinned a sardonic grin. "It's not too hard when you're invited."

Julie looked at him blankly.

His mouth twitched. "Didn't you notice how big Tracy's purse was on Friday night?"

"At the reception," Rigg muttered. "And then, after you and I left . . ."

"She went into my office and left them there," Julie concluded quietly.

Craig glared at Rigg. "You weren't supposed to be there Friday! The mugger was supposed to get Julie alone."

"You . . ." Julie whispered.

"Not me! I don't like to get my hands dirty with that sort of stuff. Let's just say I have a few connections."

"And the message on Julie's mirror?" Rigg asked.

"Just the first in a series of scare tactics. We kind of hoped you'd take the hint."

"But the videotape," Julie said. "The message on the mirror was different. Why? And why did you make the tape at all?"

Craig shrugged. "Another brainchild of Tracy's. Like I said, we didn't know what we might have to do to throw you off kilter. We didn't know exactly how we might want to use the tape. But Tracy knew it would scare the hell out of you if we did. That was why she filmed a question mark. We didn't know what our message to you would be then."

"But why did you send the tape to Texas?" Even as she spoke, Julie wondered why she was asking any more questions. Their rationale was so completely deranged. And yet, she was still morbidly curious about everything that had happened to her.

"We had you running and figured it would be the final blow. We hoped it would convince you to give up the audit—someone else would rush it through the final stages and then we'd be home free. Tracy figured the tape would make you think that if you came back to New York you'd be walking right into the midst of a dangerous situation. She was counting on Rigg to talk you into staying with him in Texas."

Craig peered intently across at Julie. "You haven't asked about the roses. They were my idea. You really got upset when Rigg didn't call after the roses came, didn't you?"

"We're the ones who get to ask the questions, fellow!" Rigg snarled.

Julie stared glassy-eyed at Craig. Suddenly he reminded her of Jack Nicholson portraying one of his weird characters. So the roses had been their doing, as well . . . not Francine's at all.

Julie's buzzer sounded and she rose to answer it, Asset still in her arms.

"Police officers, ma'am," a voice announced.

With a weary sigh of relief, Julie buzzed them in.

WILCOTT WAS THE LAST to leave. Julie closed the door behind him and leaned against it, not completely trusting her legs. Rigg reached for her, wrapped one arm firmly around her waist and led her to the couch, drawing her down beside him.

He hugged her tightly to his chest. "It's all over, Julie. The police have both of them; you'll be safe from here on in."

Julie pulled back a little and smiled at Rigg. "You see," she teased gently, "it never was New York that was so dangerous, it was only your employee and her friend. Every single thing that happened to me was part of their crazy scheme—the mugger, the call to my mother, Craig's black van."

Rigg's arms drew Julie firmly back against him and he nuzzled her neck. "Tell you what, Julie. I'll admit New York isn't quite as bad as I've been making it out if you'll admit the ranch has its good points."

Julie listened to Rigg's heart beating against her ear, realizing she'd admit to just about anything at the moment—anything that would keep the two of them together. "It has all kinds of good points, Rigg. The air is fresh, the scenery's beautiful, it has the best roastin' ears I've ever tasted . . . and it has you."

"Well," Rigg said slowly, "it has me part of the time." He shifted so that he was looking into Julie's eyes. "That's part of what we have to work out, isn't it—the fact that you don't want to be on the ranch when I'm not there."

Julie nodded, barely breathing.

"Look, Julie, aside from all the other problems Tracy and Craig have caused, the Stanton Group has suddenly been left without anyone to manage its finances. Even if Tracy gets out on bail, I'm certainly not crazy enough to let her anywhere near my office!"

Julie closed her eyes, forcing herself to keep silent, breathlessly waiting to hear the rest of what Rigg had to say.

"Julie, I'm going to have to spend a lot more time in New York...at least in the short term...at least until I'm positive Neil really is on the straight and narrow, that he was just an innocent victim of Tracy's scheme. But I really believe that has to be it. I'm sure if he'd been involved, Tracy and Craig would have been only too happy to blow the whistle on him." Rigg shook his head ruefully. "Neil's a valuable man; he knows New York real estate inside out. But if Tracy could slip all those payments by him, he's obviously no financial wizard."

Rigg paused to gently kiss Julie's lips. "Julie, if I'm spending more time here, I want every minute of it to be with you. What if you managed the eastern division's finances for me? What if you left G and K, came to work for me? What if we hired an assistant for you so that you could get away from New York whenever you wanted ... whenever your husband wasn't here, whenever he was on his ranch? What do you think, Julie? Marry me? We'll have two homes; we'll have the best of both worlds.

And we'll be together all the time.... It would hardly seem right for my wife to be working for some other company when I had a perfect job for her in mine."

"I think," Julie said softly, "it wouldn't be only a perfect job. I think it would also be a perfect happy ending."

ATTRACTIVE, SPACE SAVING BOOK RACK

Display your most prized novels on this handsome and sturdy book rack. The hand-rubbed walnut finish will blend into your library decor with quiet elegance, providing a practical organizer for your favorite hard-or soft-covered books.

Only $9.95

Approximately 16" x 8" when assembled

Assembles in seconds!

To order, rush your name, address and zip code, along with a check or money order for $10.70* ($9.95 plus 75¢ postage and handling) payable to *Harlequin Reader Service*:

Harlequin Reader Service
Book Rack Offer
901 Fuhrmann Blvd.
P.O. Box 1396
Buffalo, NY 14269-1396

Offer not available in Canada.

BKR-1A

*New York and Iowa residents add appropriate sales tax.

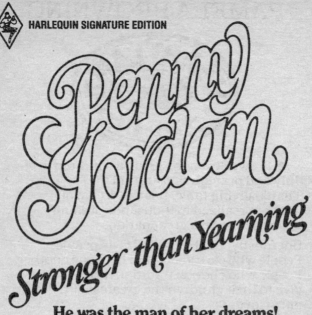

Penny Jordan

Stronger than Yearning

He was the man of her dreams!

The same dark hair, the same mocking eyes; it was as if the Regency rake of the portrait, the seducer of Jenna's dream, had come to life. Jenna, believing the last of the Deverils dead, was determined to buy the great old Yorkshire Hall—to claim it for her daughter, Lucy, and put to rest some of the painful memories of Lucy's birth. She had no way of knowing that a direct descendant of the black sheep Deveril even existed—or that James Allingham and his own powerful yearnings would disrupt her plan entirely.

Penny Jordan's first Harlequin Signature Edition *Love's Choices* was an outstanding success. Penny Jordan has written more than 40 best-selling titles—more than 4 million copies sold.

Now, be sure to buy her latest bestseller, *Stronger Than Yearning*. Available wherever paperbacks are sold—in June.

STRONG-1R

PAMELA BROWNING

...is fireworks on the green at the Fourth of July and prayers said around the Thanksgiving table. It is the dream of freedom realized in thousands of small towns across this great nation.

But mostly, the Heartland is its people. People who care about and help one another. People who cherish traditional values and give to their children the greatest gift, the gift of love.

American Romance presents HEARTLAND, an emotional trilogy about people whose memories, hopes and dreams are bound up in the acres they farm.

HEARTLAND...the story of America.

Don't miss these heartfelt stories: American Romance #237 SIMPLE GIFTS (March), #241 FLY AWAY (April), and #245 HARVEST HOME (May).

HRT-1